¶

Also by Ruben D. Gonzales

The Cottage on the Bay
The Lake Nebo Murder

A solid, believable murder mystery
Well plotted, solidly constructed, simply told mystery. Those who enjoy whodunits with a strong, independent, and capable female protagonist will enjoy this book. Will keep you guessing up until the end. Highly recommended!

5.0 out of 5 stars Entertaining storytelling!
A suspicious death. Powerful small-town family influence. A persistent protagonist with an unusual sense of auras. Straightforward storytelling and dialogue. Mr. Gonzales adeptly weaves all of this together into a very entertaining read!

Great mystery
I love the plot and the author's descriptions of this quaint mountain town. I love the main character and hope to read more of her adventures in the future. I recommend this book to anyone who enjoys a good crime mystery.

Insightful and entertaining
I really enjoyed this book. The author incorporates his knowledge of the region into the story making for a realistic read. The characters were fun to follow. Great book!

¶

Murder on Black Mountain

By

Ruben D. Gonzales

Deep Indigo Books
Published by Indigo Sea Press
Winston-Salem

¶

Deep Indigo Books
Indigo Sea Press
302 Ricks Drive
Winston-Salem, NC 27103
This book is a work of fiction. Names, characters,
locations and events are either a product of the author's
imagination, fictitious or used fictitiously. Any resemblance
to any event, locale or person, living or dead, is purely
coincidental.

For information regarding bulk purchases of this book,
digital purchase and special discounts, please contact the publisher
at indigoseapress@gmail.com

Cover Design by Pan Morelli

Manufactured in the United States of America
ISBN 978-1-63066-552-4

"To Sue Ann Lapp...editor, partner, wife, love."

—Ruben D. Gonzales

¶

Chapter One

Return

I broke a heart or two, burned some bridges, and made Pa mad when I left home years before, so after my long absence I hesitated when I got the word about the accident and I'd have to visit Black Mountain. Knowing the appearance of his little sister would be expected, I swallowed my pride and made the trip into the foothills of the Blue Ridge Mountains to bury my big brother, Early Shaw.

I arrived in the midst of a welcomed Indian summer that descended over the dark hills to break an early cold snap. A spectacular scene of the season greeted me as fall leaves covered the forest landscape in orange, yellow, and brown blends. An occasional red hue crowded in the oak foliage, nature acting like a mad painter working from half a palette, finding only earth hues staring up at her.

After the long drive, I sat in my Jeep in front of the house of my brother's new widow, delaying the inevitable, hoping that if I waited long enough maybe I'd awake from the bad mountain dream.

My whole life the mountain seemed to call to me, and I tried my best to ignore the voice. I escaped the persistent cry several times; first, going away to college with the thought of maybe after graduating I'd move to New York to be a photojournalist. But like an old hound dog that follows a raccoon in the night, the incessant howl followed me no matter where I went, so there I sat, back home.

Becky must have heard the Jeep's tires on the gravel drive that led up to their house nestled in a clearing in the woods abutting the Pisgah National Forest. Coming out on the porch, she stood waiting on me.

Becky had followed Early to college, but she made him wait before she'd agree to marry the wild man. They'd been going with each other since high school, and she knew him like a book, so knew he needed time to settle down. She graduated, then stayed over a year and got her teaching certificate. She took her time moving back home, ignoring the call, teaching a year in the city.

In the meantime, Early started work at the Black Mountain Town Police, but she gave in after he asked her for the hundredth time, maybe wanting Early more than wanting to stay away. I was doing a tour in Afghanistan when they ran off to Myrtle Beach to get married.

I climbed out of the Jeep and walked on a brick paved path toward her.

"Girl," she said to me, "what took you?"

"I came on as soon as I could," I answered, climbing the porch steps. When I got within a few feet she surprised me and rushed into my arms. "Not like you live around the block," I told her, feeling uncomfortable in the arms of my brother's widow, wondering if we would still be some type of sisters without Early to bind us.

Becky and I were never close. Her star just shone too bright in that town to try to match, so I resented her and her hold on my big brother. Short like me, she kept her dark hair long, and more times than not like me, braided and hanging long down her back. Everything she wore looked neat and trim on her, whereas, I favored the jean, boots, and frumpy look of the local mountain woman…but I can clean up okay, if needed. She carried a face full of freckles, and even though the years added a few lines to her face, she somehow maintained a trim figure without the aid of a gym membership, while I jogged semi-regularly to keep the extra pounds at bay.

"I can't believe it," I told her, pushing back from her, tears filling my eyes.

"I know," she said her voice steady, her dark blue eyes dry and focused straight on me. "Like a bad dream that sucks the air out of your head and forces you awake."

She let me go, and turning about in the entryway, said, "A real nightmare." Walking through the short hall toward the kitchen and family room beyond, she added, "I feel like he's going to come home any minute and sit down and pour a cup of coffee."

"How are the boys?" I asked, following, taking notice of a faded red energy aura trailing behind her, a sign I knew for an unsettled soul.

Mama explained to me about my ability to read energy auras when I turned five years old; up until then, I just thought everyone could see them. Mama told me they are a result of a problem birth I went through, and the treatment from Louise Looking Bird, an old Cherokee woman midwife, from Laurel Ridge. Louise and her family farmed an old homestead on a narrow bluff overlooking the southern bank of the Swannanoa River. People say Louise and her people been living up there since before the first settlers came into the valley, and everyone knew Louise knew the native magic of herbs and potions.

I use my gift of aura reading in my portrait photography. I learned to capture the essence of a person in a photo by clicking the shutter of the camera right at the moment of the aura's brightest glow. The resulting image of the person pulses energy, almost alive, like they are about to take a breath and move. My newspaper editor thinks my photos of erstwhile interesting farmers and the downtrodden area citizens sell enough papers to justify the meager salary they pay me. He says my photos captured the real essence of a person's soul. I wouldn't go that far. I mean, I love my work, but there are other things important about being able to read auras.

One of the side results of my gift is being able to see the familiar dark pink aura of a person. When I see that, I know people are lying.

"The boys are over to Mama's," Becky explained about her and Early's four boys. Becky looked as much the pert teenager she used to be. She wore black slacks, black flats, and a black sweater, but her beauty transcended her attempt at mourning.

She took a seat in one of the high stools that surrounded a long, white granite-topped island that separated the kitchen from the new family room addition. The kitchen sported modern stainless-steel appliances and white cabinets with matching granite tops, and I wondered if the granite came off the mountain, and how did Early pay for the addition on his small-town salary.

"I didn't want them in the middle of this," she explained about her boys, looking over my head, maybe looking back into the past. "Growing up, I loved the farm. You know it's peaceful there, and Little Earl has been the adult man around here for a while, so he'll talk to the others." Snapping back to the present, she smiled wide at me and said, "I'll go over there again tonight. We've been sleeping down in their basement, on the foldout in sleeping bags, in front of a fire. It's been fun."

Bookshelves lined the family room and housed a vast collection of their four son's photos; boys in football uniforms and holding baseball bats. Assorted trophies, plaques, and medals rounded out the display. A gun cabinet with glass door stood in a corner of the room, its contents full to bursting. Memories of Early settled over the room like left over clouds from a winter storm.

"So," I said, getting to the question that had been bothering me since I heard about Early, "what all happened?"

"Well," she began, getting up and moving to the counter where a drip machine held a pot of dark coffee. She picked up the pot and waved it at me. I nodded my head and she pulled a clean mug down from a cabinet and filled that one and another on the counter. "Well, like I told you, looks like Early drove his cruiser off Moore's Curve."

"I don't know how."

"Just an accident." she said and returning to the island put my coffee mug down in front of me.

"No, ma'am, I don't see Early driving through that curve just like that. I'm sure Early drove that curve twenty times a week since his teenage years."

"Well, you know it can be tricky at night."

"Not for Early."

"What else?"

What else indeed, I thought, what else could it have been, but an accident. Still…

My brother Early Shaw fit the image of the southern "good ole boy". He smiled bright and wide, showing off a full set of teeth. He kept his hair buzzed like some Marine; although he didn't serve because of his busted knee he earned playing football. He took after the Shaw family men—tall, with piercing gray eyes; his body big and heavy with muscle, though with age, he softened up some. Early liked to joke; he liked to joke a lot. He thought of life as a game; like football, like college, like love; just games, and once you knew the rules, you could play to win. Early smiled easily and laughed his way through trouble and I loved him, more than I should.

"Well, I'd like to find out a bit more about this so-called accident. In the meantime, is there anything I can do?"

"No, not much, town fathers are taking care of everything since he died on city time and all."

"You mean, Granddaddy Shaw!"

"Who else?"

The Shaw family ran the lumber mill in Black Mountain and most everyone worked for the mill, did business with the mill, or somehow served employees of the mill. As far as mill people were concerned, your life began and ended at Shaw Mill. There are Shaws all over the valley, my pa included. Folk in town call the head of the Shaw family Granddaddy Shaw, although for most, it is *not* a term of endearment, but respect.

The current Granddaddy is Lawrence Shaw, father to his four boys, Franklyn, Randall, Mathew, and Miller, who run the town, but they call him "Granddaddy" now like everyone else. I know it's childish of them, a relic of the past, from a time when people thought the old worth listening to.

Back during the Depression, a lot of folk moved up to Black Mountain to work at the Shaw's lumber mill. Soon, all the men who worked at the mill became Shaw men. I guess taking the Shaw name was just easier than trying to explain a past that didn't exist anymore.

"So, what's happening with the investigation?"

"Well…"

"Well, what?"

"Well, like I said, they figure Early got to driving fast, faster than he should have, so there's nothing to investigate. Besides, there are only two other officers and they can't investigate anything."

"What about the other officers?"

"There's only two others."

"Two?"

"That's right. The town cut the department's budget last year and let the four oldest officers go, leaving the two newest. Early kept one in the office and one off, rotating them, but he performed the real leg work."

"How does the town expect to run a department with three men?"

"I don't know, Emma, but seemed like the town budget director kept on Early's back, like trying to make him quit."

It took a few years, but Early moved up the ranks at the BMPD and got to a level where it paid enough to start a family. He used a home design package to build their rancher, hiring a dozer to blaze a road connecting the house site to the paved frontage. He situated the front of the house west so he could watch the sun set in the evenings. The kitchen took up the back of the house, and Becky could see the sun rise over the mountain through the sliding doors from her breakfast table. When Chief Harold Shaw retired after his thirty years, Early took over, although it didn't pay much.

"Okay, okay," I said, somewhat agitated, storing that information for later, but trying to stay focused. "I just don't understand it," I said. "Early was too good behind the wheel to have an accident like that."

"Well, he hadn't been himself for a while now. Not as sharp."

"What do you mean?"

"Oh, his work and all, and lately he'd been getting these headaches. I tried to get him to see the doctor, but he'd just laugh at me and take some aspirin."

"He could be stubborn."

"Like all the Shaws."

"I guess..."

Early and I grew up with the Shaw name, and although I tried to ignore it, Early embraced it. Though older than me, Early and I got along fine. More than a brother, he looked after me, dragging me all over the mountain. I think he wanted to prepare me for life when Mama and Pa wouldn't be around.

We grew up poor, but loved, in the backward little town— running in the mountains, fishing, playing. Early and I used to run with the local Cherokee youth, tracking, camping out. I learned to shoot a rifle from Early, learned to fight back when needed, and learned to be independent, be distrustful. Unfortunately, being wary made for a lonely life, made me miss opportunities at love that I maybe regretted. I'd find it hard to admit that to anyone, anyone in Black Mountain.

When I got old enough, I plotted my escape from town, to something else—anything else. Black Mountain released its native progeny begrudgingly, smothering them in tradition, hoarding them like a hound dog stockpiles bones for gnawing on later.

Mama wanted me to go to college. I think she thought I'd

7

meet a rich boy and get married, since I'm cute and all, but that hasn't worked out yet, although I came close one time.

I interrupted my college years following a boyfriend and joining the National Guard, and deployed with my unit to Afghanistan. I know, I know, but you know how love works. My mama said on a list of dumb things I could have done it stood pretty high up the ladder, but you know how mothers think. I think Pa was right proud of my service since he served in Vietnam, although he didn't like to talk about it.

After my commitment ended, I'd seen enough death, so I didn't re-enlist. I went west. I worked traveling between all the national parks taking pictures, enjoying the peace and quiet of nature again, and trying to forget everything I saw while serving. I sold a few photos to nature magazines to finance my gas; and, living out of my Jeep, managed to stay away from my home state for several more years. About ten years ago I surrendered to the mountain's call and moved home to finish up my college degree. I discovered there was more to growing up than just running off.

After graduating I split the difference between the mountains and the sea and took a gig at the big newspaper in the Piedmont where a friend of mine worked as an assistant editor. Assigned to the sports department I shoot stills of the big games, video for the paper's web site, and on occasion, I fill in on the crime scene beat. I wasn't entirely clear of the mountains, but far enough away I didn't hear the incessant sound.

"So," Becky asked me, bringing me back to the present, "are you thinking about looking into it?"

"I might. I just don't see it—an accident, I mean."

"You'll have to deal with Granddaddy Lawrence, you know."

"I know."

"Well, I guess you been told."

After we both stayed quiet for a minute, she asked me, "So, how's your pa taking it?"

"I don't know," I confessed, returning my thoughts to the present, feeling guilty. "I haven't seen him yet."

"Emma!"

"Now, I came here first thing."

"Well, you need to look in on him."

"I know, I know…I'm going over there next."

"Look, he's cleaned up now."

"Has he?"

"He has, last time he came over to visit the boys, I think he even took a bath."

"That is a change."

"You know he's gone back to the church."

"I think I heard that."

"Yep, he's even doing some preaching."

That, I hadn't heard.

Chapter Two

Home

The mountain where we grew up stands at the southern end of the Blue Ridge range, holding grand along the horizon, and dwarfing the little town. The mountain's southern exposure is covered in thick laurel, crowding out any other plant growth, leaving its face a dark green, masked sentry over the town.

The big interstate connector bypassed the town back in the late 70s, leaving the town residents in a blissful time warp, back before the internet brought the world crashing onto Main Street like a parade you weren't invited to, but still had to sit and watch. To tell the truth, the town folk liked it that way. The night sky filled with stars as the evening hue turned from gray black to pitch. The mountain filtered out the ambient light, and folks living on the north side could view God's nightly heaven in its entirety, lighting up eternity.

It'd been some time since I'd been to Pa's. On a previous visit to town, I stayed with Becky and Early and didn't even see the man. Since Mama died, I just couldn't bring myself to visit. Her memory hovered over the house and me. Pa let himself go, stopped bathing, letting the house go to decrepit. I couldn't stand the mess and dirt, and this from a gal that doesn't know one end of a vacuum from another.

I approached the dirt road that marked the beginning of the family land. From the bend in the road at the top of the little rise, I could see a bright light coming from the kitchen window at the front of the cedar-slat sided small house. I pulled up the drive and stopped next to his beat-up brown truck. I pulled my old back pack with my personal stuff from the back seat and walked up the gravel path to the wooden steps that led up to the narrow front porch that Pa built for Mama when we were young. Pa opened the door before I knocked.

"I wondered when you'd come," he said. The night shadow engulfed him, a silhouette between the past and present. I couldn't mistake his voice, deep like a country music singer that somehow found a range below base, or his unique orange aura that claimed his troubled soul.

"Hey, Pa!" I greeted him, going into his arms.

"Well," he said after we held each other for a short spell, wiping back his own tears. Stepping out on the porch and to the side so I could pass him through the doorway, he said, "Come on in, if you're going to."

The sitting area and adjacent kitchen appeared as I remembered with a host of memories of bright, happy days filling the space. The rooms stood spotless, which surprised me, since as far back as I could remember, Mama did all the house cleaning. Fact is, I don't recall Pa did anything in the kitchen besides eat.

"Crazy thing!" he said closing the door after I entered and then leading me to the kitchen table where a coffee mug stood on a checkered place mat. The bare bulb light above shone down on a small Bible sitting open. I sat opposite his place as he retreated to the short counter.

Used to be Mama carried the only Bible in the family. People knew if you met her on the sidewalk in town then you'd better be ready for a mini revival on your life of sin and the forgiveness that awaited those who confessed. People knew in town that if Mama prayed over you, good things would happen—if you believed that kind of thing. Oh, she could drag us off to preaching Sundays, even get me to put on a dress, but more times than not, Pa would find a way to be off somewhere, hunting or fishing.

Mama would tell him, *"You know, the Lord is fishing for men, I'm sure if He caught you, He'd be keeping you."*

Pa would say, *"He better bring a strong net, then, Darling, because I'd like to wiggle out, if not."*

"Too late for coffee," he offered me, breaking my reminiscing.

"No, I'm so tired nothing could keep me up."

He filled a heavy mug with a dark brew from an old percolator, placing it in front of me. "I'm glad your mama wasn't here to see this."

By the color in his face, I could see Pa had been taking care of his self, and by the red in his eyes, I could see he'd been crying.

"I know," I said, sipping from the cup, holding back my own tears, "it would have broken her heart for sure."

"You pretty as ever, girl," he said with a slight smile. He wore a shirt that, though clean, appeared as wrinkled as possible. I could see his white sock-covered feet and worn bedroom shoes beneath his faded, drawn up blue jeans. A belt, taken in a notch or two, attempted to hold up his pants. "Life in the city okay with you?" he asked, and tried to smile through a weak grin, grown taut, I imagined, with the worry over Early's premature demise.

"Sure, I love my work, but you know me and the next job opportunity are only an adventure away."

"Just remember, next time you run off, try to stay closer to home."

"I will…I'm not against you Pa."

"Just the Mountain?"

"Is doesn't hold me like before."

"You and your brother used to like the mountain camping out," he said taking a seat. "It used to worry your mama sick, you two by yourselves, you a girl. Do you know," he said, laughing, "she made me follow you out first few times you two camped overnight by yourselves?"

"What?"

"Yes, ma'am, oh, I stayed a ways off each time, close

enough to keep an eye on you all, but not so close you would know. She didn't worry about your brother, but she worried over you. One time, it took to raining, and I about come down with pneumonia staying out in it all night."

I didn't know that, although I knew Mama worried.

"Yes, sir, she loved you two, alright, and did her best by you. This would have killed her, losing Early."

Of course, Mama's memory still rested heavy on the little house, like a birthmark you might wish away but reality keeps it planted deep. Mama sewed the cover for the chair cushion I sat on and wove the area rug underneath my feet. The china hutch held her collection of plates she brought up from her mama's house, and two rows of photo albums crowded the lower shelfs. A bunch of framed photos of Early from his playing days, a couple of others from our graduations, and one of me in uniform crowded any vacant spaces. An assortment of framed needlepoints filled the lone inner wall. One read, *"You Only Live Once, So Live in the Mountains!"*

The pretty roll top desk she loved stood where it stood for twenty-five years. Made of oak, it belonged to her father, and she kept books and writing stuff in there for our schoolwork.

One spring evening during high school, after the night cooled the air, we were sitting at the kitchen table. Darning an old pair of socks and drinking coffee, Mama asked me about my homework. I told her about the assignment our English teacher gave us.

"What assignment?" she asked.

"We're studying a dumb play."

"What play?"

"Romeo and Juliet."

"Now, Emma Louise," she said, putting down the socks. She liked to include my middle name when addressing me on something important. "That's a wonderful story. You know, undying love between man and woman. How they love each other so much that they can't bear the thought of living

13

without each other, so they would rather not live at all. Now, that's real love."

"You ever feel that kind of love, Mama?"

Her elbows were resting on the tabletop and her hands held her chin. She looked pretty as a teenager with a hint of starlight in her eyes and a lavender aura enveloping her.

"Yes, Emma Louise," she said with a smile, sipping from her cup, and getting back to those old socks, "about your pa, you bet, since we first met…but just don't tell him, or he might get a big head."

When we were young, Pa worked up at the mill at night, and by day, farmed the land for corn and soybean we used for feed for the few cattle we kept. Mama scratched out a vegetable garden in season and took in laundry year-round. She liked to grow tomatoes, and in season, she combined the slices of a red Cherokee Purple with leaf lettuce on white bread for her favorite sandwich.

I'd forgotten how quiet the night could be around the house. A memory rushed at me. A memory of Mama, humming some tune as she worked at the sink, a contented smile on her face as she stared out the window at the sunset and the end of another hard but successful day of just living.

"So did you hear what happened?" Pa asked me, breaking my memory tour.

"Some. Becky told me. Have you talked to the police?"

"No, I can't get anyone to return my calls. Like they're not interested in explaining it."

"That's kind of what I gather. What have you heard around town?"

"Just that he went off Moore's curve and drown."

"I can't figure it like that," I said, sipping coffee. "I sure don't see Early just going off that curve on his own."

"I know. Early been driving that curve his whole life. I bet he could drive it blindfolded."

After we both stewed for a while over the circumstances

14

of Early's accidental death, Pa asked, "You talk to Becky about the arrangements?"

"I talked with her before coming over here, but she said the town is handling the details."

"The mayor?"

"Him and Granddaddy," I said, getting up from the table and stretching my arms out and up over my head. "I'll be going down to town to talk to the mayor in the morning; got a few questions for him. But for now … now, I'm ready for bed."

"I doubt you get much out of them."

"Why's that?"

"Early and the Shaws been at one another for a couple of years now."

"About what?"

"Well, sometime ago, two years or more now, Granddaddy Shaw up and shot a fellow up at the mill."

"He what?"

"That's right, shot him bad. They caught this shop manager up there with his hand in the petty cash, and Granddaddy Lawrence confronted the man in the office. Hear tell the man, high on drugs and pills, charged Granddaddy. Well, Granddaddy pulled down the old squirrel gun they keep in the office, you know for the coons and those coyotes we been seeing the last few years, and anyway, when the man came at Granddaddy, he shot him once in the chest."

"Kill him?"

"Not right off, but the man up and died few days later."

"What happened?"

"Well, the man's people put up a stink and called on Early to investigate. Early looked into it to please them, even though he knew it wouldn't amount to anything. The mayor didn't like it, Early going around asking the family questions and interviewing everyone up at the mill. Things turned bad between the Shaws and Early that day and stayed that way till now."

"Till now?"

15

"Yeah," Pa said, getting up from the table and leading me down the short hall to my old room. "Looks like the Shaws won't need to worry none about your brother anymore."

My room looked like it did the day I left for State, only smaller. Several shelves lined the walls and held an assortment of my high school memorabilia. A red State bedspread covered the bed, and a quilt of many colors that Mama made lay across the foot of the mattress.

"I put clean sheets on your bed, Emma," Pa said, moving in front of me and switching on a small light sitting on a narrow table by the bed. "I thought you might stay over."

I reached out to my pa and we hugged again. It'd been a while since he hugged me like that.

"You know, Pa," I told him, "you can't blame yourself for Mama's dying. It wasn't your fault. Don't take it so hard." Mama and Pa told me a thousand times I was the biggest and best surprise when I came along. I think Ma and Pa liked having a daughter, sort of a balance with Early, so they loved me more than they should.

"I know. I've been trying harder, and Pastor Bennett's been helping."

"Say," I said to him, using the sleeve of my sweatshirt to wipe tears from my eyes, "what's this I hear about you taking to preaching?"

"I speak a spell now and then. Pastor lets me lead our Sunday school class. You know—the old people group."

"I'd like to hear that, Pa. I'd like to hear that for sure."

"Well, maybe Sunday next."

"I don't know about this week," I told him. "With everything going on and having to deal with the Shaws and all, come the end of the week, I might be up to my neck in sin."

Chapter Three

Mama

Growing up in Black Mountain, you could count the things for kids to do on one hand. The boys played football on the mill team and the girls got to play softball. Some boys played on the high school team, while girls could play volleyball— although being on the short side, Coach told me to stick with softball. A few of the boys from the high school team got to play in college.

Mama worried she birthed a boy. The opportunities for a boy in Black Mountain didn't amount to much unless you counted working third shift at the mill as a career move. Year before Early went to Black Mountain High, a boy named Todd McCoy went on to college because of football. A big old boy that played center on the team, and slow as a snail, but he earned a football scholarship.

Football took on a whole new meaning for Mama after hearing that. She figured it could be Early's ticket out of there. She thought I'd marry young, since I'm smart, pretty, and all. She thought I'd marry someone well-off, so didn't worry about me.

Well, from then on, she made sure Early attended each football practice and wanted to know his game schedule. For a long time, she saw every game he played. When Early made the high school team, she wanted to know everything she could about football.

In the beginning, Early couldn't break into the starting lineup. Although big enough even then, at a good two hundred pounds, a senior kid, outside linebacker too, Denny McBride played ahead of him. A lot of college coaches made the trip into the mountains to scout him, and he wasn't about to give up his position.

Then, one Friday night, halfway through the season, McBride knocked himself out on a hard tackle and Early went in the game to take his place. Early played pretty good, but everyone assumed the McBride kid would start again when he came back.

The next week on Monday, Mama asked Coach Carter for a playbook. She spent that evening studying it at the kitchen table. After a couple of hours, she got up and handed it to Early.

"You finished?"

"That playbook's no good," she said.

"What do you mean?"

"I mean it's full of your team's plays."

"Right."

"Well, that ain't gonna help you any when you play Pinnacle High School Friday night. What you need is the Pinnacle playbook. That way, you'll be prepared to stop their plays."

"Mama, the coach over at Pinnacle isn't going to give me their play book."

"No? Well, maybe we'll have to see about that."

The end of that week, Thursday night before the Pinnacle game, she came in the house.

"Here," she said, handing Early a stack of papers.

"What's this?"

"Those are a bunch of plays that Pinnacle uses. They like to run it, and it looks like they go right most of the time. That's to your side, Early."

"I know what side I play on Mama. Where'd you get this stuff?"

"Old man Magruder, over in Pinnacle."

"Who's that?"

"He's the game day janitor over at the stadium there. He's

been watching the games Friday nights for twenty years, so he knows real well what plays their coach likes to run. Early, you make sure to study everything there because I expect you to make ten tackles on Friday night...or I am going to be real disappointed."

"How did you get this stuff?"

"I told Magruder I'd pray over him if he'd help me out."

Early listened to Mama and studied. That Friday night, Early made twenty tackles, and from that night on he played first string. Every Thursday night, Early and Mama would sit down at the kitchen table and study the next team he'd be playing. From then on, without exception, when Early stepped on a field, he knew more about the plays the other team were going to run then the team itself. Opposing coaches wondered how Early anticipated so well, like he stood in their huddle, listening to the plays called. We wondered how Mama got all that information.

During Early's senior year, the State coach signed him. He'd been all-state three years running, and they were happy to get him. Mama liked the way it all worked out.

Chapter Four

Monday

In the morning, I rolled over, and reaching out from the bed, grabbed my cell phone. I pulled the covers back over my head and tried to open my message app, but I'd forgotten our old house didn't have cell service or internet. I didn't mind, though. In fact, I smiled at the thought of being off the grid for a while.

Freezing when my feet hit the cold floor, I grabbed my old house coat that had been hanging on the back of the door. It possessed that outdoor wind freshness you get when you hang washed clothes out to dry on a line under the sun on a clear fall day.

I found Pa sitting at the kitchen table reading the Bible, a cup of coffee in one hand and a piece of buttered toast in the other. Rivets of light beams from the dawn sun seeped through the worn window covers like honey dripping through a honey cone, and I expected another warm Indian summer day.

"You want some eggs for breakfast?" he offered, putting down the Bible after pulling a sliver of red ribbon between pages to mark his place. "Though this time of day, you might be thinking more about lunch."

"No, thanks," I told him, ignoring the time quip, "just some coffee for now."

"You'll get hungry."

"Thanks the same, but I'm going into town and I'll grab a bite at the diner."

"What's on your mind?"

"Don't know for now," I told him as I moved to the counter to pour a mug of coffee. "But with what you and

Becky tell me, it sounds like Mayor Shaw had it in for Early."

"What did Becky tell you?"

"Oh, she filled me in on Early's department getting cut back and all. I'd like to find out what all happened and why."

"If something's happening, you know Granddaddy's behind it,"

"No doubt."

"You figure to talk to him?"

"I figure."

"You sure you want to snoop around?"

"Who's snooping?"

"Look, girl," Pa advised, "you a grown woman now, and I can't be telling you much, but you know the Shaws won't take it well if you start asking questions."

"I know."

"Then, I guess you've been told."

I finished the rest of my coffee in a huff and went back and spent a few minutes taking a fast, unsatisfactory shower. My hair looked like a nesting place for small critters, so I shampooed it out and blew it half dry, the hand-held hair dryer filling the house with a high-pitched wind. I combed the dark mess out and pulled it back in a ponytail, holding it in place with a scrunch. I put my ball cap on to cover my handiwork. I searched through my backpack for a clean sweatshirt and slipped into the pair of jeans I wore the day before, reserving my best clothes for the funeral proceedings. I put on clean socks and my hiking boots and went back out to the kitchen.

It'd been a while since Pa and I spent a morning in each other's company, and I hated to start my visit with an argument. I don't know why, maybe a leftover memory of Mama hanging in the air like a mist over warm water, but I went over and bending down, gave him a kiss on top of his head. He smiled up at me, a grin short a couple of teeth. Leaving Pa reading his Bible at the kitchen table, I took the Jeep down the hill into town to look into the matter of my dead big brother.

♦◊♦

The early morning light bathed Main Street in soft shadow, hiding the structural blemishes of the old buildings. I cruised north along the street and the store fronts that housed a hodgepodge of businesses. The plumbing supply appeared closed, but the hardware store looked open. A sign in the window of the one-time TV repair now displayed a computer service shop, and the former Shaw Travel agency now housed a tourist information center. The Fish and Game shop stood proud with American flags waving bright out front, but Saunders Photography Studio looked shut up, a tattered "closed" sign hanging in its window. It appeared as though most of the local businesses managed to stave off the competition from the big box stores located on the new highway bypass near the county seat, Morgan.

I drove past the lush Town Park grounds, lined with antique lights sitting on posts that used to funnel gas for the flames before the mill started feeding electricity to Main Street. I made my way on up the street where the small Black Mountain City Hospital sat; a white-washed albatross from the past where near everyone in town started their lives and near everyone went for their last days. A morning crowd filtered in and out of a cute coffee shop that looked new to me, *The Coffee Bean*. It looked conveniently located across from the hospital. Circling back along the opposite side of the street, I found much of the same mixture of old and new businesses.

I worked my way back down the street to Town Hall situated on the other side of the green public square. Eight Romanesque columns held up the grand two-story portico of the building, stretching the length of the 100-year-old granite edifice to better times. Whereas other local counties and towns took their names from Civil War heroes like Johnston, McDowell, and Ransom, Black Mountain took its name from a rock.

I drove east to the edge of town and paused, hesitating, letting the Jeep idle. I needed to go to the funeral home. I needed to see for myself about Early, but a wave of heat crept into my face as I recognized the flush of emotions that would bring. I thought old man Gilmore would be up working his trade. I knew it sinful of me, but I hoped the man had other customers to work on and hadn't yet started to prep Early.

Gilmore's took up a large corner lot at the end of Main Street. The grand Victorian home had seen better times. Its façade tried hard to look kept and clean, but I could see faded, peeling paint, and a detached downspout hung over a flower bed, threatening to squash a row of mountain holly.

I parked along the curb in front of the entrance and climbed out of the Jeep cab and approached the doorway. For the first time since hearing about Early's death, I began to feel a true certainty that Early was dead and I was about to see for myself.

Mr. Gilmore heard the Jeep, because he met me at the door and said, "That you, Emma Louise?"

"Yes, sir," I answered the old gentleman.

"I'll be darn," he said, standing in the doorway. His short, squat body was adorned in a full-length black rubber apron and thick rubber gloves, a blue surgical cap covering half his head. "You about as pretty as ever, I'd say."

"Well, thanks." I told him as I extended a hand to greet him proper. Mr. Gilmore showed a dark gray aura that more times than not I gathered to mean a foreboding over life in general. Of course, in the business, as such, I shouldn't have expected anything different.

He took off the gloves, and tucking them under his left arm, grabbed hold of my hand and with an iron grip, shook it, rattling my teeth. "Still haven't grown any."

"No, expect not."

"Sorry about your brother, Emma, hell of a thing."

"Without a doubt," I said to the man. He carried a flat

expansive nose and sleepy eyes that somehow fit his profession.

"You been working on Early back there?" I asked.

"Not much," he said moving aside and inviting me in. "Just poking around a little."

"Good, I wanted to take a last look, you know, before you prepped him, one last look as I knew him."

"You sure you want to?"

"No," I admitted, beginning to fight back an onset of tears, "but I need to."

"Okay, if you're up to it," he said, and waved to follow him.

The Gilmore family had been putting people down to rest in the Swannanoa Valley for over two hundred years. The job of the town undertaker evolved over time, but remained a difficult, painful task. In the days of the first settlers into the valley, many towns didn't have a specific person for the job. The first pick for undertaker in a community fell to the town furniture maker. He did double duty as a logical choice that townsfolk turned to since a good carpenter owned the tools and a supply of wood to make their coffins. It is a sad, morbid business, but the Gilmores were known as excellent carpenters.

The first Gilmore carpenter followed the first settlers and syphilis over the Blue Ridge into the valley in 1812 and set out to bury mountain folk and Cherokee at about the same pace. It didn't take long for disease to clean out a good deal of the native population, and then after the war, the farmers and mill workers came.

When formaldehyde came along with tuberculosis, the Gilmores switched professions entirely to undertaking. Unfortunately, modern antibiotics and the declining town population began to put a hurt on the funeral home business in Black Mountain.

Gilmore led me down a short hall of the old mansion to a newer structure that housed the preparation lab. The physical condition of this area of the business looked to be newer by years, and appeared scrubbed clean and sturdy in walls and floor.

A series of four refrigerated bins lined one wall of the 24-by-24-foot room. Two stainless steel tables occupied the center of the room under an array of fluorescent light stands on wheels. A row of stainless-steel counters and a grouping of sinks lined the opposite wall. A white sheet covered a body resting on one of the tables. It didn't surprise me that a dim memory aura still flowed from the body, Early's body, strong as he could be. A strong energy aura will emanate from a powerful person a long time after the person has passed. Early's aura flashed between brown and black and the yellow of optimism, a manic fluctuation, a life uncertain and unsettled, a troubled soul. I guess his energy still hung tight to this world, stubborn about giving up.

Gilmore approached the table, and nodding to me, waited. I pulled my cap off and moved to the head of the body and stood for a minute before folding down the top portion of the sheet to reveal his face. Early's body stretched across the table, but still in full form. Usually a beast in perpetual motion, his body still exuded power like he could pull a breath and climb down off the table and move on to get the workday started.

I tried to fight them, but as tears started to roll down my cheeks, I said, "I hope he didn't suffer any."

"Well, I'm not an expert," the man said, hesitating, handing me a red handkerchief, "but signs here tell me the force of the crash killed your brother instantly."

"What do you mean?"

"There's not much water in his lungs so he died before he went under."

"He must have been going fast."

"Yep, real fast."

I wasn't sure what Gilmore was getting at, but since the whole thing seemed a real mystery to me, I needed to know what the old man thought.

"I don't know what you're getting at, Mr. Gilmore, but if you're thinking something more than a random accident, here, then I want to know how my brother got himself killed."

"Well, your brother just didn't roll off the road and slide down that bank. His cruiser ended up way out in the river. I'd say he must have been going a hundred to end up that far out. I mean he must have been airborne for a good ways before he came down. That's the force that killed him. It's like hitting cement at that speed, and if he wasn't wearing his seatbelt...well, it would have snapped his neck. He just didn't turn upside down in the river and drown."

I looked down at Early through a wave of his dark aura and I half expected him to look up at me. When I first began to understand my ability of reading auras, I wondered how it all worked; so I went up and met with Louise Looking Bird and she counseled me that my aura visions were created by the energy in a person's body. Depending on how strong a spirit a person possessed, that energy hung heavy in the air around them, and if I concentrated in a quiet space in my head, I could capture them. I can't see everyone's auras. For some, a deep distrust and a secret nature can suppress their aura, but not many people are like that—at least, in my travels.

"Like a dream catcher?" I asked Louise, referring to those circular objects made of yarn and feathers.

"It is something like that, but in your vision." She told me the Squawroot medicine she used during my birth made me see the visions. She said Squawroot looks like a small

26

pinecone and lives underground on the roots of the many oak trees in the forest. Some of these oaks go back several hundred years, even before the old Cherokee. The Cherokee used Squawroot for many cures, including treating babies and menopausal women. The treatment and the combination of the squawroot and a tea potion brewed from the mountain laurel, creates the ability to see the auras.

Louise explained that the mountain laurel tea can put you into a deep sleep, to the point of death. Mountain laurel in a certain potion can be poisonous; but used correctly, laurel is known to affect vision. The combination of new vision and deep sleep at birth creates the magic, if you believe in that kind of thing.

I looked down at Early's great body. He'd put on some weight, but his arms and chest stood barrel strong.

When finished, I slid the sheet up and over my brother's body and over his calm face. I didn't know if I'd see Early again. Depended on whether or not Becky decided to go with an open coffin.

I stood at the table for a minute longer, drawing Early's memory aura from the space but the vision in my recall appeared blurred, faded, like a forgotten dream. It seemed even Early's body energy had run its course.

I walked over to a sink hanging on a wall and splashed cold water on my forehead, and taking a couple of paper towels from a single sheet dispenser, dried my hands and blotted the water from my face. I found a metal folding chair near Gilmore's desk and wobbly sat down.

"Feeling light-headed?"

I hated to admit it, but nodded my head.

"Sorry." Getting to his feet and crossing the room he opened a window a crack and let in a cool breeze.

After I recovered, I got up and we walked out of the lab and retraced our steps out to the public area.

"Becky said the Shaws are taking care of the particulars?"

"Yes," Gilmore said, following me out, "I talked to the mayor earlier and he said not to worry, that the Shaws look after their own."

"Least they could do."

"I'll get the personal things up to the house, though. I'm sure Becky will want them."

I stepped out the front doors, and plopping my cap back on my head, stopped on the porch landing to take a deep breath. My head cleared somewhat and I said, "Looks like it will be warm today."

"That's the Indian summer for you, warm in the day, crisp at night. I hope it lasts a while!"

"Me, too."

"Where you off to?"

"I thought I might maybe catch the mayor in town."

"Well, if it's the mayor you're looking for this time of day then take a look in the diner. The mayor eats breakfast there every day, and you might catch him just finishing up."

"Thanks, I think I will," I said, not sure if I could eat just then.

"And I'll tell you one more thing about all this, Emma."

"What?"

"I'd be careful about asking questions about this thing."

"What are you saying?"

"Just be careful where you stick that pretty little nose of yours."

Chapter Five

Diner

Shaw's Diner gets the town's food, convenience store, and gas business. You can get a plate of eggs or old donut and a pretty strong cup of coffee in the morning—a hot dog with decent chili at lunch, and a case of beer and a fill-up at night, although everyone knew you overpaid. The modern franchises located along the interstate tried to siphon off convenience and food business, but the quaint oddity of a country diner had something they couldn't duplicate: gossip. With gossip its prime product, in demand by the locals and tourists alike, Shaw's still packed them in.

Cars and trucks filled the parking lot in front of Shaw's Diner but I pulled around to the rear of the building to find a spot. Taking off my cap, I looked at my hair and face in the rearview mirror, and pulling wild strands back behind my ears, I got out.

When I started in the diner, two big men came out and did their best to molest me there in the doorway, laughing, making me squeeze by between them. I smiled through the ordeal, but when one of the men put his hand on my rear-end, I grabbed hold of one of his big fingers and yanked it full over trying to break it. When the men pushed their way by me, I smiled at the man and released his hand. The man took to hopping about holding his hand up to his mouth and sucking on the joint that needed tending.

"Holy cow, lady…" the man said as he hopped about.

"Why, you must have got your hand stuck in the doorway here. You know you should be careful where you stick those hands of yours."

As to be expected, the men went off a bit less jovial than when they started the encounter.

I waited at the checkout area behind a couple of other groups before a spot at the food counter opened up for a single, and I took it.

"Coffee?" the teen-looking waitress dressed in white and a red checkered apron asked, waving a glass pot at me. I couldn't see her shoes, but I hoped they'd be sensible for the pace of work since she carried extra pounds around.

I nodded, and she pulled a mug from somewhere and filled it. A small stainless-steel container of real cream stood nearby, along with a glass sugar pourer. Artificial sweeteners packed in a straw basket were within reach. The coffee was good and I watched the woman drift down the counter filling mugs and putting down breakfast checks as customers came and went. When she made it back to me, she smiled amidst a muddy yellow aura, signaling a tired persona, and asked me what I wanted to eat.

"What do you recommend?"

"Stay away from the grill if you want to keep that pretty little figure of yours."

"Is the oatmeal good?"

"Mama's recipe," she said, "with blueberries?"

"Why not," I agreed, thinking my stomach might be able to handle that after my morning visit with Early.

She nodded yes, and called out the order to someone in the back grill area while writing in a little pad. I noticed the name 'June' stitched into her shirt over her left breast. I remembered the name from somewhere out of my past and she looked familiar, but couldn't place the young lady. June wandered down the other end of the counter where she took up with a couple of men who looked like truckers, and from the easy banter and laughter, they sounded like regulars.

An assortment of customers filled the booths along the front glass wall, and in the last booth, four men in suits and ties talked animatedly between mouthfuls of food. Though out of place by their dress they fit right in by their size, three of them going well over 250 pounds and showing every pound stuffed in shirts too small for their girth. The third man, though he could be as tall, looked to be slim as a rail. A murky brown aura cloud hung over the group, its color a sign of character that hovered between suspicion and greed.

I dimly remembered what Mayor Franklyn Shaw looked like. Though older, he ran some with Early, but I talked to him from time to time. I remembered a fat kid that no one made fun of because his family ran the mill and a stray insult could land your pa on unemployment. I didn't recognize the thin man wedged against the window or the man sitting to his right, but I did recognize the fourth booth occupant, Cousin Randall Shaw, Town Attorney since getting his law degree from Wake Forest about twenty years ago.

A bell dinged in the service window, and June appeared. Grabbing a big, steaming bowl, she put it down in front of me while topping off the coffee mug. After laying down a spoon wrapped in a single white paper napkin she asked, "You don't remember me, do you?"

"Sure, I do," I lied, unfolding the napkin, "you're June."

"No, but it's okay, I'm June Oliver, Stacie Oliver's little sister?"

"Oh, Stacie, of course, I thought you looked familiar."

"Everyone says we resemble, I could see you were looking at me close. I get that a lot from Stacie's old friends. They can't figure how Stacie stayed so young looking."

"So, how's Stacie doing?"

"She's doing okay, married now, got a couple of pretty little girls and a boy. She works with Mama some at the parlor in town."

"Oh, well, I'll drop in on them, see what she's been up to."

"She'll like that. I'll let her know you're back."

I added honey to my oatmeal from a miniature glass pitcher on the counter and dug in, discovering an appetite. I just about made my way down to the bottom of the bowl, where several blue berries tried to hide from my spoon, when the four men in suits wiggled out from their booth and lumbered my way. Mayor Franklyn Shaw, recognizing me, spoke first.

"Emma Louise Shaw," he said, loud enough for the others to hear, "is that you?"

"No other," I answered, revolving around on my seat and getting to my feet, the mayor towering over me.

At the mention of my name, the diner became quieter.

"How's it going, Franklyn?"

"I've been fine," he said. "But just terrible about the chief." Mayor Franklyn Shaw continued, reaching out and offering his right hand, "We are real torn up by it all."

I took the mayor's pudgy hand and returned a firm grip and said, "Thanks, Franklyn, I appreciate that, but of course it's a little hard to believe."

"What is?"

"That Early would have an accident like that."

"Oh, well…unlucky, I guess."

"Now, Franklyn, you and I both know that Early was the luckiest man in town."

"Maybe Early's luck just ran its course!" the large man I didn't know said with a smirk.

"Yeah," Randall Shaw added, "no one's luck lasts forever."

I moved my attention over to Randall. Tall like the others, he looked to weigh about 240 pounds, but he didn't show any signs of working out in a gym. He possessed the Shaw pointed nose, sagging cheeks, and same receding hairline that made all Shaw men foreheads look like landing strips for small planes.

"Now, now," Mayor Shaw smiled wide to his brother, "we're all family, here," he said. "Emma, you remember Brother Randall."

32

I didn't need to shake the man's hand since it wasn't offered.

"Sure," I said. The group's collective aura exuded an array of brown that branded the bunch as bad news and made me quiver and look forward to stepping out in the sunshine. "Just one big happy family."

"We try to keep it that way," Mayor Franklyn said.

"So, who are the rest of the cousins?"

"I'm sorry, Emma," he said. "This is Wendell Banks, the town budget director, and Dr. Miller Shaw."

Miller Shaw, a younger, thinner version of the others, sporting more hair in his youth, smiled and nodded hello to me. By some freak act of nature, in size and build, Banks could have been a family relation, although I knew he wasn't. I didn't offer my hand to either of them.

"Well, Emma, we've just been discussing the arrangements for the chief."

"You were?"

"Yes, ma'am."

"Are you discussing the arrangements without the family?"

"Well, we didn't think Becky or your pa would be up to it."

"So why didn't you get in touch with me? "

"We tried to track you down, Emma, but you know we've been a little busy."

"Too busy to give me a call?"

"I don't know that we had your number, Emma. You haven't been much of a resident around here the last few years."

"Okay, so I'm here to speak for the family now."

"Well, you know, Emma, we all think of you as family, so we told Becky we'd take care of things."

"What's the hurry?" I asked. "You all not trying to hide anything, are you?"

"What's that supposed to mean?"

"Well, Franklyn, if you don't mind, I have a few questions about all this."

"Sure, sure," he said, looking about the now quiet diner, every table listening to every word. "But not here, Emma, not here. Shouldn't we do it in private?"

Taking a look at all the eyes in the quiet room fixated on us, I figured the crowd would be interested to hear that discussion, but I agreed with the mayor and said, "Of course. Your office?"

"Sure," he said, looking relieved. "I'm off on a couple of errands right now, but what say we meet about noon?"

"That'd be fine."

"Okay," the mayor said, and leading the big-bodied pack up the aisle added, "See you at noon."

The mayor and cousins lumbered to the exit, dragging their combined muddy brown aura with them and didn't bother stopping at the register on their way out. I wondered if they left the hard-working waitress a tip.

I glanced up and down the aisle and the customers started back to the business at hand, eating. The conversational din picked up and I turned and sat back on my seat, grabbing my mug of coffee. June came by to top it off, and smiled at me, her aura flashing from dark blue to violet, a sure sign of a happy soul.

I finished my coffee but stalled, trying to avoid my next errand. I picked up my check, put down three dollars for a tip, and reluctantly strolled to the register to pay my tab so I could head out to where my big brother died in his so-called accident.

Moore's Curve swerved right to left at the bend in the road and the protective guard rail there sported a new gap. I pulled off the paved frontage at the location and climbed out of the Jeep.

A length of that yellow crime scene tape stretched across the hole in the wooden fence like a band-aid.

Looking down over the edge of the ridge, I saw a big wrecker with a winch hauling Early's cruiser out of the Swannanoa. I could understand that a vehicle going straight on could crash through the flimsy safety barrier, but Early's cruiser made the hole in the rail well before the actual bend in the road.

The river ran fast through this section of town and at least thirty feet of beach shore stood between the edge of the road cliff and the dark water. Early must have been doing over a hundred miles an hour to launch his vehicle that far out; that, or he got a little push for help.

I figured it might be useful later, so pulled my camera from the Jeep and started snapping off photos of the scene around the hole in the barrier and up the road a bit where I saw a few skid marks. To get a closer look, I stepped over the police tape and scooted on my rear down the slippery slope to the river bank below.

"Hey, lady," a man yelled at me when I got close to the wrecker, "just what do you think you're doing?"

"You talking to me?"

"Yeah, I'm talking to you, dumb broad," he continued, as a couple of his friends came around the truck to join him. "What are you doing snooping around here?"

"Who says I'm snooping?"

"If you don't have business here then you're snooping. Who are you?"

"Well, I'm Emma Shaw, Chief Shaw's sister."

"That right?" one of the other men asked, surprised.

"Yep, that's right," I explained again. Three shades of a black aura filled the area around the men, emitting an unmistaking evil. "I've come home for the week, you know, to settle a few things and all. Thought I'd come out and see the spot where my brother died. Course, people here about know me, but I don't recall seeing you three, so who are you all and what's it to you what I'm doing?"

"Doesn't matter who we are, little lady," the first man said with a little less intensity. "You need to clear out of here if you know what's good for you."

The three looked enough alike to be brothers, big with fat stomachs, but I didn't think they graduated at the head of their class.

"I won't be leaving until sometime after the funeral," I explained. "You know…family matters."

The man doing all the talking looked at his comrades and smiling at them, lunged at me. I moved to my right, and grabbing his outstretched arm, pulled hard. I stuck my hip into him, and using his weight, yanked him over and onto the ground with a judo move I learned in the Guard.

At my sudden movement, the two other men stepped back, surprised, leaving the talker and obvious leader on his own. Recovering from his fall, the man struggled to his feet and crouched ready, about to charge, likely to bowl me over. I didn't think the brief hand-to-hand combat course they made me take during basic training would enable me to fight them all off, but I hoped if I could make enough noise maybe someone would hear me and come to my rescue.

Just then, someone *did* come to my rescue, sliding on the same path I came down and joining the little crowd on the beach, like maybe we were all going to have a picnic.

He stood as tall as the other men, although they all weighed much more, but he stepped between me and Loudmouth. Having been thwarted by little old me, Loudmouth wasn't in a mood for talk, and swung wildly at the man. My new friend saw it coming and ducked, and as he did, he brought his left fist up into Loudmouth's kidney area, bringing the man down to his knees.

It happened so quick the other two were caught off guard and stood flat-footed. Before they could get themselves organized, my hero waved a finger at them. "Hold on boys," he said, "take it easy, or you'll be feeling poorly like your friend, here."

The two held their ground and turned to check with each other, like looking for direction. My rescuer friend took his foot and pushed the first man over on his side.

"Take it easy, big fella," he said to the guy, rolling him on his back and looking down at him. "So, tell me, who's giving you orders?"

"Go to—" the guy on the ground gasped.

"Ah, ah, ah…" my friend said, shaking a finger at the man. "How about you two?" he asked the two men as he approached them.

"We were told to keep everyone away from here until we finished cleaning up the mess."

"Told by who?"

"*I* told them," a voice from behind us said.

When I turned around, I found Wendell Banks standing on the river shore, his wing tip shoes covered in mud.

"What's the deal with Early's car?" I asked the man.

"That's the whole deal," the man said. "We're going to haul it over to the yard and maybe see if we can salvage anything. I told these men to keep the public out of the area so they could get done. They're getting paid by the hour."

"Okay, so I'm sure you didn't mean the chief's sister, just looking after her dead brother's affairs."

"I mean anyone. This is official town business, and you two don't count as official, so why don't you be on your way?"

I thought about arguing, but I didn't see anything more to gain by hanging around. So smiling up at my mysterious friend, I shrugged my shoulders and we headed off.

"Well," I said to the man, "I guess you saved my life."

"Oh, I don't think those three meant any harm."

"I don't know," I said taking a good look at my hero, trying to place his voice, because a thick beard hid his face. "They looked on the harmful side to me."

"Well, Emma, I don't think they'll be bothering you anymore."

"Oh no," I said, recognizing his midnight blue eyes behind the dark beard.

"Well, don't strain yourself," he chuckled.

"Jeff Carson…" I shouted out, rushing into the arms of my old high school sweetheart.

"About time," he smiled down at me, showing off a mouthful of white teeth. "Have I changed that much?"

"So sorry, I was kind of preoccupied."

"That's okay, I guess I *have* changed some."

"Well, well," I said, welcoming his light blue aura in the dull surroundings, "I guess I owe you a kiss or something for rescuing me."

"That's okay," he declined, and I couldn't help feeling a bit disappointed that he turned down my lighthearted offer.

"So, what *are* you doing out here?"

"You, too?"

"Now, don't get all riled up," he said, raising his hands in a defensive position, "I'm just curious, is all."

I smiled at him then, recalling our high school days, all pleasant enough—at least, until I went off to college and left him behind. Jeff and I were the same age, and one of his brothers use to run with Early.

"Sorry, those three put a scare into me."

"Oh, they're just some boys working on orders."

"So, what about you? You like saving women in distress?"

"I heard you back in the diner where your conversation with the Shaws interrupted my breakfast."

"Oh…"

"Yep, I'm always interested in what the Shaws have to say."

"Why so?"

"Oh, let's just say I have a business interest."

"That's a little mysterious."

"Is it," he said, turning about and leading me off toward the muddy bank.

He led the way up the steep incline, and reaching back, held out his hand for me to take, which I did, feeling a familiar shock. I gripped his hand hard, holding on, although I didn't need to. I'd been climbing steeper banks than that one near all my life, but I appreciated the gentlemanly offer and wasn't about to refuse, holding on to him for the entire climb up to the road's edge…holding on to the past, and the memory of young love.

"Well," he said when we reached the road, grasping my hand a bit longer than necessary, "do you need anything else?"

"No, no, I appreciate the help," I said, as I released his hand. "So, what have you been up to all these years?"

"Just working steady in the shop."

"Is your pa still working there?"

"He's semi-retired now, although he comes by now and then to check on the place."

"How's Caroline?" I asked after his sister, a one-time good friend of mine.

"She does the books, but mostly stays at home with her kids."

"I see her posts on Facebook. She's got a bunch."

"Five of them, at last count."

"I'll have to call and catch up with her, now that I'm home."

"You should, I'm sure she'd like it."

"How about you? Married, kids?"

"No…you know, still looking, I guess."

"That's surprising, fellow like you."

"How about you? Are you still chasing that rainbow?"

"Yep, I'm still chasing it."

"Haven't tired yet?"

"I might be slowing down some, but I've still got life left in the old legs."

"I can see that, still got your spunk."

"What do you mean?"

"I saw how you handled those two goons back at the diner and the big fellow there. I can see you haven't lost your way with men."

"I take that as a compliment."

"So, what are you doing out here?"

"I don't know. Just curious, is all."

"About what?"

"I don't know how Early could just blow through that rail. He must have driven this way a thousand times, so I just don't see it."

"Then, what?"

"That's kind of what I'm looking in to."

After a long pause, during which I expected another warning about snooping but didn't get, I changed the subject. "Say, maybe we can get together, I mean now that I'm home for a spell."

"You plan to stay long?"

"Maybe. That depends."

"Depends on what?" he asked, ending the talk and walking off toward his red truck, leaving me standing alone on the edge of the cliff.

Well, I'll be, I thought, watching him drive off, wondering about the man. I turned back to the cordoned off area. The scene stood bleak, and when I tried to return to the task of analyzing the crime scene, the memory of Jeff Carson, heart throb from my youth, rushed in and dominated my thoughts.

I made it a point to remember to drop by his sister's place and see if I could get a bit more information on her brother and what he'd been up to all these years.

With no plan for the next couple of hours before meeting

with the mayor, I decided I'd take a chance and try to catch Becky and my four nephews at her mom and dad's place. I figured the boys would be home from school, staying close by; you know, with their daddy dead, and all.

Becky's mom and daddy lived on the edge of the town limits on 200 acres of rolling land that used to be the biggest dairy farm in the county, back when her grandparents ran the place. When her grandparents died, her dad turned it into a mix use farm and survivalist camp. John Bernard Davis, or JB as his friends called him, ex-Vietnam vet, kept a small herd of Jerseys for the milk, cream, cheese and the occasional table beef they provided. The dairy played first fiddle in JB Davis's plan, a means of survival when, he thought, the feds would come in and try to take his guns.

The Davis's story and a half Cape Cod sported a fresh coat of battleship gray paint. On the east side of the house, one of those steel buildings covered a new looking RV that stretched over 50 feet. A canvas covered boat and a couple of jet skis were parked nearby, while several old trucks and run-down cars shared the yard on the west side of the house.

Early's oldest son, Little Earl, stood under a square open-sided metal building working on a beat-up red Jeep. Using a flat knife, Little Earl carefully applied bonding filler to a deep dent in one of the front panels, using the knife edge to fan out the thick goo. Most of the faded finish paint on the Jeep had been sanded smooth and covered by a layer of gray primer. Early's three other dark-haired boys, ages 14, 12, and 10, busily worked on various other sections of the old Jeep, sanding them down for a smooth finish of primer. The dust from the sanding covered the boys in a white mist, making them appear ghost-like.

"Shouldn't you all be wearing a mask or something?" I

41

shouted to the group after I parked between a new-looking silver SUV and an old red pickup.

The youngest of the boys, Johnny, came running when he saw me get out of the Jeep.

"Aunt Emma!" he yelled, leaping into my arms.

"Johnny Shaw," I hugged the boy as he came close to toppling me over, getting white dust all over me, "looks like you grew a foot since last summer. What's your ma feeding you?" I kidded the boy who looked and filled out like his mama, light and whimsy.

The other three boys came jogging up and I tussled and prodded William and Larry, each in turn, like sizing up livestock to buy.

I reached out with my right hand to greet the oldest boy, Little Earl. Taking my hand in his he squeezed hard and pulled me towards him then he jabbed a left-hand finger into my right ribs, a gag move his daddy liked to play on unsuspecting parties and family members with short memories. I shook it off, grabbing him by the shoulders, and after manhandling him for a bit, stood him up to me, back-to-back, and saw he stood a foot taller. He carried a Shaw build, muscled and full, unlike his shorter mom, filling it out to a maximum. Although I hadn't seen it firsthand, I knew the boy could play football, too.

The second boy, William, stood equal in height and looked like a bull. He showed a face full of freckles like his mom.

The third boy, Larry, grew into a mix of the families. He wouldn't grow quite as tall as the Shaws, but he was built like a horse and kept a smile going as wide as his face could allow.

"So, you all working hard on that Jeep?" I said to the group as a whole.

"You got to get the wrinkles out in the dent filler," Little Earl said, "if you want a smooth finish. Otherwise, it looks like an amateur job with all those bumps."

"But what about those masks?"

"Oh, Grandpa gets after us about it," Little Earl said, "but we forget."

The dairy barn sat at the far back of the makeshift work site but within a short walk of the house. As I discussed health issues with the four boys, Becky and Mr. JB Davis came out of the barn, heading our way. Although strong as a mule and mean as a cat, Mr. Davis wouldn't dress out at more than 150 pounds sopping wet. His whole family grew on the slight side, short and wirily—Becky too—and all with auras racing across the rainbow spectrum depending on circumstances. Becky joined her boys and said, "So, did you see your pa last night?"

"Yeah, all squared away."

Mr. Davis caught up to the bunch of us and we all walked toward the house, but before we got there, Mother Davis called out to the boys to wash off with the garden hose before trying to enter her clean kitchen. Broad and strong, Mother Davis bore three children, but her two boys both died young; one in Afghanistan fighting for his country, and the other driving fast through the hills trying to outrun the County Sheriff. She blamed the government for both of her boys' deaths. In many ways, I didn't blame her.

Mrs. Davis smiled at me and said, "Good to see you, Emma Louise," as we watched the boys spray water on each other, "although I'm sorry about the circumstances."

"Yes, ma'am, I know," I answered, following everyone up the back steps, as Becky and the boys finished up with their garden hose baths.

"Yes, Emma," Mr. Davis said, "we are sure sorry about the chief."

"Thanks, JB," I answered. "Are you still in the milking business?"

"I keep twenty or so cows," he said, moving on to sit in a porch chair. "I trim the old girls out once in a while and keep the best. I can get twenty gallons a day out of some of them, good cheese, too. Man over in Hickory comes by and picks up the milk. He operates some type of organic food company. We calve three or four a year and I pull the oldest girls out to butcher and put the meat up. These boys can go through some beef."

"Are you making any money?" I asked the man as the four boys and Becky scrambled up the steps and headed through the back door that led to their grandmother's kitchen and food.

"You know it's not about the money, Emma, but the independence," he said, stopping and pointing out to the planted fields. "I can grow all the corn and soybeans I need for feed. I got apples to spare and put up for the winter. I've got more potatoes in the cellar than we could eat in a year, and Mrs. Davis cans everything out of the garden we don't eat fresh. Between the old cows I butcher and the deer I bring down out of the mountain we have enough meat to last a spell."

"Well, I can see you got it all figured out."

"I try to take care of my responsibilities."

"I wonder if Early saw to his responsibilities, if he made arrangements for Becky and the boys."

"Well," he said, and continued with what I would describe as a smirk. "He seemed like he was making out alright."

"What's that supposed to mean?" I asked him.

"I'm not the one to say things."

I didn't like the tone or direction of the conversation seemed to be heading, but I said, "Go on, you started it, what's eating you?"

The man shrugged his shoulders and getting up he looked through the back porch screened door, checking on the family.

"What's on your mind?" I asked again, a dirty gray silver aura forming about him, denoting skepticism on life.

JB walked back, and sitting down, said, "Emma, seems like Early got into something here, lately."

"What do you mean?"

"I think you know what I mean."

"Mr. Davis, sir, I don't much like what you are saying."

"Emma," the man said, addressing me with a stare," I don't know that I care what you like, when it comes to that little girl in there. That's my little girl in there, and I'd kill the man that put her in danger."

"What are you saying?"

"Early started running with a mean crowd, lately."

"What?"

"Yes, ma'am, backwoods boys, running drugs back in the mountains."

"I don't believe that, Mr. Davis."

"I didn't, either, but I asked him about it one day."

"What did Early say?"

"He didn't deny it. In fact, he threatened me, throwing his position at me, being Chief of Police and all. Heck, you know I don't have much use for the law out here. He told me to stay out of his business."

"Maybe you should have."

"He got himself into something, Emma, and it cost him."

"What are you talking about?"

"Something he'd been making extra money on."

"What do you mean?"

"Early knew where the dark things grew and he'd go in and get them. That's why he was so good at his job, and I'll tell you another thing."

"What?"

"I'd leave this matter to rest, if I were you."

"What matter?"

"This looking into Early's accident."

"Who says I'm looking?"

"Words around town, but it's better to let this be."

"Why?"

"Early's dead and gone now, nothing we can do to change that, no need dragging up the how and who. Becky would be better off, too."

I didn't know about Becky and whether she'd be better off or not. Depended on what I might find out. What I didn't know was how the word spread so fast that JB Davis knew all about it. I needed to get into town and see what the mayor had to say.

Chapter Six

The Mayor

On the drive down to town, I re-played the conversation with JB over in my head but wasn't convinced of the crazy old man's accusations. I'd have to hear from Becky myself before I'd believe it. For all his faults, I just couldn't believe my big brother would get into anything illegal. I'd have to have a sit down with Becky and hash it out.

A few minutes later, I pulled up in front of Town Hall and parked next to a bright, silver Mercedes I surmised belonged to the mayor, and a big older model red Cadillac that, except for needing painting, looked pretty nice. I used to dream about owning a convertible like that.

I turned the engine off and paused for a minute, steeling myself for the meeting ahead. A cool air greeted me as I pushed through the building's tall doors into a quiet foyer.

The mayor's office suite contained an outer room with a counter in front of an administrative area. A small conference room visible from the glass double door entry stood to the rear of the area next to a private door that I'm sure led to Franklyn's office. Several plush looking pieces of furniture crowded the little rooms. Surprising, a pretty blond lady sat behind the counter. She looked up from her smart phone and greeted me with a smile as I came in. The sign attached to her desk counter identified her as Shelby Stone.

"Good morning, ma'am," she said, in a northern accent not familiar to the mountains of the Blue Ridge. "May I help you?"

The woman was dressed in a tight-fitting black dress with long sleeves, cut extra low in the front. "Yes, yes, I'm here to see the mayor."

47

Ruben D. Gonzales

"Well," she said, thumbing a page over on a desk calendar, and continuing in the same demeanor and accent added, "I don't see an appointment for him for this time?"

"Are you sure," I smiled at her, seeing a blue pastel aura surround her, like a fine mist over water, denoting a sensitive nature.

"Yes, his appointment schedule is right here, but I don't see any appointments for him right now."

"Well, you see," I began, shaking the dim image from my head and taking a good look at the woman. I thought her dress a bit tight for office wear, she holding a few extra pounds, but remembering the mayor, I'm sure he enjoyed it. "I ran into Franklyn this morning at breakfast, you know, and maybe he hasn't had a chance to tell you. He might have sent you a message."

"Well…" she said, picking up her phone and fumbling with the screen, "he could have, but I don't see it. It could have got hung up in transit. The service around here is pretty slow."

Just then, Mayor Franklyn Shaw opened the inner door and spurted out.

"Emma," he called across the room before reaching me with an outstretched hand. "Right on time, I see."

"I like to be punctual, when I can."

"I see you've met my assistant." The mayor nodded in the direction of the lady behind the counter.

"No, we haven't met."

"Emma, this is Shelby Stone, Banks and Sister Evelyn's daughter. Shelby, this is Emma Shaw."

"Pleased to meet you," I greeted the pretty woman. After the introduction, the mayor grabbed me by the arm and tried to direct me away toward his office.

"You're Emma Shaw," she asked with more interest in my visit, "Chief Shaw's little sister?"

"Yes, I am, did you know the chief?"

"Of course, she did, Emma," Mayor Franklyn Shaw said,

48

interrupting, "they worked across the hall from each other for close to two years, now."

"Sure," I said, pulling my arm away from him and returning my attention to Shelby Stone. "Did you know him well?"

"He talked about you some."

"Oh, yeah? What did he say about me?"

"He said you were a hippy artist!"

I laughed and said, "He did, huh? Well, that's more right than not on that point."

"Oh, he didn't say it in a bad way."

"No?"

"No, more like…"

"Like what?"

"Like…like he envied you."

A large assortment of paraphernalia from Franklyn's college days dominated the walls and bookcases in his inner office. A couple of diploma-looking framed documents stood out among the batch, but their fancy, elaborate, cursive writing made it difficult to read. As far as I could tell, Franklyn earned something between a Doctor of something and the number one salesperson award for the month of August 1999.

I took a seat in front of an expansive desk across from the mayor and said, "That's quite a secretary out there, Franklyn."

"Administrative assistant."

"Oh, is that what they call them now?"

"Don't be crude, Emma…not like your brother; it's not in your nature. That's Bank's daughter, from a previous marriage."

"I'd be careful what you say, Franklyn. I'm not in a great mood to start."

"Look," he said, leaning back in his chair, his aura fluttering about him, fluctuating in the dark pink range of untruthfulness. "Everyone is sorry about Chief Shaw and we are going to do right by his family, but the man's gone and we can't do anything about that. He died in an accident."

"I don't think so."

"You don't think so what?"

"I don't think he died in an accident."

"What makes you say that?"

"I went out and looked at the scene of the wreck and it doesn't add up for me."

"What?"

"The way his car went through the barrier there and landed way out in the river."

"What doesn't add up?"

"If Early rolled through that curve at a normal speed, he would have maybe slid off the bank as he rounded that turn, ended up down there on the shore maybe. But the way he burst through that rail and ended up way out in the river…well, I just don't see it. Early would have to had to be hitting a hundred miles an hour to launch that heavy cruiser out that far."

"Maybe he was in a hurry?"

"That could be, but only in a pursuit, like in a job-related pursuit. That's why. Gilmore said the force of the car hitting the water killed him."

"Why does he say that?"

"He said he died when he hit the water because there was no water in his lungs, so he didn't drown."

"Gilmore," he laughed, "since when is old man Gilmore our resident forensic expert?"

"He's the closest thing in town without Early around. And while I'm on the subject, what are you going to do with Early's car?"

"His what?"

"You heard me. His car."

"We are hauling it over to the yard. We've got a crew over there now, fishing it out. It's pretty much a total but I'm hoping to sell it for parts to recoup some expenses. Old back country boys will buy just about anything."

"Why so fast? You need to keep it for the investigation."

"Look, we took a look into it and that's it, he died in an accident."

"Well, that's interesting," I said, noticing his aura veering into the pink range. "As I see it, with Early gone, I don't see much experience in the department to come to that conclusion, and since we are on subject, just what about all these cut-backs?"

"There've been some cut-backs, sure, what local government hasn't in these challenging times to balance the department's budgets? We tax at what the state allows, but we still come up short, so we tighten the belt when we have to."

"Including cutting the police department?"

"I'd cut the library budget if I thought I could get away with it, but the literary guild would have my hide for sure if I tried that. But things are looking up."

"How so?"

"We just got approved for a Historical Renovation Grant from the state for the old water mill on the river. We got the mill on the Historical Places list and it's eligible for a big grant. We have an elaborate plan to renovate the thing and turn it into a tourist site with a museum, a gift shop, even a petting zoo. Once we get operational and start to charge entrance fees and markup in the gift shop, we might be able to ease off the pressure on the departments. All we got to do is get the funds in here."

"What's holding it up?"

"Oh, these grants come with a load of paperwork; certificates, bonds, audits, estimates, you name it. Banks is working through everything, and says he's close to finishing. Until then, it's tighten up your belt."

I rose from the chair and paced across the room to a window that overlooked the front lawn of Town Hall. A large magnolia tree shaded this side of the building from the sun, lucky to keep its leaves year-round, though during the winter it didn't fare well with the mountain snow. Turning back to the man, I said, "Look, Franklyn, I want to see this thoroughly investigated. Now, I understand the staff on hand is real short on experience, manpower, and apparently, interest; so I am going to take a look into Early's so-called accident."

"Do you think you're more qualified?"

"I couldn't do worse."

"Well, Emma, let us worry about that. I know we might be a little hillbilly town to you, but the resources are here to handle this. Randall put in eight years with the State Prosecutors Office before coming back here to be Town Attorney, so we've plenty of experience on board. Now, we've looked into it and are satisfied Early died in an accident, so you need to stop your snooping."

"What are you telling me?"

"I'm telling you to stop this amateur investigation of yours," he said waving the ruler at me like a schoolteacher, his aura pulsating between brown and dirty brown, denoting, among other things, a certain disposition to insecurity, "and let us handle it."

"Or what?"

"Or you'll find yourself in a heap of trouble. You don't belong in Black Mountain, anymore, and we don't like outsiders poking their noses where they shouldn't. You need to drop this and finish up your personal affairs and put Early to rest."

"Listen up, Franklyn," I said, moving to the front of his desk and looking down at the man. "I'm here for the week and it's only Monday, so you're going to be seeing a lot of me around town. Now, you don't have enough men to run an investigation, so I'm going to be looking into the matter of how my big brother died…and I'm telling you to stay out of *my* way. I've advised my paper I'm here and would be spending some time poking around, and there's a chance a story could run on little Black Mountain. So unless you want a color spread in the biggest paper in the state, then *you'd* better be careful."

"I wouldn't do that, Emma; you might be sorry."

"What are you talking about?"

"Emma, you know, your brother…he knew how to get what he wanted, and he wasn't afraid to cut a few corners if it suited him. I don't know what got into him these last few years, likely all those hits he took playing football. He could be hard to deal with, and not everyone in town will be sad to see him gone."

"I don't see it that way, Mr. Mayor."

"Look, Emma, Early ran that department as his own chiefdom. The less I knew about his dealings, the better I liked it. To tell the truth, as long as he kept crime down in town, it didn't matter to me. He could have at it."

I didn't respond right away, caught a little by surprise by the insinuations, but stood my ground.

After a long pause, he said, "Now, you put this to rest quiet like and we'll see to it that Becky and the boys are taken care of, way past what Early arranged for them. We don't have to, but the Shaws look after their own. You keep this up and the only one coming out of this bruised is your brother."

I stood there, not sure what to say, anger welling up in me, along with disappointment. What did he know about Early? "Look, Franklyn, I know you and Granddaddy have discussed this. Maybe Early wasn't a saint, but he deserved more, and I'm going to find out what happened, no matter what Granddaddy says."

"You leave Granddaddy out of this."

"Glory, Franklyn, no one makes a move in this town without Granddaddy approving it and you know it."

"Emma, I'd be careful about sticking that nose of yours into things you don't know anything about."

"Why?"

Ruben D. Gonzales

"Because you may not like what you find out."

♦◊♦

The Shaws thought they were due what they owned or controlled in Black Mountain, arriving among the first families into the Swannanoa Valley. Before Hernando DeSoto, who came through around 1540, the valley belonged to the Cherokee. DeSoto and his men left behind tuberculosis and measles and after the Indian population thinned out, mountain men came in trapping and trading. Pioneers heard tales of the mighty Smoky Mountains to the west of the coastal regions and explored the valley. After the Revolutionary War, the lands along the Swannanoa Valley opened to settlers. Samuel Davidson started the settler movement, coming across the Blue Ridge in 1784.

The first Shaw, Walter Shaw, bearing a land grant given for his service in the Revolutionary War, came close behind. He brought his family and several slaves across the Swannanoa Gap around 1788. Frontiersman Daniel Boone came through the valley and married a local woman before heading further west and settling Kentucky.

Other families followed, and although faced with the hardships of pioneer life, they thrived on the rich land, wild game and fish, nuts and berries, greens, and honey from bee trees. Roads built in the early 1800's brought wagons into the valley carrying more settlers.

With the increase in population came the increase for trade, and the Shaws recognized the opportunity and set up a general store in 1850, and the lumber mill in 1890. The mill met the needs of the growing communities in the valley and then the railroad that began to service the mountain towns. Fed by an assortment of local prime hardwoods a furniture industry blossomed, along with the industrial revolution. Until the oak in the mountains ran out, and the industry started to use a variety of veneers for tabletops, the Shaws ran the town of Black Mountain pretty much like they owned it.

Starting with Walter on up to the seventh generation Lawrence, the current Granddaddy of the family, the Shaws have dominated town business and politics. Oh, no one says it out loud, but you know they know your business and anyone's business is Shaw business.

In addition to the mill and diner, the Shaws own the town bank, the local real estate company, the general store, and the grocery franchise, as well. If you build, tear down, buy or sell, or got to run to the ladies' room, the Shaws know about it.

Before leaving Town Hall, I poked my head into the Police Department office. I opened the heavy door and stepped into a bright though silent office setting, right out of a 1950s B movie.

"Mighty quiet in here," I said to a lone town officer sitting behind an ancient computer monitor. "Shouldn't there be more going on?" I let the door close behind me. A dark wood railing separated the administration work stations from the small public waiting area. The rear wall of the office suite housed two identical doors, each with a different title stenciled in black paint on the upper half of the door; 'Chief Shaw' and 'Storage'. "Like an investigation," I explained to the man."

A series of old photos hung on the interior wall forming a gallery of the LMPD. Officers from different generations proudly smiled at the camera capturing them in time.

"You must be Chief Shaw's sister," the young man said, standing up from a small metal desk, guessing my identity as I let myself in.

"That's right, and you are ...?"

"Officer Carter," he said. "I heard you were snooping around."

"You heard?"

"Well, you know, small town and all," he said with a smile that disappeared when he remembered. "Sure sorry about your brother."

"Thanks, I appreciate that," I said as he sat back down in his chair, looking sad enough.

The office hung heavy with Early's leftover energy aura.

"One tough guy," he said. "I'll give you that."

"Yeah, Early could be a hard man when provoked."

"How's Becky Shaw taking it?"

"Oh," I paused a second, wondering at the young man's interest in Becky. "She's doing about as good as can be expected."

"Well, tell her I asked about her if you see her."

"Say, Carter," I said, getting back to the subject, watching his aura pulse in the orange range of confidence, "were you the officer that found the chief that morning?"

"That's right." He got up from his chair and crossed the narrow room to a set of file cabinets. "How did you know?"

"Well, with two of you, I had a 50/50 chance of guessing."

Officer Carter put a file on top of the cabinet.

"So you were the first one on the scene?"

"No, Mr. Banks arrived first, then I pulled in just before the Doc."

"Doctor Shaw?"

"He put in an appearance," Carter said, returning to his desk and sitting down, "although he didn't stay long."

"When did the mayor show up?"

"He came next, and then Randall Shaw."

"That all, no one else?"

"No."

"Who reported it?"

"A trucker went by the spot and saw the hole in the guard rail and called 911. Officer Green took the call and relayed it to me. I hustled out and saw the Chief's cruiser upside down in the river. I waded in and pulled the chief out, but he'd been under a good hour so…" He stopped his dialogue for a spell. "Anyway, old man Gilmore came out about an hour after that and the mayor told him to get the chief up and take him in."

"They took him right to the funeral home…not the hospital?"

"No, everyone knew the chief died in that river."

"Tell me, Carter, did Early have his seat belt on when you found him?"

"No. No, he didn't."

"Was that unusual for Early?"

"It would be unusual for the chief…he stayed on to us to buckle up. He must have left out in a hurry that night if he didn't buckle his seat belt."

"Did you get a chance to survey the area for any other clues?"

"Survey?"

"Yes, investigate. You know, look around."

"No, ma'am, Ms. Shaw, I didn't pick up on much, you know, lot of water out there."

"So no one took a look around?"

"Well, everyone seemed to be busy, but I think the mayor and Randall Shaw looked over the scene."

"Okay, Officer Carter," I said with a little less rancor, "do you think I can take a look at the file?"

"What file?"

"The file on Early's accident."

"Well, I don't think there's a file or anything, more like a report."

"Well, okay, can I see the report?"

Officer Carter reached down to his desk and picked up a piece of paper, holding it like weighing it for value before handing it over.

I took the sheet of paper from him and it took me seconds to scan the report.

"Is this it?"

"That's it."

"Kind of thin, isn't it?"

"Well, the chief was the one who investigated cases. He took care of all the complex stuff."

"What about you and Office Green?"

"Oh, we took the Police Science course over at Morgan Tech, but it was all book stuff, nothing practical. The chief handled any real investigations and kept his files in his office; he could be secretive."

"Okay, Carter, I'm not accusing you of anything. Say," I said, handing him back the report and changing the subject, "are you kin to Coach Carter, coached the high school football team and girls' softball back when?"

"That's right, he's my grandpappy."

"Sure enough?"

"Yes, ma'am."

"Is he still coaching?"

"He stopped full-time coaching a while back. He helps out with the football team part-time for no pay."

"Oh, who's coaching now?"

"Brandon Shaw's been the football coach for the last couple years."

"Brandon?"

"That's Randall Shaw's son."

"Don't believe I know him."

"He played at Guilford and came back here to teach right after finishing school. He worked as the assistant under Grandpa then took over when the state made faculty members get their teacher certifications."

"That's a shame."

"He got in his thirty years to retirement, so he didn't mind."

"Oh, well I'd like to talk to him about the old times."

"You can catch him at the diner if you hurry. He's there on the weekdays for lunch."

"I might do that."

◆◇◆

The lunch crowd came early, so by 1:00 the diner appeared empty when I passed through the doors for the second time that day. June ran plates of food to a couple of people along the counter and nodded her head at me as she went by, but more than half of the booths stood empty.

I recognized Coach Carter in one of the booths, his bright yellow aura pulsing his capacity at playfulness that you'd associate with a coach. He sat opposite another man about the same age and size, whose aura remained hidden, although I could see an outline of black signifying un-forgiveness. Coach filled out his side of the booth, although he didn't look like he carried any more weight than the last time I saw him.

When Early played in college, coach and several town dads made a frequent Saturday trip east to watch the games. Early would round up as many non-conference game tickets for them as possible, and the men brought a tail gate of barbecue and beer. If Early couldn't get enough tickets for everyone they'd draw lots for the stadium seats and the rest of the men would stay in the parking lot eating and drinking, listening to the games on the radio.

"Hey, Coach," I called out to the man, approaching his table.

"Emma Louise!" he shouted back, sticking out his hand. "You're as pretty as ever." He smiled up at me, but then his smile faded as he figured the reason I found him. "Sure sorry about your brother."

"Yeah, well, bad stuff happens."

"Have a seat," Coach offered, sliding over against the window.

"Thanks, Coach…" I sat down and got comfortable. "I hoped to catch you here."

"Oh," he started, but remembered his booth mate. "Sorry,

Maury, this is Emma Shaw, Chief Shaw's little sister. She used to be a spunky second baseman on the softball team."

"I remember Emma," the man said, holding out his hand, his aura making a quivering appearance, showing a dull black. "Early played with my boy, Mikey Wade."

"Sure, I remember, Mikey played on the line for those championship years."

"That's right."

"What's Mikey up to, he still up at the mill?"

"Well," he said letting my hand go, his aura turning the gray sign of distress, "he put in about twenty years, but sorry to say, Mikey passed away last year."

"Oh, I'm sad to hear that."

"Yeah," he said wiping his mouth and picking up his check, "well, shit happens."

"Sometimes."

"You know, Emma," the man said, "we were all sorry about Early."

"Well, like we were saying."

"Yep," he said to me as he stood up and turned to the register, "real sorry."

He half-waved at us as he made his way to the counter to pay his bill.

"Coach," I said, "I didn't know about Mikey."

"Oh, ain't your fault girl, it's still a little soon for Maury. Maury and his wife only had the one boy."

"How did he die?"

"Cancer."

"Oh, no…"

"Yeah, came on real fast."

"What caused it?"

"I don't know but..."

"But what?"

"Well," the man said lowering his voice and looking around to see how close the nearest customers sat. "Rumor has it that it's something up at the mill."

"What do you mean?"

"There've been others up at the mill to come up sick."

"Where did he work up there?"

"He worked in the glue station."

"Did anyone check into it?"

"No, you know the Shaws wouldn't allow anything like that. Besides," he said, picking up his coffee mug and taking a swallow, "too late for Mikey. You should have seen the way he wasted away, like overnight. Tough to see him there in the hospital bed, all of a hundred pounds at the end. 'Course, the mill took care of everything for the family."

I paused a minute. I hadn't heard a hint of anything improper going on up at the mill. Breaking the silence, Coach said, "So you were trying to catch me? How'd you know I'd be here?"

"Your grandboy told me."

"Stevie?" he asked.

"Yep, I saw him up at Town Hall and he told me you ate lunch up here every day."

"Now, that ain't exactly true," he defended, laughing about it. "I don't come up here on Saturday or Sunday, not unless Mrs. Carter takes a hankering for waffles."

"So how are you?"

"Not bad for an old retired guy."

"Stevie says you are still coaching a little?"

"Oh, they keep me around as a mascot, a relic of the glory of Bronco Football."

"Who's this 'they' person."

"The Shaws."

"Granddaddy in particular?"

"In particular, but Brandon likes to remind the team that championships are in the town blood."

"How's the team doing?"

"They beat up on the out of conference teams but since

61

then 3 and 3 and heading into the last couple games on the regular season schedule. Could still make the playoffs if they finish strong."

"Tough season?"

"It's hard to play with a squad of twenty-five players."

"Short roster?"

"I'll say, all the boys going both ways. By the end of the third quarter, their tails are dragging, and they can't finish. Oh, Little Earl and Wil can keep the team in a game, but even they can't do it all. It's not like when Early played, when the mill worked four hundred men and we'd dress out 60 or 70 boys."

"I suppose tough times at the mill mean tough times everywhere."

"Nothing's changed there. Young families moved out a long time ago or commute to work. Only the old folk left."

"Who do you play Friday night?" I asked changing subjects.

"Lenore's coming in." he said, brightening. "You need to come out to the game. Everyone does, even Granddaddy."

"What are your chances?" I asked the man, storing the information that Granddaddy might be at the stadium come Friday.

"Good, I'd say, 50/50, although it's a large school now. After the furniture industry sank, the town branched out and went high tech. A lot of new families moved into the county from out west, California kids. All the families seem to build around the lake so the high school is stocked with players."

"You'll give them a game, though, right Coach?"

"Sure, we will," he said with enthusiasm. "By the way, the school's trying to set up a commemoration of some sort for Early at the half. Maybe that will get the boys fired up for a strong finish!"

"You think William and Little Earl will still play?"

"Oh, I hope so since the other quarterback on the team is Hunter Shaw."

"Hunter Shaw?"

"That's Mathew Shaw's youngest son. He goes both ways, too. He's an alright corner but he can't throw a lick."

"Would Early want the boys to play?"

"Well, it is what Early would expect, hard on his boys as he could be—especially Little Earl. They stood at odds on a lot of things, but no one could stand up to Early for long. Yep, Early would expect it, but that's not the reason Little Earl needs to play Friday."

"What then?"

"Little Earl has to play because if he doesn't, we'll lose for sure!"

"I bet Becky will have them play, then."

"So, you going to look into all this?"

"What makes you think that?"

"Oh, there's talk in town, you know how it is."

"I see nothing's changed about that."

"No, and another thing…"

"What?"

"I'd be careful what closets you shake up."

"You too?"

"Just be careful, young lady. The Shaw family still runs this town, and they don't take to people meddling in their affairs."

Chapter Seven

The Mill

I drove north on the Mill Road, a steep winding grade, with as many curves as the pieces in Early's case. Coach Carter added his warning to the list I started accumulating since coming to town, and I knew it would be foolish not to take his counsel.

Hidden in a perpetual mist, Shaw Mill, like an ancient castle, its shadow dark and oppressive, sat on a bald bluff above the north shore of Swannanoa River. Earlier in its history, the river flow turned a heavy breast shot water wheel that powered a big saw, but when the mill grew they converted to a back shot wheel and put it to turning a turbine to produce electricity.

With power generation, the mill operation added several more saws and moved up the ridge to its current location. Black Mountain log poles carried the lines that funneled the power to a hodgepodge of tin-roofed buildings covering ten acres of site that at one time employed several hundred men from the town.

When a coal burning plant down in the piedmont funneled cheap electricity into the town, the waterwheel power lines were directed into the houses along mill row until power generation came under regulation. Since then, the town took its power from a statewide grid with the waterwheel set to evolve into a tourist attraction, complete with a gift shop and I'm sure a Shaw-owned bakery.

A newer looking cedar shingle covered building stood guard at the gate to the compound, and I pulled the Jeep over and parked in one of several graveled parking spots. Three late model trucks sat side by side in the lot and I wondered if Granddaddy Shaw owned one of them.

I pulled the Jeep sun visor down and flipped open the cover of the little vanity mirror there to check my look. I took a brush and ran it through my hair a couple of times, then pulled the long strands taut and redid the scrunch. I dug a lip gloss out of the glove box and went over my lips hoping the little shine would smooth out the cracks and soften my look.

A couple of tractor haulers stood in line waiting to unload, their diesel engines idling loudly. A giant crane with claw attachment snatched the raw logs off the trailers, two and three at a time. With a roar, and twirling 180 degrees, the crane dropped the logs into a pile with a crash. A front loader pecked through the pile, sorting the logs into some division of quality I wasn't sure of, packing flat beds full, pulling forward and reverse with a backup buzzer sending a warning through the air.

At intervals, another truck powered its way out of the mill and, hooking up a trailer, hauled a chosen stack up into the mill proper where the saws waited. The noise from the big saws could be heard even above the racket in the yard.

The office building sported a nice porch and a massive double oak door welcomed visitors. I skipped up the steps, and muscling open the door, stepped inside, closing the door behind me and shutting out the yard din.

"Emma Shaw," a large man called to me as I crossed the threshold. The voice belonged to Mathew Shaw, or at least someone that used to be Mathew Shaw. The bald head and about 100 extra pounds separated him from the slim quarterback that, during his playing days, roamed the field eluding would be tacklers and throwing pin-point passes at clumsy receivers.

Although a couple of years ahead of me I kept up with his on the field exploits. Mathew Shaw, the youngest of the Shaw sons, and I dated for a couple of years before he walked on at

Western and quarterbacked for two years. I used to think we might end up together, but when he went up to Western, he stopped writing and I lost interest and started dating Jeff Carson.

"Mathew," I returned the welcome, entering the space and taking the room in. A black iron wood stove poured heat out into the office area, and a thin layer of soot and sawdust covered the wood floor and the spartan furniture. "Long time!"

"Sure has been," he said, struggling to get to his feet and waiting for me to cross the room. He hitched up his worn jeans as he waited. "So how many years has it been?"

"I couldn't count them," I said, reaching him and offering my hand.

"Is that all I get?" he asked, opening his big arms, waiting for me to respond. I didn't know what I expected after all the years, since I knew the man was married now and had a bunch of kids.

I gave in and let him hug me and tried to ignore his hand slipping down my back and over my rear end. "That's better," he laughed, giving me a squeeze, his earthy green aura ebbing between bright and dim. The noise from his laugh appeared to start from low in his fat belly and erupt up like a volcano spewing lava.

"So how are you, anyhow?" I asked, pushing him away.

"Well," he said, ending his smile and sitting heavily behind his thick metal desk, "up until couple days ago, things were pretty quiet around her. I tell you Emma, we are sorry as can be about your brother. Heck of a thing."

"Thanks," I said, taking a seat in a metal folding chair set in front of his desk. "I appreciate the sympathy."

"Well, sure, you all been like family, and I know Granddaddy Lawrence about cried when he heard. You know our daddy loved your brother."

"A lot of people felt that way, Mathew, so dying like that is a mystery."

"You don't think it an accident?"

"No, he knew that road like the chin he shaved."

"So, what are you thinking?"

"I'm thinking he was chasing someone, all out, foot to the floor fast, and somehow lost control and went through Moore's, but not just accidently.

"Well," he said rocking back in his worn green office chair, "I don't know if you know or not, Emma, but drug traffic has picked up a lot, now-a-days. These backcountry boys grow and run the weed over the mountain like their daddies used to run liquor. They go tearing through the back roads at night, dodging the sheriff and the ATF boys. There's no respect for the law, the old ways, manners—and no conscience. Early knew the trouble; he came across them all the time, right here."

"What do you mean?"

"He seemed to be running in one of my men for something at least once a week."

"Anyone in particular?"

"Girl, Early locked up half the men on the compound at one time or another. I can't tell you how many times a month I bailed some dingbat out so we can keep the place running. What with the men out sick half the time and Early picking up the other half for possession, it's a wonder we kept the place operating at all."

"That bad?"

"You bet… Early had a regular little thing going for him."

"What are you talking about?"

"Nothing, nothing," he said, a smile forming, "just that Early booked a bit aggressively when it came to a little weed possession. Now, don't say anything, Emma, not to Granddaddy in particular, but for costs sake, I wish they'd make personal use legal. That would save Shaw Mill a lot of bail money."

"Mathew, what are you implying?"

"Well, I'm sure you'll hear about it, but Early and the town magistrate, Walker Shaw, worked a deal where he'd get a return on each fine the town collected. It made a nice little monthly bonus for Early."

"Sounds legal enough."

"Oh, sure…"

"Did the mayor know about this?"

"Yes, ma'am, everyone knew; cost of doing business is all."

"Well, I'm looking into this, and what happened that night."

"How can I help?"

"I want to talk to Granddaddy, Mathew, find out why Franklyn has it in for my brother."

"What do you mean?"

"All the cutbacks and cutting his department and all. It seems a shame treating Early like that after the years he put in."

"I wouldn't know about that, Emma, and neither would Granddaddy."

"Oh, come on, Mathew, we both know that Granddaddy knows everything that goes on in this town. Let me talk to him."

"Sorry, Emma, he's not here today. Fact is, he doesn't spend a whole lot of time up here, anymore. These days, he stays out at the farm working the vineyard."

"Vineyard?"

"You didn't know?"

"Know what?"

"Granddaddy's in the wine business."

"You're kidding me!"

"No, serious, he and Rusty Burton took about 50 acres of rolling land along the southernmost ridge of the farm and planted vines. Brought them in from God knows where."

"How's it going?"

"Tourists love the place."

"I'd like to see it," I told Mathew.

"We even built a tasting room out of one of the barns, open to the public."

"So do you think I could talk to Granddaddy out there?"

"No, he'd not be up to talking to you."

"Why not?"

"Granddaddy's getting on in years, Emma, he doesn't get out much these days."

"So who's running things now?"

"I'm running the mill, Franklyn looks after the businesses in town, and we got a man that runs the vineyard."

"So, how is the mill business these days?" I said, trying to change tacks. "I hear different stories around town."

"We get by alright. Few years ago, we converted from hardwood dimension lumber to third grade sheeting."

"Plywood?"

"Grade B for roofing and subfloors. Housing industry provides the demand, and the supply of tall, straight pine is still abundant in the mountains, here, so we can buy local. We're working on a contract with a big box home improvement center, and if that comes through, we'll be sitting pretty."

"Did it cost you, converting over?"

"Some, we owned some of what we needed, and had the space. A lot of old timers squawked, of course. We put in the rotary saw for peeling the veneers and beefed up the dryers. Getting the press area built set us back some, but the trouble comes with the bonding process, and the government EPA regulation. Something about the formaldehyde in the resins we use. Getting to a point a man can't make a decent living with the government red tape in place."

"What kind of manpower are you down to?"

"That's the beauty of the newest technology, Emma, less men are required to run the mill."

"So what are you down to?"

"Give or take, we're down to 100 men on the payroll."

"That's down from a couple of hundred?"

"More, in the old days."

"That must be tough around town, that type of cutback."

"We tried to go in phases, a few here and there. The old timers aged out and we stopped hiring new years ago. Granddaddy could see the furniture industry going to veneers so he looked to the best opportunity left."

"Did the housing bubble burst hurt you?"

"Oh, sure, but construction grade sheeting is in demand across the industry. A hurricane or two a year helps. You should have seen us during Katrina—we worked three shifts."

"Can I take a look around the new operation, see what you've done?"

Mathew Shaw paused before answering, then said, "I guess so." Picking up a desk phone, he said, "Let me call the plant foreman to give you a tour."

Putting hard hats on and stepping through a rear door of the office building, the foreman and I crossed the log yard and entered the veneer mill. A steady noise from a wide saw peeling the thin veneer from a long, straight pine log filled the metal building and made talking difficult. Conveyer belts circulated the veneers off in the direction of the back of the building, where, I assumed, they would be cut to size before drying.

We left that building and walked across the yard, heading to the dryers. About halfway between buildings, one of the crew, carrying a clip board, intercepted us and the foreman stopped to answer a question. I waved at the foreman, motioning that I wanted to go on and he nodded his approval back.

Taking a quick left turn, I hustled to the rear of the mill and found the doorway of another section of the giant building. The smell of resin or glue filled the space, and though large fans pulled air out of the area, I still gagged and coughed from the fumes. I couldn't imagine working in there, breathing that stuff for a long shift.

Pulling a large handkerchief from my pocket, I covered my nose and took a real good look around. A section of the floor contained giant heavy tables where the pre-cut dried sheets of veneer were glued together before they were fed into a press. Several workers using a lift on wheels guided the wide sheets into place, where a machine sprayed something I assumed to be glue, evenly across the surface of the sheets before pressing another veneer layer into place.

Satisfied with my little side excursion, I started to back out of the door when I bumped into someone, the surprise making my heart skip a few beats. I turned and found Mathew Shaw staring down at me. The plant foreman and another worker stood behind him, their blended group aura fluttering between brown, black, and darker.

"Enjoying the tour?" he asked me.

"Now, Mathew," I said, stuffing the red checkered handkerchief back in my rear pocket, "I only wanted a look around."

"Looking for anything in particular?" he smiled.

"Okay, Mathew," I said, and lurched into the whole thing bothering me since I heard about Early. "Here it is. I don't think Early just drove off that curve by accident. Someone ran him off, and I'm looking into it."

Mathew motioned to the two men that they could leave, and turning back to me, asked, "That why you're snooping around up here, because you think we're hiding something?"

"Well, according to Becky, Banks and Early hadn't been getting along."

"Yeah, okay, maybe Banks is a bit of a jerk, but that was between them, not the family."

"Oh, glory, Mathew, you know no one around here makes a move without Granddaddy's approval."

"Still, the family had no beef with Early, at least nothing big enough to kill him."

"What about this EPA thing?"

"What about it?"

"I understand formaldehyde causes cancer."

"Emma, I'm going to ignore what you are saying, this time. Granddaddy cried when he heard about Early. We are all sorry about that, but you shouldn't come up here and imply we're hiding something, or we're involved in some way with his death. Heck, if I wanted to kill Early, I just would have shot him."

The Shaws bonded together, tighter than that resin they use in the plywood they make. I knew it sure would be hard to get anything incriminating out of any of them.

"Well," I said, leaving the building, "Granddaddy hit it right thinking like this with the plywood and the vineyard."

"Oh, there's nothing wrong with his head," Mathew said, following me, letting out another big laugh, "he's just getting old."

Chapter Eight

Main Street

The mill and the din of the yard faded behind me as I drove down the mountain into a thick mist, like being reborn into the silence of the forest. I rolled down the window and welcomed the wet breeze. Not able to see Granddaddy Shaw gnawed at me some, but I figured I'd catch up to him before long.

I put on my ball cap to hold my hair in place and motored down towards town. The mountain road wound tightly around blind curves and I fought the steering wheel for control. The sound of the tires on the crushed Shaw Road drowned out the wail of the engine. The Jeep's transmission fought the steep downhill grade and its echo off the granite walls masked the roar of a descending logging truck approaching from behind.

In the rearview mirror, the logging truck snaked out of the heavy fog, its lights leading the way and blinding. I hesitated speeding up, still unsure of the road pattern, and instead looked for a turn out to let the truck by.

The road held tight to the forest tree line and the shoulder on either side lay deep after decades of erosion from heavy spring rain, leaving me no opportunity to turn off the road and get out of the way of the barreling-toward-me-from-behind truck.

The big rig and I burst completely out of the fog bank and into a morning sunshine that brightened and appeared to straighten the road at the same time. The logging truck lurched forward and whacked the back bumper of the Jeep, sending me fishtailing in the gravel, but I gained control and hit the gas pedal, trying to put some distance between the logging rig and my out-manned vehicle.

Approaching the bottom of the mountain, the "Y" intersection where gravel road and paved road merged rushed to meet me, and I hauled the wheel over and headed east, pulling over to the side of the road as it widened where the paved road took over from the gravel.

In the rearview mirror, I saw the logging truck turn opposite, west towards the interstate, and disappear around a curve where the road hugged a bend in the river.

In the quiet of the cab, with the engine settling into a steady idle, I wondered about the circumstances of the truck almost sending me off the road. During the descent, I didn't have the time to think about who and why, but now in the shadow of the town's outskirts, I did weigh the probability of the encounter being only chance.

Surely the trucker saw me; maybe regretted rear-ending me. Then again, since he didn't stop and offer an apology, maybe he only regretted not sending me off the road for good, like Early.

With my heart still beating in my breast, like a bass drum in a marching band, I looked both ways up and down the road and pulled out and headed to town. I stopped in a parking space on Main Street, but not sure of my next move, I got out to just walk up the street, trying to calm down. I passed the Fish and Game Shop and Saunders' Photography Studio, which still looked closed up, and got to Miller's Fine Clothes. Deciding it a good diversion, I went in to see if they had something on sale.

Miller's fine clothes occupied a convenient two-story space on the corner of Main Street and 4th Street. The Millers lived above the business where they raised several children, all girls, the count of them I couldn't remember. Several generations of town church goers found dresses, suits, ties, and shoes for everyday and special occasions there. High school senior boys rented their prom tuxes there. The girls could order a fancy gown from a catalog, and the funeral home could get you a nice black suit for your last public outing before they put you in the black earth of the mountain.

I waved to Mrs. Miller sitting behind a counter, leafing through a magazine I supposed the newest fashion edition, keeping up with the latest trends. We weren't the only ones in the shop as I found Shelby Stone looking through a stack of scarves. Over her dress, she wore a red sweater that possessed the ability to cling to her body, revealing the full curve of her breasts. Her hair layered down from her head across her shoulders and she wore a pair of dark glasses, tinted a shade of blue.

She turned around to me with a bright red silk material like scarf and holding it up to her neck asked, "How does this look?"

"Well, shows off your color," I said, and meant it, too. Her aura pulsed into a warm rainbow glow I'd only seen once or twice before.

"I think so. I just love red."

"I'm partial to blue," I told her, riffling through the scarves on the counter. "You know, makes my blue eyes stand out."

"You want one of those scarves?" Mrs. Miller called from the counter.

"Yes, ma'am," Shelby called back, waving the red scarf and then wrapping the red silk around her neck. As she walked to the door, she said, "Put it on our account."

I watched the pretty lady saunter, no, more flounce, out the door, and when she left the shop, a palpable void took her place in the space, hanging heavy like unfinished words.

"That lady's nothing but trouble," Mrs. Miller called out from the counter.

"You think?"

"Watch yourself around her."

"I'll try."

"So, you going to buy anything, or just looking?"

"Hey, Mrs. Miller," I said to the older woman, taking off

my cap and putting on a smile for her, despite her woeful attempt at warm customer service, "I haven't seen you since high school."

The woman slowly made her way around the counter, and approaching close, slipped on a pair of bifocals. "Emma Louise," she said, "why I hardly recognize you, it's been so long. You still a pretty thing, though."

"Yes, ma'am, thank you, it's been a while."

"Probably a good ten years, as I count them."

"Maybe more, but I appreciate the compliment."

"Sure sorry to hear about your brother," the lady said, giving my arm a squeeze with a bony grip, her aura beating a steady orange-red glow. "Bad stuff happens!"

"Yes, ma'am, it sure can."

"Well, what can we do for you?"

"I need a couple of things for daily wear," I explained. "Looks like I'll be up here longer then I planned, so need an extra thing or two."

"Sure thing, Emma," the woman said, "take your time."

"So how is business these days," I asked as I returned to my task of finding something to wear besides the extra clothes I brought for the funeral services.

"It could be better. 'Course, the downtown business is up and down with the sawmill, but we're getting more and more tourist traffic, people coming up to see the fall colors, and now, the Shaw Vineyard. We put out those bonnets, and flannel shirts the city folk think we all wear around here, and it makes for a nice little sideline. Been thinking about bringing in cowboy boots, but the inventory cost is a lot to carry."

I ended up buying a sweater blouse I might need to go with the skirt I brought along, in case the Indian summer ended sooner than I thought.

Leaving Millers', I turned left, and lugging a bag, walked up the block passing the still closed photography studio, Carson's Fish and Game, Shaw Hardware, and Nadine's

Boutique. I just about made it past Nadine's when Nadine Oliver pushed her shop door open in front of me as she swept out the remnants of the last customer's hair. Seeing me standing there she said, "Emma Shaw, is that you under that cap?"

"Mrs. Oliver," I greeted her. The big woman with small hands wore her hair in a thick bouffant no one outside of town would dare wear. I took off my cap and smiled at the long-time town stylist known to have coifed every woman's head in town at least once.

"June texted us you were in town," she said. "So good to see you, except…"

"Right, I know."

"So sorry, Emma dear, seems bad things happen to the best of us."

"It sure does. So, is Stacie around?"

"Not right now, but I'll send her a message, and she'll be down right away."

"I'd love to see her."

"She'll love to see you, too. June told us you were back in town for a while?"

"Just to attend to Early's affairs."

"Well, since you're here, would you like me to shampoo out your hair, maybe take off some of those split ends?" she offered, pulling a pair of shears from a pocket and flashing them at me. "I've got an opening right now."

"Well," I said, conscious of my mess of hair, and going into her shop I said, "I'm probably due.

"How's business up and down the street?" I asked the woman after I settled in a soft chair and she unbraided my hair.

I leaned back over the wash bowl at her station and she set to gently wash my hair, saying, "The tourist business is up, makes up for the slow in-town business, so we're hanging in there."

"I don't know," I said while getting comfortable, the

gentle massage of my scalp making me sleepy. "I don't think I saw a single vacant store front up the street."

"No, not at first glance."

"What do you mean?"

"Well, several shops were barely squeaking by, harder to make ends meet, so a few sold out to the Shaws."

"Sold out?"

"Sure," she said, helping me to sit up and blotting my hair with a fresh towel. She then combed out my hair. "Now they rent, trying to get by. The Shaws don't charge much, and keeping the store fronts open helps us all."

"The Shaws don't own enough of the town as it is?"

"Well, only half the town, Emma; they may get to 100% ownership one day, but not yet. 'Course, they run a couple of things themselves like the new coffee shop."

"The *Coffee Bean*?"

"Yep, May and Randall Shaw's place."

"Does the Carson family still own the Fish and Game Shop?" I asked.

"Oh, sure," she went on casually while combing and clipping at the ends of my hair with a pair of sharp scissors, "that's one business in constant demand up in the mountains; guns and ammo! I doubt the Shaw family could get hold of that property, though, at least not while old man Carson's alive. Carson used to own two or three other businesses in town, but the Shaws bought them out. Jack Carson just hates the Shaws."

When Mrs. Oliver had snipped the last split end standing, she took out a hand-held blower and started to dry my hair. Caught in the chair with no escape, I got out my cell phone and went through several unopened messages, including one from my editor who wished me condolences. I had just hit the delete mode when Stacie Oliver blew into the small shop, filling it with her presence and her energy.

"Emma Shaw!" she yelled, seeing me in the chair. "Get

that skinny butt of yours out of that chair and give me a hug."
And before I could climb all the way out, she yanked on my
arm and dragged me into a bear hug, her big arms smothering
me into her wide, soft chest. "So how come you see June first
before you get around to seeing me?"

"I ran into her at the diner," I said, pushing myself away
from her grasp. "I didn't know she worked there."

"Oh, yeah," she said, releasing me and giving me the once-
over look. "Say, I know it can't be possible, but you look
smaller than ever."

"Thanks," I answered. Stacie's aura yo-yo'd between the
yellow of a carefree person and the ruby red of a person that
loves life.

"No, I mean it's good that you stay small. Seems like the
rest of us up here put on about five pounds a year."

"Speak for yourself," her Mama said as she got me back
down into the chair.

"Another few years, and we'll need a truck to get around
in."

"You look the same to me," I lied.

"You're lying, but that's okay. Yeah, June didn't want to
go into the family business, so she started working over at the
diner. She says the tips over there are better than what she can
make here. Besides, over there, she don't have to worry about
putting up with Mama."

"That's not the main reason."

"I know, Mama; the real reason is you don't pay enough."

"Well, who's shop is it, anyhow?"

"Now, Mama, she is your daughter."

"Well, Stacie, you know darn well that June would have
come in here if there'd been room, but you were working back
then and there wasn't another chair, so she started over at the
diner."

"Well, when I had Amy, she could have come in then."

"By then, she was settled over there with regular

customers so I can't blame her any."

After blowing my hair dry and fluffing it out, she spun my chair around so I could look at the results in the big mirror on the wall.

"Do you still braid your hair up, Indian style?" Stacie said to me. "You know, like you used to when you were young."

"Just when I feel the urge."

"Well, it looks better, full out like this. We aren't kids anymore."

"So, how's that ole Mark of yours? Is he still up at the mill?"

"Where else? He's been there I guess close to twenty years now."

"And your kids?"

"Little Mark started high school last year and Rebecca and Amy are in middle school. Amy just started. I promised Mama I'd come back to work when Amy started middle school but I'm only up to a couple of days a week and Saturdays right now."

"No hurry," her mama said. "There's barely enough regulars for me."

"That's because you haven't kept up with the trends, Mama. I've told you that before."

"Oh, sure, I see them lining up at the door for you."

"Just wait until I get back in here full-time. This place will be jumping."

Well," Mrs. Oliver said, "this should hold you, gal. Get you through the week, anyway."

"Looks good," I told the lady, and meant it.

"So," Stacie said, "are you going to have time so we can catch up?"

"I'll be in town a while, so we'll get together."

"You going to look into this Early thing?"

"Who said anything about that?"

"Come on, girl, I figure that'd be the one thing to keep you around this place."

"I don't know, there's another reason or two."

"Does Jeff Carson factor into your plans?"

"Now, why would you think that?"

"Come on, girl, this is Stacie you're talking to."

"Well, we did run into each other, the other day."

"Oh?"

"Yes, but just by chance."

"Come on, Emma, that man has never gotten over you!"

I shook Mrs. Oliver's hand, and giving her a twenty for the cut and a five-dollar bill as a tip, I put my ball cap into my new clothes bag, and with Stacie following, I left the shop.

Out on the sidewalk, Stacie took hold of my arm and said, "Girl, I know you, you back in town and all, but just be careful."

"Careful about what?"

"Come on. June told me about your run-in with Franklyn and your kin down at the diner."

"How'd she get to you so fast?"

"Ah…text messaging?"

"Okay – so the mayor and I had a few words."

"Look, you just be careful about dealing with the Shaws."

"What do you mean?"

"You just be careful, Emma. The Shaws still run this town, nothing's changed about that."

Chapter Nine

Fish and Game

I left Stacie with a promise to try to meet later and walked up the street in the direction of the Fish and Game Shop. I wondered about my old friend Jeff Carson, so decided to face the inevitable and drop in.

Jeff Carson and his family had run the fish and game store for generations. History tells us that Carson's great, great, great granddaddy was the original gunsmith in town, come over with the first settlers in 1809. Way before the Shaws.

I walked the few paces to the Fish and Game Shop and passed Saunders Studio again. Stopping to look at the shop's sidewalk display window, I could see Mr. Saunders hadn't been keeping up his work. Several old photos hung from the inner display, but faded prints and curled up corners meant he hadn't bothered to replace the old layout; some photos looked as though they were taken back in the 70's.

I wondered about the studio, but moved on to the Fish and Game Shop. I pushed through the door that sported thick wrought-iron bars. Similar bars backed the windows giving the place a jail look from the outside, but bright fluorescent lights bathed the welcoming retail space and the display cases.

Jeff Carson and another man, older than Jeff, but about the same size, appeared busy working. The older man stood on a stepstool arranging boxes of ammunition in some order. Jeff sat at a worktable behind one end of the counter.

Using his left hand, he pulled down on a lever of a hand loading machine. A box of fresh yellow hulls sat on one side of him and a plastic container of a black powder mix and another container of buck shot sat on the other. When he sealed the casing top, he took the newly loaded shell and placed it in a new cardboard box.

Getting up, he moved down the counter and placed the carton in a neat row with others. Before turning to me he recorded something, on a sheet of paper on a clipboard.

"So we meet again," I said, walking up to the counter, glad I just had my hair washed and combed out. "My hero."

"Hey, you were doing okay on your own, I just helped out."

"You busy?" I said, half flirting, seeing his familiar blue aura.

"Depends." When the other man walked down the aisle behind the counter to join us, Jeff introduced him. "Emma, this is my older brother, Bobby."

"Ma'am," the man nodded at me, but didn't smile, before moving a little down the aisle, dusting counters, his dark brown aura in tow.

"What are you doing, loading your own shells?" I asked, bringing my attention back to my old flame.

"Well, we got to save when we can, Emma."

"So anyway, thanks again for saving me the other day."

"You're welcome again."

"Yeah, who thought I'd get so much attention looking into this thing."

"So you *are* looking into it?" Bobby Carson asked me from ten feet away.

"Right," I explained, trying to measure his interest. "You know, I just don't figure Early running off the road like that."

"Well, that's a tricky curve, hard to take when running fast."

"Not for Early."

"Even Early ran into things hard to handle from time to time."

"What's that supposed to mean?"

Bobby didn't comment further, but left the counter and

went into the back of the shop.

Jeff waited a beat then said, "Maybe you should be taking all this up with the town police?"

"From what I hear, they're not interested in another explanation."

After an awkward pause and with his brother gone, Jeff switched topics and asked, "Can I do anything for you?"

"Oh," I said, and smiling wide, added, "like what did you have in mind?"

"No, I meant, show you something."

"I don't know, do you have anything worth seeing?"

"Now, Emma Shaw," Jeff said, embarrassed, "you know what I mean."

"Well," I started to say, trying to come up with a logical reason I dropped in there besides taking a good look at a one-time love interest and making fun of him. "I've been thinking of buying a handgun," I told him off the top of my head. "You know, for protection."

"This doesn't have anything to do with those three guys at the river?"

"No, it's not that." I plopped my bag up on the counter, then thought, but why not? "I've been thinking about it for some time."

"Well, what did you have in mind?"

"Not a clue. Why don't you make a suggestion?"

"Here," he said, pointing down at a glass-topped cabinet a few feet away. "Take a look at these."

The display case contained a sleek line up of handguns from a smaller derringer model on up to a large magnum type of pistol with a long barrel that looked to be heavier than I could lift—much less, shoot. Serving with the Guard and being raised with an older brother and father who liked to hunt, I knew about rifles and shotguns, but I knew little about handguns.

"I guess I need something small, maybe something that could slip into a purse?"

"Well, be careful about carrying a concealed weapon without a permit, but for a woman I'd recommend the Lugar SR22. It's light, easy to shoot, and easy to clean. The 22 caliber is a great first choice for anyone just getting into shooting because of the light recoil. Some people complain that the 22 lacks stopping power, but the truth is, that in any self-defense situation, it's better to feel comfortable with the gun than to have something that's hard to shoot due to recoil, and only allows you to get off one shot."

"What about one of these automatics?"

"They have more firepower than you'll need, Emma. Lot of police carrying these Glocks now, basically a plastic gun with a big magazine. I think for women, all you have to do is flash the gun and most muggers would be scared off, anyway."

"Most?"

"Yeah, the others, the hard-core, well, you better learn how to aim for them."

"Did Early get equipment from you?"

"Sure, he ran up a tab here, bought a new gun last year."

"I'd think the town would provide everything Early would need…"

"Oh, the town reimbursed Early for his work-related purchases, but he ran up a tab on a few personal items. Pa let him charge what he needed, but Early always settled up."

"Like what kind of stuff would the town reimburse him for?"

"Different things," he said.

"Like what?"

"They're in the book if you want to see."

I nodded and followed him over to the checkout counter. Pulling a ledger from somewhere beneath the register, he opened it, and thumbing through, found the pertinent page.

"Let's see, okay, here we go. What do you want first?"

"Start at the top and work back."

"Well, let's see," he said as looked over the book. "We brought in a new vest for him back a few months."

"Vest?"

"Yeah, body armor, concealable, light with ceramic inserts, like the Army uses. That cost $550.00."

"Wouldn't the town cover that?"

"The town provided a heavy model, old style. Chief wanted something to wear under his shirt, not noticeable, for undercover work."

"Okay," I said, "what else?"

"Let's see…ah, last fall…last fall he ordered a new shotgun for Early junior; a 20 gauge Winchester. Nice gun with solid walnut stock, no plastic."

"How much?"

"Gun show demo I got him for $200."

"What a deal," I said, only half kidding.

"Yep, that gun sells for $499 at the Gun Pro Shop."

"Did he buy all the boys a gun?"

"Not yet, just Early Junior, when he turned 18. He said a dad should give a son his first gun when the boy turns 18."

"Oh?"

"To hear his granddaddy tell it, the boy's the next thing to Daniel Boone around here. I wish more fathers still thought like that."

"What do you mean?"

"Oh, in the old days, lot of fathers bought their kids rifles and shot guns. You know, rite of passage, good for business. But now days, guns have been handed down from dads and grandfathers to offspring. No demand for new hunting guns these days. Plus, the young people only want those military style guns, and we don't carry any of those since the inventory cost is high."

"What else in that book?"

"That Glock is in here."

"Why'd he want another gun?"

"Early said he wanted a more effective weapon for going up against the bad guys."

"Now, that's something the town should have provided."

"No, the town issued a .38 caliber policeman's special, but Early wanted more power, so he had to pay for that himself."

"What else?"

"There's lots of ammo and some hunting gear. Just stuff for the family, but Early came in when he could to settle up for his personal stuff. The balance stands at zero now; kind of fitting."

"What do you mean?"

"Oh, you know, now that Early is…"

"Oh, yeah, I get it."

"Sorry…"

"Anyway, that's quite an account."

"Early was a good customer. I wish everyone in town spent money in here like Early did."

Feeling guilty about the business in town, I picked up a couple of logo shirts; one white one and one red one, and after paying with my credit card, I added another bag to my load.

"So," Jeff said as I walked to the exit and he opened the door for me, "maybe we can go out later in the week, you know, after things settle down?"

"Like a date?"

"Sure."

"Okay," I said, staring up at him, tongue-tied, "I'd like that," and lamely added, "after things settle down, that is."

I went out and climbed in the Jeep, thinking about Jeff Carson, but before leaving town, I made a last stop at Shaw's Market where I planned to pick up a few toiletries.

When I entered the store, I saw Shelby Stone at the checkout with a twelve-pack of soft drinks and an assortment of snacks. A pretty blond teenager stood next to her, bored. The teen girl wore a short dress, so short I could see a line of red underwear, and both her thumbs worked her phone as she rapidly texted, probably sending out a distress signal to her posse about being detained by an overly protective mother.

Her red aura fluttered up and joined her mother's in a rainbow kaleidoscope.

"Supplying up for a party?" I said to her, coming up from behind.

"Just a little something for the evening," she said, smiling wide, looking down at me through a pair of pink-tinted sunglasses.

When the clerk rang up her order Shelby told the man, "Put it on the family account, will you?"

"Say," I told her, thinking of accounts, and reaching out and touching her arm before she got away. "Could you do me a favor?"

"I don't know," she smiled, "that depends."

"Mother!" the teen girl moaned at being delayed.

"Just a minute, Sugar," she said to her and to me she said, "I apologize for my daughter, Holly, she's only this way like…always. So, what do you need?"

"Could you run up an account of all the reimbursements Early submitted over the last couple of years."

"Why?"

"Just something I'm working on."

"I don't know that stuff is in the budget department."

"It should be public record and all, and I'm the public, so it's allowed."

"Oh, it's not that, it's that I can hardly make heads or tails of those accounts. They're all on computer, on that Excel thing. I'll have to order it from Wendell, and it might take a few days."

"That's okay," I told her. "I'm not going anywhere for a while."

"Why doesn't that surprise me?" she said as she made her way to the exit.

The clerk and I watched Shelby and Holly leave the shop. We both stared at them through the store front windows as they sauntered across the parking lot toting the twelve-pack and bag of snacks, an orange aura trailing after them. The two pretty ladies climbed into a yellow VW bug with convertible top down, in spite of the chill in the air. I knew we were staring for different reasons.

Chapter Ten

Tuesday

Growing up, we knew Pa and small talk didn't go together. I doubt he said more than two sentences in a row, best I remembered, but along with his newfound religion, he discovered a gift for gab. We ate through an extensive late breakfast of eggs, biscuits and gravy he prepared, and after I filled him in on my question on how Early ended up in the river, we chatted up several unrelated stories that did more than enough to lift the mood of the morning.

"So," I asked him to be clear on his idea, "you're thinking about opening up the fields again, for corn?"

"That's right, I've been working the soil some. You know—waking it up."

"But isn't the price of corn low? How will you make money?"

"That's the thing, Emma, I'm not going to sell the corn, I'm going to give it away."

"To the poor?"

"Them, and anyone that needs it. There are a lot of folk in need, Emma, many right here in the valley. I've been thinking of a way to give back."

"But how are you going to pay for it?"

"Now, I haven't worked all the details out just yet, but the extension service has a program that will reimburse a fella for seed costs. I don't have all the answers, but it could work. You know me, I don't mind the work and I have all the equipment and the land. It seems a shame to let the land just sit there idle."

"Well, it sounds like a great idea, Pa. I'm not much of a businesswoman, but if you can make it work, then why not?"

In the late morning, a cool wind started down the mountain. Until then, I'd forgotten the fall and enjoyed the Indian summer, but the weather could change on a dime in the mountains, the weather or a man's life. After looking through the wardrobe I brought, I recognized I didn't bring enough stuff for getting outdoors. I asked Pa whatever happened to my old clothes. He answered by climbing up into the attic.

"I think your mama saved all your old clothes," he said as he worked his way down the attic ladder steps, hauling a big cardboard box. "You should find something in here. It doesn't look like you filled out any since."

"I'm counting on that."

I rummaged through leftover teen attire and memories of my high school years, all I thought I had left behind. In addition to several worn pairs of jeans, which now would be in style, I found three or four long-sleeved plaid blouses that must have been the rage back then, one black skirt, and my old pair of calf-high boot moccasins I used to hike the mountains in. In addition, I found a treasure of athletic socks and old but usable underwear. The bras may have been wearable, but I couldn't squeeze into them with their small cup size. I remembered going off to State well before I matured out so…

I changed out my better outfit for a pair of the worn jeans that fit me perfect, which I half expected, or maybe, hoped. I slipped on a flannel shirt, tied it with a knot in front and to finish off the Ellie Mae Clampett look, I put on the soft leather moccasin boots.

With the viewing of Early's body waiting on us that evening, we spent the day together. Pa showed me all that he had done around the farm and fired up the old tractor and we rode through the fields while he shouted out his plans above the roar of the old diesel engine, the dust of Black Mountain covering me.

About 5:00, we hurried back to the house to dress for Early's viewing. After I hogged the bathroom for an hour, I put on black slacks, matching sweater blouse, and flats I brought for the occasion. Pa took a fast shower, put on a dark blue suit, and hard shoes.

We took my Jeep and drove down the mountain to Gilmore's. A long line of cars backed down the road from the funeral home, but a Gilmore attendant in a dark suit and tie spotted us, and directed us to a family parking space where other cars of the immediate family were located.

Like all Blue Ridge towns, Black Mountain took its funerals seriously. I'm sure there are some deep-seated emotions wrapped up in the whole spectacle. I didn't know how I felt about a public viewing. Although it put to rest any notions of whether or not a dearly departed had, in fact, departed, it still evoked a primitive skepticism about the thin line between life and death. Some people liked to see a body before they'd believe a loved one passed. In Early's case, doubly so—since I'd seen my big brother Early's body and I still couldn't believe it.

Town folk, hunched against the cold, lined up at the door and stretched down the porch and well down the sidewalk. Gilmore hadn't opened the main doors yet, giving the family a chance to enter through the office door for a first see.

Becky and her boys arrived before us and with Mother Davis and John Davis, sat up front in a grouping of fold up chairs. Dutifully, we walked up to the open casket and paused a moment to look in on my big brother. He looked better in his youth, of course, but at that moment, he looked every bit as I knew him, still strong and still broad. I closed my eyes for a moment, hoping to catch a memory aura of him, a dull haze hanging in the area. Leftover auras from troubled dead people and their kin filled the space with a mud-like miasma, a morbid color of lifelessness. The atmosphere reminded me why I hated funerals.

I wondered what Early would say about my snooping into his death. Knowing him, he'd approve. I thought if I didn't succeed in solving the mystery he'd come back and haunt me. I held back a sniffle while thinking that would be just like him.

Pa paused a while longer at the casket, but I turned to Becky, her folks, and the four boys.

Just then, Mr. Gilmore came in and asked the family if he could open the doors for everyone, saying, "There's quite a line out there. Mrs. Shaw, are you ready?"

Becky looked up, and then faced her boys, and smiling wide said, "I guess we are as ready as we are going to be, right boys?"

The four boys nodded in unison, all with tears in their eyes.

The line of visiting friends and distant kin snaked through the hall and made its way down the receiving line. The greater Shaw family came first; the mayor and brothers, Officer Carter, assorted other Shaws and town's well-known citizens.

Wendell Banks and his wife were there, and Shelby, as well, dressed in a dramatic tight-fitting black dress and spiked heels so she towered over everyone except the tallest Shaw men. Dark glasses hid her eyes and her blond hair, pulled back from her face, flowed down her back. A few other town women shed tears, as well, but as befitting a hard town in hard times, mourners walked stoically past Early's body, shook hands with the family, said a few words, and then left as promptly as they could manage. Mama's three sisters came through towards the end and brightened up the room with a constant chatter and carrying on about Early's boys, not seeing them in a few years. Their shared rainbow aura swung in the bright warm ranges.

A few notable townfolk neglected the affair—Granddaddy Shaw for one, and the Carson family, as well. It disappointed me that Jeff Carson didn't show.

The last of the visitors went through the line and left the immediate family in silence.

Mr. Gilmore came into the room, and with a nod of her head, Becky gave him permission to lower the lid on Early's casket. I imagined that would be the last time I'd see him, and felt a hollow in my stomach. Gilmore walked over to Becky, and, holding both her hands in his, said a final few words.

Emma and the boys left the welcoming room, followed by Mrs. Davis and Pa, but I hung back for a minute, tears running down my cheeks. I put my hand up on Early's casket, and wished him well, thinking it would be the last time we'd be alone. I promised him I'd find out what happened out on the road that night, promised both of us.

"Do you think he hears you?" Jeff Carson asked, surprising me with his appearance.

"What do you mean?"

"You know, praying for his eternal soul. I'm sure he'd appreciate it."

"I don't know about Early and the Good Lord."

"Well, if it's a comfort to you in all this, I'm sure Early was doing right the night he died."

"Why are you so sure?"

"Just something about the way he did his job. He knew right and wrong."

"I've heard different."

"Be careful about who you listen to, Emma. This old town holds secrets, more than we know."

Jeff smiled at me, and after a second, turned and walked from the room. I followed him with my eyes, and stared a while at the exit door where he'd left through, wondering about what he said.

"Everyone set?" I asked as I walked out and joined the others.

Becky stepped forward, and for the family, said, "We want you to come up to the house for a spell."

"I don't know, Becky, Pa's here."

"Now, we've discussed it and it's settled. Logan said you can drop him at the house, since he turns in early, before coming over. So, you go on and drop him off and come on out to the house for a while. We'll snack some on Mama's desserts and you can sit and squirm over coffee, while I tell everyone tales of you and Early and your adventuresome youth. It will be fun."

I couldn't disagree with Becky and her plan about visiting. Any diversion would be welcome on the eve of Early's funeral, but as far as talking about Early and me growing up, well, I could call that conversation a lot of things, but fun would not be one of them.

Chapter Eleven

Wednesday

Wednesday morning broke cloudless with a leftover bitter cold gripping the mountain; a perfect day for a funeral. We were looking at an 11:00 o'clock graveside service, followed by lunch in the fellowship hall, prepared by the church's women's club. There'd be fried chicken, pulled pork and ham for sandwiches, potato salad, three bean salad, deviled eggs and lord knows a bunch of diet-busting pies and cakes for desert.

We'd had a nice visit the evening before. Becky took it easy on me, leaving out the embarrassing episodes of my growing up in Black Mountain, although there were enough tales to get everyone laughing. It did everyone good to laugh out at the youthful high jinx of Early and me. When heads around the room started to droop around midnight, I excused myself and drove to Pa's for the night.

I went back to my room for bed, but spent a minute or two going over the mysterious circumstances of Early's so-called accident. I eventually fell asleep and dreamed about Jeff Carson.

The next morning, before the excitement of the day, I put on my moccasin boots, jeans, and my jacket and grabbing my camera, rushed out to catch a few shots of the sun coming up over the mountain. There's nothing quite like the morning sunrise in the mountains. Like a giant rousing from a deep slumber, the shadow of the mountain lifts until it dwarfs the valley, and then disappears, leaving the light of day.

When I returned from my walk, I found Pa sitting at the kitchen table with a cup of coffee and his Bible open to a passage.

"What are you reading, Pa?" I asked him as I put my camera down and poured a mug of coffee.

"Psalms 23:4 – 'Yea, though I walk through the valley of the shadow of death, I will fear no evil: for thou art with me; thy rod and thy staff they comfort me.'"

"You know," I said taking a seat across from him. "I wonder if Early thought of dying."

"Every man thinks about dying, Emma."

"You think?"

"Yes, every man thinks about dying; some more than others, but even Early."

About 10:00 in the morning we climbed into my Jeep and left for the Davis place. We found the boys dressed in ill-fitting suits, but Becky wore a light blue blouse over a black skirt and tall heels, looking a bit sexy for the funeral occasion when compared to me in plain black and flats. The Davises rode down in their old red truck, Little Earl and William in the old Jeep, and Becky and the other two boys in her new SUV.

In town, we pulled up behind a shiny long black hearse of indeterminable age, parked at the curb in front of Gilmore's funeral home. Becky told us they'd be loading Early's coffin into the hearse and we'd follow it over to the graveyard located a few steps from Pa's church and Mama's grave. Becky picked the four boys, Pa, and her daddy as the pall bearers.

At the church cemetery, Reverend Shaw said some kind words, and then the large group paused in quiet for a minute. I sat there with my eyes closed trying to remember. Tears rolled down my cheeks and I used a red checked handkerchief to wipe them off.

I could see several memory auras of the recently departed hanging quiet in the still of surrounding area, all emitting a sadness I'd rarely felt.

When the service ended, the Reverend Shaw invited everyone to go on over to the church basement and begin with the lunch. I told the others to go in, but I wanted to stay a bit longer, maybe wanting to extend my time with my big brother.

Before lowering Early down into the mountain earth, each member of the burial crew came by to tell me how sorry they were. They explained how Early endeared himself to the families down in Mill Town, even the black families.

One of the men asked me if I remembered him. "Howard Whitaker," he said, "I played alongside Early."

"Howie," I said, placing the face with the name. Howie Whitaker played defensive end on those high school championship teams. His family ran the city's lone junk yard. "Sure, Howie," I said, extending my hand, "it's been a while."

"Sure has," he said, taking my little hand in his two big ones.

"How's your pa?"

"He's good, retired now, you know, spends his free time fishing."

"You looking good," I complimented the man, seeing his muscles bulging out of his blue work shirt. "What are you doing here?"

"Gilmore put me on here part-time. I guess he thought with a Whitaker on staff, a little black business might come his way.

"Look, Emma," he said, "we were all sad to hear about the chief."

"I appreciate that, Howie, and I'm sure Early would appreciate it, too."

"Yes, ma'am," he continued, his aura beating a darkening pink, a sign he was circling about the truth. "Yes, ma'am, a real shame about the way they treated your brother these last few years."

"How do you mean?"

"Oh, you know, just about the mayor."

"What about the mayor?"

"Well, you know, Emma, things pretty much soured

between the mayor and the chief there at the end. Don't know how your brother stood for it."

"So I've heard something, but what exactly happened?"

"Well, I can't say for sure, but there's gossip."

"Gossip about what?"

"Oh, folks say Mayor Shaw wanted to fire Early, but Granddaddy stopped it."

"Why'd the mayor want to fire Early?"

"Oh, seems he had a little something going on the side and the mayor warned him, or else."

Oh, oh...I knew Early liked a good scheme, but I figured he'd keep it below the radar so it wouldn't get in the way of his job.

"Are you sure about this, Howie?"

"Come on, Emma, this is a small town and nothing much goes on around here that you don't hear about."

I stood back as the men lowered Early down into the ground and watched as they shoveled in the first of the dark mountain soil. Early loved this mountain and the town, and I hoped he slept soundly in his eternity, but feared for his eternal rest. If what Howie said turned out to be true, about Early running some scam, well, I didn't think Early would get much eternal rest buried there next to Mama.

The lunch spread looked large enough to feed a brigade and then some. Though I'm partial to pulled pork and macaroni and cheese, I seldom pass up the opportunity to stuff myself with home cooked fried chicken when the pastor's wife is serving it. Back in high school, the softball team would crash a funeral lunch just to get the chance to eat a piece or two of Mrs. Bennett Shaw's fried chicken.

Light gray walls encompassed the basement hall and several rows of fold up tables crowded in with enough fold up metal chairs to accommodate eighty or so mourners. I carried my loaded plate in two hands and made my last stop the drink table where a pretty young girl with purple hair handed me a red solo cup filled with sweet tea.

"Wow, Aunt Emma," Johnny said when he saw the pile of food on my plate, "Mama told us to not make pigs of ourselves."

"Now, Johnny," Becky said sharply, popping the top of his head with her finger, "I only said to take it easy."

"But I'm still hungry!"

Becky looked around the table at the other boys and they gave her a glance that said much the same. "Alright, you can make a second trip through the line, everyone looks fed and happy."

The four boys jumped up and disappeared in a gaggle around the food table like black crows picking at fresh roadkill.

"Growing boys, there," I said, as I sat down on the hard chair at the table.

"By the looks of that plate," Becky said, "they aren't the only ones."

The lunch crowd began to taper off. The guests began to stop off at the table to say goodbyes and maybe a final condolence before they left to return to their lives after the brief respite from their own problems and challenges.

After the lunch, the family rode out to the Davis place; Becky and Mother Davis in the SUV, the four boys in the Jeep, and JB bringing up the rear in his truck, while I rode Pa back to the house with the promise to visit back with them after getting Pa settled.

I pulled my Jeep around to the side of our house and we got out. The path along the east end of the house sidled up close to the wooden fence line that separated the field and the few grazing cattle Pa kept from the line of Mama's peach trees.

I stopped at the fence and looked out on the small orchard.

"You know," Pa said, "I planted those trees for your mama the year we built this house."

"I know. Mama told me."

"Did she tell you we argued over them?"

"No."

"Well, we did. One of the few arguments we had. She just had to have peach trees. I told her apple would be best, high up like we are, but she wanted peach. She said everyone grew apples up here and she wanted something different. Oh, I tried to talk her out of it, but she insisted on peaches. She said anyone could grow apples, and wanted to try something different. She said she liked the challenge, and all. She liked to see how the trees struggled to sprout buds and then blossom, high like we are.

"Oh, she'd get a handful of peaches now and then, just enough for a pie or two. She baked a peach pie for the fall festival, right proud to show everyone that she could do it."

We went in the kitchen of our little house that looked much like it did when Early and I used to sit there having a meal. The sparse counter held the kitchen equipment needed to feed our small family. The table, heavy on thick legs, sat expectantly, like a bull at pasture waiting for a mate. The chairs, equally sturdy against rough wear, yet with smooth seat bottoms, worn by double and triple duty of meals, school studies, and occasional Sunday school lessons, looked like they did years before.

I went back to my room and changed out of my Sunday attire into more comfortable jeans, flannel shirt, and my moccasin boots. I stopped in the bath to freshen up before heading out, and when I came back, I found Pa reading a passage from his Bible. Though reading in general seemed a foreign enterprise for Pa, reading the Bible verged on mystery, like why the sky is blue and who made the stars.

"I'm studying more than reading," he explained when I asked him.

"Studying for what?" I asked, taking a seat opposite him.

"I lead our Sunday school class before service, and we study a different reading each week."

"What's the reading for this week?"

"*Mathew 19:23* – 'Again I tell you, it is easier for a camel to go through the eye of a needle than for someone who is rich to enter the kingdom of God.'

In many respects, Pa differed from his old self, but reckoning his newfound spirit with the old gave me trouble. "I'm sure the Shaws love that verse."

When I got out to the Davis place, Mother Davis fed me a dinner of meat loaf and creamed potatoes and after the excitement of the last few days, we enjoyed a quiet afternoon out at the farm. Just before nightfall, I made up an excuse to get away into town to check out the new coffee shop over by the hospital.

"*The Coffee Bean*?" JB asked.

"Yes, looks like a nice place, Doc Miller Shaw's place."

"Doctor Shaw?"

"Yep, he and his wife opened it."

"If you got a hankering for a cup of coffee, I can pour you one here."

"It's not just that, I want to visit with Doc Miller," I said thinking of more than just visiting. I needed to get to a service location so I could check my messages in private, and while there, I thought about following up on the EPA thing up at the mill.

The Coffee Bean occupied a nice spot that once belonged to the old appliance store, within walking distance of anyone downtown and convenient to the little hospital across the street.

City Hospital, the only hospital or clinic in Black

Mountain, stood proudly on the same spot for over a hundred years. I'm sure someone from every family in town spent at least one night sleeping in the worn visitor's room, waiting on word of a family member in treatment, or in the middle of an operation. The ancient cafeteria served up home-cooked food three meals a day to patient and visitor alike, and bad coffee through the late night and early morning, as needed.

I parked right in front of Saunders' Photography Studio and wondered about its continual closed sign out front. Mr. Saunders had been the sole photographer in town all these years. I couldn't imagine many weddings in a town the size of Black Mountain. Plus, a chain photography studio at the Morgan Mall attracted all the young people and their fast spending appetite.

Back in high school, Mr. Saunders took all the yearbook photos and he used to let the yearbook club work out of his shop, putting the book together. Mr. Saunders caught the first glimpses of my photography that showed promise. He told me many times I'd turn out to be a real artist, the first to suggest I go into photojournalism. Of course, it was different times back then, back when print development meant something, like art, back before digital. Mr. Saunders gave me my first good camera, an old Minolta 35 mm single reflex shutter, a nice camera back in its day, back when film was still king. We all learned to develop our pictures here, in his dark room, learned other things in there, too.

I continued down the walk and when I pushed through the entry doors of The Coffee Bean, the warmth and aroma from a wood-burning fireplace greeted me.

Several groups of young teens cradling mugs of one concoction or another occupied the tables scattered about the dimly lit comfortable room. With eyes fixed on phones or tablets, no one noticed me when I went in.

A large flat screen TV filled out one wall of the area and a grouping of love seats and reclining chairs framed the immediate space in front of the dark set. An agile young lady scurried about the seating area delivering orders and dodging the occasional foot and chair in the aisle.

Doctor Miller Shaw stood behind the counter scooping coffee beans into a grinding bowl. I assumed someone's selection for the next round.

A long display case, backlit with a bright light, fronted the work counter and contained a selection of pastries and pies that I hoped were homemade.

"Emma," Doc Miller greeted me when he noticed me salivating over his display case. "What brings you out this evening?"

"I heard you were branching out as an entrepreneur, Miller, so I thought I'd check it out."

"This is all May's idea. She's wanted to do something like this for years. She hates that the young people make the drive over the mountain to Asheville to find something to do."

"I don't know. I can see a few gray hairs in here."

"Yeah, they've kind of adopted the place," he said, looking around at the diverse crowd, "less grease in here, if you know what I mean."

"Well, hey, Emma," his wife May greeted when she recognized me, "Miller said you were in town."

"May," I nodded at the good-looking woman carrying a sheet of fresh-made cookies for the display case.

"Those smell delicious enough to eat," I said.

"They are," she smiled at me. "I make these from my mama's recipe, oatmeal chocolate chip. I like to bake a batch about this time to whet everyone's appetite. We don't sell much in the afternoons, otherwise, and these get everyone thinking a little and the teens love them."

"I tell you what," I said, "you can fix me up a cup of French roast and one of those bear claws and I'll be in heaven."

"Find a table, then, we'll bring it over when it's ready."

I paid for my order, picked out an empty table near the front windows, and settled in. With time before my order arrived, I took out my cell and checked my messages. I found several from office colleagues, all passing along their sympathies. The waitress came to the table and interrupted my fingering back thank you messages, carrying the coffee on a tray and holding a small plate in one hand. She slid the plate in front of me and then put the coffee mug down. A selection of real cream, real sugar, and a little straw woven basket of artificial sweeteners adorned the table. I made a show of doctoring up my coffee with a choice of cream and a variety of other things.

"How's the coffee?" Miller Shaw asked as he approached.

"It's great," I said realizing it with the first sip. "Congratulations, I like this place. Here, sit down."

"Well, like I said," he repeated as he sat in one of the empty chairs, "it's May that deserves the credit. I work the night administration part-time over at the hospital so stop in to make a nuisance of myself."

"You pull the night shifts over there?"

"I do. Banks in budget ran some numbers and recommended to the hospital board to contract out the daytime administration to save money. Since its slow nights, I signed on part-time to stay involved."

"How about last weekend?"

"Last weekend?"

"Yeah, you know, the weekend my big brother turned up dead."

"I worked that shift," he frowned, his aura wavering between red and dark red, the colors associated with men trying to hide something, I'm sure not looking forward to the direction of the questions.

"You didn't see anyone come in maybe injured in a wreck?"

"No, no, I didn't. Why?"

Ruben D. Gonzales

"Oh, I don't know, Doc," I said, taking a bite out of my bear claw, feeling the immediate effect of the sugar rushing through my blood stream. "I figured that maybe my brother got involved in a collision or something so maybe someone needed treatment."

"No, we didn't treat anyone for an accident that night or over the weekend. Saw some cases with the flu, but no accident cases, but you know as well as I do, Emma, that half the men up here would treat themselves first before coming to the hospital."

"You still take care of any medical needs up at the mill?"

"Oh, sure," he said, looking relieved to be on familiar ground, "accidents mostly."

"And Granddaddy Shaw, you see to the family personally?"

"Sure, he's my number one patient."

"So how is Granddaddy?" I said, working my way around to the point I'd been wondering about since coming to town. "I haven't seen him at all."

"He spends his time out at the farm these days, tending his grapes."

"I heard about that. So how's it going, the wine business?"

"It's going well. We carry our Cabernet here in the shop, quite an operation out there."

"I'd like to see that."

"Sure, I'm sure Granddaddy Lawrence would like to show you, but fact is he's been under the weather with a bronchial infection of some sort, coughing wheezing, you know. I'm giving him antibiotics to try to knock it out, but it's been a stubborn infection. He stays close to the house these days, but I imagine he will come out on top of it."

"Maybe it's the formaldehyde up at the plant?"

He eyed me with a doctor's examination stare, like he wanted to give me a hysterectomy. "The what?"

"Formaldehyde, you know, the stuff that comes off that

106

resin glue they use making the plywood up at the mill. I hear it can make people sick."

"Not necessarily, depends on the exposure," he explained, his aura veering into the dark gray range.

"What kind of exposure are we talking about?"

"Well," the man said, his aura spreading through the pink range, "we are talking about much more exposure than what is up at the mill. Formaldehyde is all around us in plywood and particle board and doesn't bother us."

"But in concentrated form?" I asked.

"Well, of course, in concentrated form, anything could harm you. Eat enough of those bear claws and you could end up over in the hospital, too."

"Concentrated," I continued, "like in the resin they're using up at the mill to bind those layers of veneer together?"

"Yes, yes, it is concentrated, but not over the regulated limits. We monitor the air quality and it stays beneath the EPA thresholds."

"Tell that to Mikey Wade."

"Who?"

"Mikey Wade, he died from cancer last year, worked in the glue section of the plant, remember him?"

"We take the necessary precautions."

"But formaldehyde is a proven carcinogenic," I pointed out to the good doctor. "What are the EPA guidelines to use it?"

"Now, look…" he began, but I cut him off.

"No, you look. You know you're operating out of health compliance up there and I believe Early found out about it."

"No, Emma," Miller Shaw said, his aura lowering down into the pink ranges of untruthfulness, "fact is, the EPA lets production continue with resins containing formaldehyde under an exemption as long as it is within the set thresholds and precautions are taken, and as I pointed out, the mill is under EPA compliance. We've been inspected and the level of formaldehyde up at the mill is below the level needed to keep using it. So you can end your little fishing expedition on the mill."

"What are all the loud voices about," May Shaw asked us as she came up to the table. I hadn't noticed the level of the conversation until then, and as I looked around the room, I saw more than one table of guests looking our way.

"Sorry, dear," Miller Shaw said to his wife.

"What's this about?"

"Nothing, Mrs. Shaw," I said, apologizing. "Sorry, it's this Early thing and all, been hard on me and the family."

"Of course, dear," she agreed, taking a chair at the table and saying in a low voice, "what a tragedy. How is Becky bearing up?"

"Well, as best as possible, considering."

"Yes," she said, nodding her head, "well, make sure you tell her hello from us."

"Okay, then," I said, concluding the visit and getting to my feet. "I thank you for the great coffee and the dessert, I'll be back."

"Oh, will you be around town for a while?" May Shaw asked, looking up at me, smiling bright.

"Just a while longer, Mrs. Shaw," I said, smiling back at her and Miller, "just a while longer. I've got a few things to do including a visit with Granddaddy."

Once outside and clear of the café window, I paused to go over the conversation. Although Doc Shaw appeared to have all the answers, his pink aura meant he was hiding something. When I heard someone approaching, I looked up and saw Jeff Carson coming toward me in an easy gait.

"Hello, stranger!"

"Hello, yourself."

"I missed you this morning."

"Oh, you know," he mumbled, like a teenage kid confronted by a teacher, "I paid my respects last night."

"Well, I guess those things are more for family than anything."

"Yeah, I don't think Early would miss me."

"You've said something like that before. What got between you and Early? I thought you all were close?"

"He'd been running with some of those backwoods boys here lately."

"What do you mean?"

"Oh…I don't know for sure…he'd been keeping company with a different crowd. A crowd I don't much care for."

"I've heard that. Maybe that's what got him killed."

"You still think something not right about his accident?"

"You knew Early. You knew how he could handle a car. Do you think he just rode off that road on his own?"

"If not, then what?"

"If you're interested, I've got a plan that might shed some light on all this."

"What are you cooking up?"

"An offer you can't refuse."

Jeff stood there, solid on his big feet, and I could see the wheels turning in his head and his aura started to yoyo in the orange range of inquisitiveness. "Okay, Emma Louise, I guess I don't mind helping out a little in your little investigation. It sounds interesting."

"Well, if you think it's interesting so far," I told him, "just wait until you see what's coming next."

Chapter Twelve

Junk Yard

I'm not afraid of the dark, but I appreciated the shadowy light cast down on the junk yard at the south end of Mill Row. The yard's property began where the sidewalk ended and the paved street turned over to dirt. Ancient oaks stood tall, skeletal-like in the near winter, sentries over the road, a murky fog adding to the eerie image. The town landfill and junk yard situated about a mile outside of town, sat back from the road— and I doubted anyone driving or walking past the yard would notice two people trying to break into the place.

"We're going to do *what*?" Jeff asked me when I explained what my plan was for us. After leaving The Coffee Bean, we retrieved my Jeep and I drove south to the yard. I didn't stop in front of the gate for the fenced compound, but passed the entrance and rolled down a slope to stop beneath a stand of tall spruce.

"We are going to break into the junk yard," I repeated, answering his question.

"That's what I thought you said."

"Look," I said, switching off the ignition and turning to him, "I need to break into the yard and get a look at Early's cruiser. There's something about Early's accident that I just don't see, and I need to get a look."

"At his car?"

"Right, they towed it in here after they hauled it out of the river, remember? I think the mayor is anxious to keep me away from any evidence, so I want to take a look at the cruiser before he has it sold for scrap."

"Okay, but how do you know there's anything to find?"

"I don't know for sure, and that's why I want to see it myself. I don't know where the final pieces will fall, but I know I've got to keep looking, and this—*here*—is the next step. Come on, it'll be fun."

I hoped he'd say yes since the thought of snooping around a dark junk yard alone didn't appeal to me, but I also felt if he turned me down, I wouldn't blame him. I mean, we weren't going steady, or anything.

"Okay, Emma Louise," he said to me there in the dark. I knew he smiled at me when he said it. "I don't know why I should, but if in some way it will help you and Early's family, then I'll play along."

I retrieved a flashlight I kept in the glove box for emergencies and grabbed my camera from my bag. Climbing from the Jeep, we pushed the doors closed without slamming. We walked up to the fenced area, staying in the shadows of the trees that lined the yard and kept it hidden from the road. A dog somewhere off started a barking fit, but I couldn't tell if he got wind of us or he needed to get out and relieve himself. I hoped he wasn't running loose in the yard.

An old shack I took to be the office stood leaning at an angle on a stone foundation. I paused at a location where I could see north up the street toward town. "Look, all I want you to do is stand here and keep an eye out for anyone."

"So, I'm a lookout?"

"That's right, a lookout."

"And if I see someone I should hoot like an owl?"

"No, no, if you see someone," I pointed, "I want you to toss a stone up on the shack's metal roof. The sound will carry around the yard and I should hear it."

"Are you sure? I can do a great owl."

"Well, first off, if you did do a good owl, how would I know the real owl from the warning owl?"

"Good point."

"Okay, then." I bent down and picked up a rock, handing

it to him. "Just toss the rock up on the roof if anyone pulls up. You can see all the way to town from here."

"You sure you don't want me come along? You might need me to rough up someone."

"That's sweet of you," I told him, patting him on his cheek. "Maybe tomorrow, but right now I just need a lookout."

Leaving him with rock in hand, I stuck the flashlight in my jeans pocket and slung my camera by its strap over my shoulder, adjusting it around my back. I started scaling the ten-foot- high fence and realized I should have put some gloves on. The old chain link fence wire dug into my hands as I gripped the strands. Holding my place with my fingers, I used a foothold to step up a step at a time, moving my hands in unison farther and farther up.

The compound's fence didn't have razor wire or anything but the end cut of the wire stood up sharp at the fence top and it took me a while to maneuver my legs over so I wouldn't stick myself.

I dragged my second leg over the top of the fence, and I thought clear, but I lost my grip and started to fall. I had dropped about a foot, but my camera's strap snagged a pointed end of the thick wire fencing. I had bought the sturdy leather strap some years before while traveling out west to replace the thin plastic strap the camera came with and the strap's strength caught me.

Dangling ten feet up in the air, I thrashed about, trying to re-establish a foot hold and managed to grab hold of a handful of chain link fence and gain control of my weight.

I looked down at Jeff from where I held on and smiled at him. I pulled myself up several inches and wiggled the camera's strap free then I scrambled down to the ground.

I kneeled between the fence and the shack waiting for my eyes to adjust to the dark and to catch my breath. Though cold out, a heavy sweat ran down the back of my shirt. I held my hand up to Jeff, motioning okay, and turned to the vast yard.

I couldn't make out the layout of the operation, but the vehicle section looked like it covered the east side of the property. I crossed the distance, avoiding random piles of metal and wooden pallets, using the flashlight to guide me.

I remembered the spooky yard from our teen years and how breaking into the yard made for a good Halloween prank when we managed to goad an unsuspecting gullible kid into following us into the spooky graveyard of abandoned cars and white goods. A favorite retold tale involved a poor kid who accidentally locked himself in an abandoned refrigerator and died, but his ghost still roamed over the yard, enticing others to join him the same way.

When I reached the line of wrecked cars, I used the flashlight to examine them. I took my time circling each and found Early's cruiser at the end of the line. In the dark, it didn't look all that bad—but I knew the flash on the camera would expose any secrets.

Using the flashlight, I examined the driver side front panel and found scrapes and scratches, including red paint smears, in contrast to the tan cruiser. I snapped off several photos in the dark, the flash blinding me. I circled to the front of the vehicle and got more shots. Lost in the process I forgot about keeping an ear open for the metal rap on the roof breaking the silence in the yard. When I remembered the predetermined signal, I ran for the fence.

About halfway across the yard, I stumbled on some loose gravel and went down hard on my stomach, just as a vehicle pulled up to the compound gate. The headlights glowed above me and I thanked my good luck in tripping just then; otherwise, I would have been caught in the headlights of the vehicle like the proverbial deer.

As I hunkered down in the dirt, I heard the gate pushed open and the sound of the vehicle rolling to the shack, and voices waft toward me. Two men in conversation climbed out of an old truck, although I couldn't make out any words.

I gasped for air as the fall took the wind out of me, and like another sign of luck, the flashlight beam faded dark from the impact. I rolled over on my back, and looking up through a clearing in the trees, saw a splattering of stars in night sky. I rested there in the quiet waiting for the formless voices to retire to the office. Someone in the shack turned on a light, but no shouts or other indications that they found anything amiss made its way to me.

Struggling to my feet, I made my way to the fence without further stumbling, where Jeff looked out at me from behind the wire.

"It's about time!" he whispered as I stood, bent over at the base of the fence, trying to catch my breath before starting the long climb.

"They didn't see me," I whispered in the dark.

I put my hands up on the chain links to begin my ascent when Jeff said, "As long as they've opened the gate, why don't you use it?"

I looked at him through the wire and smiled.

I took a quick glance at the office shack and jogged over to and through the gate.

Meeting Jeff, I juggled the flashlight until the bulb burned bright again. We ran over to the Jeep and climbed in. I put the flashlight back in the glove box, released the parking brake, and putting the gear in neutral, we coasted a ways before I started the engine.

"The Whitakers must be working late," I said, as we drove away.

"Well?" Jeff asked after we drove off.

"Well, what?" I said, switching the headlights on when we were a hundred yards away.

"What did you find?"

"Well, Early's cruiser is there for sure, and it looks like there are scratches along the driver's side."

"So what?"

"So I think it shows Early ran up alongside of another car or something. There're red paint marks that shouldn't be there."

"What does that mean?"

"It means Early was in a collision that night, forced off the road, and just didn't go flying off that curve on his own."

"He didn't?"

"No, Gilmore is pretty sure the force of the cruiser hitting the water killed Early, and I'm pretty sure those scratches are evidence Early turning up in the Swannanoa was no accident."

"Unless …"

"Unless what?"

"Maybe those marks are from before, maybe even a long time ago, way before your brother ran off that road."

Of course, that was a possibility…and right then, I didn't know which of the two I'd feel better about.

Chapter Thirteen

Thursday

Mama used to say things looked better in the morning after a good night's sleep, and by and large, I agreed. After the caper at the yard, I dropped Jeff back in town, drove home, and went straight to bed. With the crisp fall air filtering through a partially open window, I slept like a log.

The next morning, I rolled right out of bed before Pa stirred awake. I put a pair of my old running shoes on and a pair of my old gym sweats. Grabbing my little camera, I left the house for a jog as the sun broke over the mountain. I'd been running most of my life, running from one thing or another, but after years of running it takes me longer and longer to warm up. I jogged on the old trail Early and I walked over when we roamed together. It descended the mountain for a couple of miles then leveled off at the Swannanoa, where a flat path hugged the river's edge for several miles in either direction.

I stopped at the riverbank and took a couple of shots of the sunrise in a cloudless sky. The first rays of the morning came over the low gap in the mountain and bounced down the narrow valley out of the east, slicing through town. The light bounced off the morning sleekness of the river flow, the water a tide of energy awakened after a night of heavy sleep under the moon.

Jogging to town, I began to warm up in the Indian summer morning. By the third mile, sweat began to drip from my forehead, and muscles waking from the long night began to loosen. I ran up a deserted Main Street, shops still closed against the night, and turning at Town Hall, huffed it back towards home.

I slowed down on the path up the mountain, my legs more use to the flat lands and trails of the piedmont, but even carrying the camera I managed a steady pace and didn't stop until I reached the house where Pa sat on the porch waiting and drinking coffee.

"You look comfortable," I said.

"Did you have a nice run?"

"There's nothing like a run in the fall morning."

"I expect you'd like a cup of water before your coffee," Pa said.

"Maybe two," I said, doubled over on the walkway, breathing heavy. I made my way into the house and after putting my camera up, pulled a cold-water jug from the refrigerator and drank straight from the spout.

"Use a cup!" Pa shouted from the porch, guessing at what I'd be doing, a leftover habit from my youth.

I found a faded plastic red State cup in the cabinet and took it and the jug out to join him.

"How far did you go?"

"To town and back," I said, pouring a cup of water and downing it in a couple of gulps. "That's, what…eight miles round trip?"

"About that," Pa said, "longer by the road, but you took the trail, right?"

"Down to the river," I said, taking another gulp of water.

"River's pretty this time of year," Pa said, as he rocked in a slow back and forth.

"Lot narrower than I remember, funny…"

"What's funny?"

"The river seeming narrower, like Main Street used to seem the longest walk. Now, it's a short jog from one end to the other. It used to take Early and me a whole Saturday morning to walk through town, and now…"

"The memory is unreliable, Emma, it can play tricks on you."

"You think so?"

"Time plays tricks on a person, too," Pa said. "You can't stop time, Emma. One day you wake up with all the time in the world, and the next day, you start counting the time left. Be careful about how you spend your time. We don't know how much of it the Good Lord has allotted us on this here earth, but don't waste it on memories of the past."

"Mama and Early earned more than the share of time divvied out to them, Pa."

"Emma, I'm not sure what the Good Lord's reasoning is when He gives out the time shares…no man does. I do know He gives everyone what is deserved."

I didn't know if I agreed with him, about the time thing. If a compassionate God awarded long life to those who deserve it, then why did children die young? I couldn't accept they deserved their short time. What kind of a God dealt out time in droplets to some and jars full to others? Two people I loved more than anything were gone, their time on this earth done, gone sooner than need be to my way of thinking; and in the case of Early, I needed to find out why.

The water from the shower head came out little better than a trickle, but after a sweaty run, it still felt refreshing. I soaped up my body and washed my hair. After rinsing, I dried off with a coarse towel that looked older than me. I slipped on another flannel shirt from the clothes box, a pair of clean athletic socks, and pushed my feet into my moccasin boots.

When I came out, I found Pa standing by the door, looking like he needed to go someplace.

"What's up?"

"Get your purse, we going over to Laurel Ridge and visit with Louise."

"Why?"

"Because you haven't seen her in a while, and she's getting old."

◆◇◆

People say Louise and her people been living up on Laurel Ridge there since before the first settlers came into the valley and everyone knew Louise knew the native magic of herbs and potions. I spent time with Louise and her people when growing up. Used to be, Early and I ran with her boys.

"Have you been to visit with Louise and her family, how are they doing?"

Pa didn't respond to my question right away as he concentrated on the road as he drove. "Oh, they're fine. They've been raising a herd of Black Angus that people say is real good beef. They sell it to a bunch of fancy restaurants down in the city that serve free range beef, you know, no hormones and such. They've been making a right good living by it. You should see the big four-wheel drive truck that Louise is driving. She has to use a ladder to get in the cab."

"She still driving?"

"Yeah, and you better watch yourself if you find yourself up on a road that way."

The Looking Bird spread hovered over the southernmost section of the Swannanoa, where the big river bent in two and cascaded through a rock formation that created rare rapids through the tame flow. Two ancient oaks framed the road entrance to the compound that identified their land, tucked in a green valley of fertile soil that produced the sweet grass that generations of cattle grazed on.

I saw not much had changed since my last visit, back in my high school days. Two lines of metal roofed houses lined the lone road through the small area. Freshly painted white clapboard adorned the small square homes and several giant oak trees fronted each home site, growing bare in the fall, heading to winter, but I knew provided a welcome shade in the summer.

When Early and I visited during summer breaks, Louise

would sit with us under the shade and tell us tales of the old Cherokee that first settled the Valley of the Three Forks.

When Louise heard the truck, she came out of one of the bigger houses and waved at us. Her long, flowing hair had turned gray, but her smile lit up the compound, and a dark violet aura, a sign of the highest spiritual level, spread out from her in welcome. Louise's dark eyes glowed mysteriously, like ancient orbs, and she spoke in a voice like song in the wind.

"My daughter," Louise greeted me, hugging my shoulders, "you have been away long."

"Mother Louise," I returned the welcome.

Louise led me and Pa off to a grouping of rough cedar hewed chairs where we sat in the glow of the morning sun.

"Tell me, my daughter, are your visions bright?"

"Yes, mostly bright."

"Then all is well with your spirit."

And then, because I needed to, not that she would be able to offer any real advice on the matter, but I still told her of my suspicions of Early's accident. I could tell Pa didn't want me to, but in the end, I felt better for it. By the time I'd finished, the midday sun had risen high in the sky and Louise asked us to stay for supper. I noticed Pa didn't say much through the whole afternoon.

Chapter Fourteen

Friday

The morning broke clear and cold although heavy dew soaked the ground, bushes and trees. I put on running shoes and sweats and plodded out the door working up an enthusiasm. Four miles of nice dirt trail stood between the Davis's place and Pa's. I surprised myself by remembering the zig zagged route between thick rhododendrons.

At about the halfway point, mile two, the trail turned downward, and I picked up the pace arriving in the Davis's front yard in less than an hour since leaving Pa's.

Four half-dressed boys and a frantic mother and grandmother stormed about the kitchen pouring orange juice into glasses and filling large bowls with breakfast cereal and milk. A half-full baking sheet of fat biscuits sat on the stove top with bowls of homemade preserves and fresh butter nearby.

"What's going on?" I said as I entered into the before-school-morning bedlam.

"We're late," Becky said from a counter where she divided a loaf of bread into stacks and layered lunch meat, cheese and sandwich spread. "We stayed up watching football last night."

The madhouse continued for another ten minutes or so until the boys were chased out the door with bag lunches in hand. JB took the two youngest boys to drop them off, and William rode as Little Earl drove the old Jeep over to the high school.

"I see everyone getting off to an early start," I said, taking a seat that a minute ago had belonged to Little Earl.

"It's like this in the mornings," Mother Davis said with a smile as she wiped down a counter.

121

"Well, is everyone looking forward to the big game tonight?"

"I guess you didn't hear," Becky said, as she washed dishes at the sink.

"What?"

"Coach Shaw told Little Earl he wasn't starting on offense tonight."

"Why is that?"

"He told him he's going to start Hunter Shaw."

"Just like that?"

"I guess with Early gone he doesn't feel any obligation."

"How did Little Earl take it?"

"He says he's looking forward to it, just playing linebacker, like his dad."

After a long breakfast, during which I managed to down several fat biscuits and a couple of eggs, we passed the time talking, but tried to speak about everything except Early Shaw. After I couldn't eat another bite, Becky drove me back over to Pa's house. I carried back several of Mother Davis's biscuits for Pa, but our place sat deserted, Pa's whereabouts unknown for the time being.

I went back to the bathroom and took a quick shower. I dried off but skipped the make-up. I pulled on a pair of old high school jeans and flannel shirt from the attic box and tried to remind myself I might need to get a load of laundry going.

Pa's house sits on a flat section about halfway up the ridge of the lower section of Black Mountain. Pa cut a two-mile trail back of the house that led through the forest stand and up to the crest. If you climbed to the crest in the early fall you could look west for miles out into the Blue Ridge, the tree canopy a golden hue of leaves, like a thick carpet, stretching as far as the mist would let you see.

Early and I would hike the trail a couple of times a week. He'd take the rifle in case we'd run a doe or coon, but we walked up there to get out in the fresh air, to feel alive. Mama liked to climb the trail in the morning. She'd slip on a pair of old brogans two sizes large for her and stomp her way up the hill in her nightgown, the light material billowing in the dawn breeze, ghostlike, a gray mountain apparition. Likely as not, it would be well past breakfast before she came down.

"What were you doing up there, Mama?" I'd ask her when she came in.

"Thinking," she'd say.

After my shower I climbed the trail and hiked along the rim into the late afternoon, stopping intermittently to rest and to take pictures of the scenery. When the sun began to ease and the temperature fell some, I turned and meandered back a different way. From the ridge line above the house, you could see Tennessee to the west, and to the east, the town, just visible in the valley mist, like a shadow on water, there and then not, like a ghost town.

The high school stadium lights were burning dim in the distance, taking hold, the clusters visible above the cloudlike mist, like floating bowls, the field itself hidden, maybe invisible to everyone but the fans.

Lot of boys came across that field there, rite of passage, boys to men, small town football, the field of dreams. Like the stadium, visible from afar, a dream at the edge of sleep.

Pa hadn't been to many games over the last few years, so he wasn't up to joining us. I drove over to the Davises' that evening and parked in front. Little Earl and William left for the game two hours earlier, having to suit up and warm up before a 7:00 PM kick off. Mother Davis packed a soft cooler with sandwiches and a healthy snack bag of candied dried fruit and apple slices, although I knew I'd buy a little bowl of nachos and cheese from the concession stand.

In the early evening, I could tell the short Indian summer

about ran its course, and I remembered to bring a coat to the game. The crisp fall night, great for the players, could be rough for unsuspecting fans. Taking the Jeep, I started down the mountain and Becky brought the rest of the family.

We found a line of trucks and SUVs backed up the road leading to the stadium, the procession flowing slower and slower. Members of a Boy Scout troop, wielding flashlights, directed traffic. The paved stadium lot filled up and the rest of us drove onto a mowed grass field adjacent to the stadium that doubled as over-flow parking.

At 7:00 sharp, the teams lined up in kick-off formation and the crowd rose as one. I pulled my camera out and replaced the 50mm lens with a variable telephoto zoom lens, right in time to catch the Broncos' kicker skip step to the line, and swinging soccer style, boot the ball into the air. I watched as the Lenore back caught the ball at the one-yard line. The player made it out to the three-yard line where a Bronco defender flattened the boy.

"Early Shaw with the tackle for the Broncos," someone in the press box announced, "first and ten, Lenore."

As I remembered his father, Little Earl played like a possessed demon, roaming the field from sideline to sideline, like a lion guarding his personal domain.

At halftime, before the bands played, Madeline Bowman-Shaw, Principal and daughter of Pastor Shaw, walked on to the turf, and using a portable mic, spoke to the crowd.

"The band, team, faculty, and staff of Black Mountain High wanted to take this moment to remember the recent passing of our friend and public servant, Chief Early Shaw, who died last Friday. It is with great sadness that we bid farewell to such a great man." Turning to the band, she said, "For those of you who don't know, I marched out here on this same field, me and my flute, the same field where I watched Chief Shaw play football for four wonderful years. Chief Shaw lived like he played—hard—and he will be missed.

Although I'm sure he wouldn't be able to stay still long enough to do it himself, may I ask that we pause in a minute of silence in his memory."

The second half of football followed the same pattern as the first with both teams unable to move the ball on offense. With seconds left and the Broncos in possession of the ball, Coach Shaw kept Little Earl out on the field to play quarterback. Little Earl took the center snap and fading back three steps launched a left-handed pass down the field.

I'm sure, in years to come, the length of that pass will come to grow to sixty, seventy, maybe seventy-five yards, but truth be told, it carried about fifty, but it hit the wide out in full stride, and he scooted the last few yards into the end zone as time expired in the game.

"Touchdown, Broncos!" the announcer's voice boomed out of the P.A. system.

Gathering up our things, we headed to the exit, following behind a happy crowd. Finding myself trailing behind Franklyn Shaw, I hurried on, and catching up to him, said, "I didn't see Granddaddy Shaw out tonight."

"No, he didn't make it," he said, continuing his slow but steady walk, the crowd moving like one, in a slow flow, like sap down the side of a tree.

"Someone said he comes to all the games," I said as a few departing fans tried to push by.

"He does," the mayor said, "but like I've told you a couple of times, he's been off his feet, here lately, so I didn't expect he'd make it out tonight; although, when he hears about this game, he'll be sorry he missed it."

"I bet. Little Earl put on a show tonight, much like his Dad used to."

"Yeah, so, now that you saw your game, I guess you'll be heading out?"

"I don't know, Franklyn. I need to see Granddaddy before I leave."

"Now, Emma, I've told you he isn't up to seeing people right now."

"He's been off his feet since when, last Friday?" I asked

Franklyn stopped his journey to the parking lot and the two of us made a wide island there in the middle of the walk that parted the exiting crowd, making them change course to avoid us, like ships trying to avoid an iceberg.

Turning full around, Franklyn looked at me and said, "Look Emma, since your first day up here you've been gnawing at something, like an old dog on an old bone, and I'd like to hear it straight."

"I want to talk Granddaddy, that's all."

"Look, Emma we told you, you can't talk to Granddaddy. Now, you've buried your brother and had your chance to visit with family. Now, you've even seen a football game…so how much longer do you plan to hang around town? Don't you have a job to get back to?"

"Are you trying to get rid of me, Franklyn? What's the hurry?"

"Oh, I don't know, I should think you'd want to be on your way and we'd all like to get back to our little lives."

Our pause in the march out of the stadium allowed time for Becky and the rest of the family to catch up to us. Mayor Franklyn Shaw looked around at the family and hitching up his pants, turned around and joined the crowd flowing along the stadium sidewalk toward the parking lot.

I didn't know where Granddaddy Shaw fit in all this, or what Early had got his self into, but whatever, I figured it got my big brother killed.

Chapter Fifteen

Saturday

The next morning, out of a clear sky, a cold wind blew down the mountain filling the valley with a chill that you met with strong coffee and a heavy coat. After toast for breakfast, two cups of my Pa's dark brew, and after he read a morning passage from Proverbs 11:12 – *Whoever diligently seeks good, seeks favor…Blessed is the man who remains steadfast under trial,* I sat on the porch a while, adding up my progress to date.

Women I know handle their problems in different ways. Some eat their way through them, and others like to clean. I like to run. After deciding the mystery of Early's death wouldn't get solved from the porch, I got up and put on running shoes, and leaving Pa's, I ran up the north trail, heading into the higher elevations around Black Mountain.

I'm a dissociative runner, and don't think about the run itself, but I let my mind roam to occupy the time. This works fine if I run on a familiar route where I don't have to think about turns and street crossings, but on unfamiliar paths, it can be dangerous if my mind is wandering when I should be paying attention to rocks and tree roots. After my second trip and near-fall, I decided I had enough. At that point, I had enjoyed the run, but to save the wear and tear on my knees I turned around and headed back, at a careful walk.

When I reached the house, I found Pa out back of the house chopping firewood. Although Pa put in electricity back when we were small, he didn't bother with heat in the house, except from what the wood burning stove in the kitchen could provide. The surrounding woods supplied more than enough fuel for winters. The three bedrooms opened up right off the

127

kitchen area, and during the coldest months, we'd open our doors and the heat from the stove would filter in and keep the rooms cozy. 'Course, if you didn't bank the fire right, it might go out during the night and you'd wake up to an icy house.

Although the evangelists say we are saved by grace alone and not works, here in the mountains we say there is grace in work. By hard work we showed our neighbors and the Lord what we are made of.

Taking a heavy maul, Pa split sections of oak in half, and then in quarters, and then in eights, until the sections were small enough to be put into the wood stove box. The logs held the cold from the night before which helped the effort, but for tough pieces, he used a wedge and the hammer end of the maul to split the wood. I joined him and gathered up and stacked the pieces as he split them. Working as a team, we spent the afternoon replenishing the log lot ahead of the next heavy winter when the previous year's stored dry wood would be burned.

"That's a day's work, for sure," I said, tossing him a rough towel when, after several hours, he looked to be done. "Are you working something out, something to talk about?"

"There's something I've been meaning to talk to you about, but just haven't been able to work out how to say it."

"About Early?"

"Well," he paused, then said, "yeah, what do you make of all of it?"

Without going into a lot of detail, I said, "I think Early had a scheme going with the Shaws, going on a year or two."

"What kind of a scheme?"

"Well, for one thing, a make-money-scheme."

"So this has something to do with his death?"

"My best guess," I said, heading toward the house.

"I don't know, Emma," he said, following me, "the Shaws may be a conniving bunch, but I don't peg them for killers."

After a quick shower, I dug old clean clothes from the

storage box to replace my dirty sweats and slipped on my moccasin boots. I grabbed my brush, and joining Pa at the table, I brushed out my hair and started braiding it Indian style.

"Pa, I figure there's a connection here between Early and Granddaddy, and until I know for sure, I'm not going to rest over it."

"I'm not the one to be giving out advice, but in this matter, you best be leaving this be."

"You're the tenth person to warn me off this thing…why?"

"'Cause you might not like what you find out."

The Town of Black Mountain closes up pretty tight come nightfall. Mill men need to get up early so they go to bed early. Women of the house face chores early in the morning so they go to bed early, too. Pa turned in about twilight. I debated whether he needed the sleep or just wanted to get to bed to read from his Bible. Since Pa didn't have a TV, and I wanted to catch some of the night time State football game, I told him I wanted to ride into town to *The Coffee Bean,* the only place with a TV, and open at that time of night.

"Do you want me to ride along with you?" he asked me.

"No, Pa, you go on to bed."

"Don't seem right, woman on her own in town at night."

"Pa, don't worry. I mean what could happen in Black Mountain?"

The bane of small-town gossip isn't so much that it can hurt the undeserving, but that it more often than not is based on some true fact. Hearing about my brother Early's lawlessness from second-hand sources allowed me to maintain a façade of hope that somehow it might not be true, although below the surface of my hope, I realized it might be true enough.

Of course, with Early dead, finding a source to confirm or

deny the rumor proved difficult.

After parking a couple of blocks down from the coffee shop, I got out and walked. I had just passed the open alley between buildings when someone reached out, and wrapping their left arm about my neck, pulled me into the dark space. By his size, I figured my assailant to be a man, and forcing his forearm up against my throat, he lifted me up so my toes barely touched the ground. He leaned down so we saw eye to eye, and then, he loosened his grip and I settled back down onto my two feet. I could tell by his strength that breaking away would be impossible, so I didn't struggle, trying to save my breath.

"Now, Pocahontas," the man hissed into my face, I assumed referring to my long, braided hair. A full ski mask covered the man's head, but his eyes shone black in the night light, shining out of two slits in the wool cover. "You've been warned about poking around town about this deal with your brother. Now, just understand, Early's luck just ran its course, and you've worn out your welcome. So," he lowered his arm from my neck, and pointing a finger at me, said, "you need to move on and leave town before something bad happens."

With his arm loose on my neck, I looked up and down the alley, judging my chances of a dash to freedom. Whether or not I would have made it is conjecture since I didn't have to chance it, because Jeff Carson came around the building right at that moment.

I suppose my attacker saw the movement, because he turned away from me, fully around, and let Jeff punch him up aside his chin, the resulting force of the blow sending the man reeling. On his way down, the man reached out and grabbed hold of my shoulder and I started a tumble to the ground with him. Luckily, before I hit the pavement, Jeff caught me by the waist.

Unfortunately, with Jeff engaged with rescuing and preventing further harm to me, the attacker rolled to his feet and made his escape, disappearing down the alleyway.

"Are you alright?" Jeff asked, holding me off the ground.

"No," I croaked out, "that guy almost broke my neck. Who was it?"

"I don't know," Jeff said, looking down the dark passage between buildings. "A mugger, I guess."

I looked up at Jeff. I wondered if I should tell him what my assailant had said to me. I don't know why I didn't repeat the man's warning; something about his bearing.

"Where did you come from?"

"I saw you from the shop window a minute ago and I hurried after you."

"Why?"

"I figured you were going to The Coffee Bean."

"Why?"

"It's the only place open in town this time of night. I like to stop in before going home, to check out May's cookie selection."

When Jeff got me steady enough so I could stand, I said, "Don't you think you should chase the guy?"

"No, he disappeared; besides, the way I clocked him, he'll be feeling bad enough. I felt his jaw break when I hit him."

Holding on to my arm, he asked me, "You feel like getting something to drink?"

I didn't know if the invitation was because he wanted to spend time with me or if he thought I might need an alcohol fix for my nerves. Either way, I nodded my head and we made our way down the walk.

"Do you want to go over to the hospital for a checkup?"

"No, I'm okay," I said, regaining my voice. "He put a good hold on me, but not long enough to cause any harm. Thanks to you, again."

"Well, I'm just happy I came along when I did."

"My hero!"

We reached the doorway of The Coffee Bean and Jeff

opened the door and let me in.

A noisy crowd filled the room with patrons packed in front of the wall mounted TV showing the State game, but it surprised me to see Shelby and Franklyn Shaw sitting in the last booth along the inside wall. Though tucked away and well-hidden to patrons sitting in the other café seats, I could see from the doorway they were having a social date as opposed to a business meeting.

Shelby wore her hair down and it splayed over a dark burgundy sweater that, as usual, clung to her form. Somehow, she managed to slip into a pair of tight skinny denim jeans and her heels shone bright red from under the table. Franklyn tried his best to look hip and casual in khaki pants and a white polo shirt, but his bulk made him look out of his element, like a fat cow trying to roost in the hen house.

"Hello, you two," I said, after I wobbled over to their booth with Jeff steadying me by holding onto my arm.

"Emma," Franklyn acknowledged me.

"You folks not interested in the game?" I asked the two love birds, their shared aura yo-yoing through a variety of colors.

"We can see the game from here," Shelby said, slurring her words a bit, the result of several empty wine glasses sitting on the table.

"Mind if we join you?" I asked.

"Look, Emma," Jeff said before I could take a seat. "I've got to be going so if you're going to be okay…"

"Sure," I said, disappointed, but not enough to give up a chance to talk to Franklyn, "sure, and thanks again!"

"What's that about?" Franklyn asked as Jeff left us. "Something happen?"

"Nothing important," I said, as my hero made his way to the door. "May I?" I asked again, pointing to the empty booth bench opposite them.

"Sure," Shelby said, "are you buying?"

"Why not," I said, sitting heavily, happy to be off my feet. I waved to a waitress roaming the floor and I ordered another beer for Franklyn, and against my better judgment, another house chardonnay for Shelby, and one for me, too.

After the drinks came and I settled in, I drank half my wine in a gulp and stated the obvious, "You two seem cozy enough."

Franklyn Shaw guzzled down his beer, and placing the empty bottle down on a cardboard coaster said, "Alright Emma," his aura quivering amidst the red hues of nervousness and anger, "you've been angling to know so let me tell it."

"Go on," I said, sitting back in the booth, happy to not say more, my head just clearing. "I'm all ears."

"Okay," he started in, his voice winding up to a high pitch of nervousness, "first off, we didn't know it would come to this. When Shelby came to work at the office, we didn't plan anything. I put her on because Banks and Sister Evelyn thought it would be good for her. Of course, it may look bad, Shelby some kind of niece to me, but she's not blood-related. She's Bank's dead wife's stepdaughter from a previous marriage, no Shaw blood in her.

"Sister met widower Banks up north and got married. Banks is a CPA, used to be a collector for the Treasury Department, and they moved down here when the budget position opened up after Uncle Percy died few years ago. Sister Evelyn wanted to move back home, so forced him to move, even though he took a big pay cut to work for the town.

"Shelby married some jerk right out of high school, but that marriage ended. After Banks and Evelyn married, they brought Shelby and her daughter, Holly, down here to live. When the position opened up, he asked if I'd put her on. Oh, sure, I'd seen Shelby around town, heck, who wouldn't notice her, she's about the prettiest thing in these parts."

"Why, thank you, honey," Shelby said, her aura a rainbow of happiness.

"Yeah, well, you know, right about then we found out about Darlene's cancer. Doc Miller tended her, and we got every specialist in the state, but she couldn't be saved. God knows, I tried."

"I'm sure you did."

"Say what you will, Emma, think what you will, but up until then, nothing happened between Shelby and me. Now, I know what all the talk is around town. I can't help that. We didn't start out to fall in love, but I did. I mean, take a look at her—and seeing her every day, well, who wouldn't fall in love with her? But nothing happened between us before Darlene passed, all that is just rumors."

"So you said. That must have been hard on you?" I said without a drop of sympathy in my voice.

"Harder than I could say," he admitted, without recognizing my tone, "but I wanted to be with her. She said not to worry, that she loved me, and could wait for everything to be settled."

"That's right, honey," she said. "I love every handful of you I can grab hold of."

"Well, Darlene took her turn for the worse, and went fast. I've had a time with the kids in college and all. I got the last one off to Clemson just this fall, and then, with the house empty and poor Darlene dead, I got around to asking Shelby out.

"Now, the rumors about Shelby and me are false. Before Darlene passed, we never saw each other outside of the office, but you know people talk when they can. Before Darlene passed, someone started that rumor that we were seeing each other, and threatened to go to Darlene. I was afraid it would get to Granddaddy. This—this man knew it wasn't true, but he threatened me, anyway. You know Granddaddy, he might be a hard man, but he believes in the marriage vows."

"So?"

"So, the guy came to me and said he would tell Granddaddy and Darlene about my alleged affair with Shelby unless I covered for him."

"Covered?"

"He was working some scam in town and needed protection. I don't have all the details, but I just couldn't let anything get out, false or not. With Darlene hanging on by a thread, and Granddaddy— Well, I told the man I'd look the other way, just as long as he kept his mouth shut."

"Why didn't you go to the police?"

"I didn't go to the police because the man was *your brother*, Early Shaw."

The State football team made a late comeback that night and won the game by an extra point with no time on the clock. Their mobile quarterback eluded several would be tacklers on the last play of the game, and when he looked up the field, he could see the end zone. Darting left and right and stiff-arming the last defender in his way, he tumbled across the goal line doing a somersault and brought the stadium, and the thirty people crowded into The Coffee Bean, to their feet with one roar. Amid the high fives and shouts of joy in the café, I sat still and quiet as I digested what Franklyn told me.

"Early was the man?"

"You knew Early better than anyone, Emma; if he found an angle to exploit, he would. Here, lately, he could go off at any minute with that temper of his, worse than ever. I say from his years of banging his head playing football."

"I don't know that I believe any of this," I said lamely.

"Heck, Emma, you knew your brother, Mr. Scam the Man."

"Were you mad when he approached you?"

"I was mad, alright."

"Mad enough to fire Early, get rid of him somehow?"

"Okay, Emma, here it comes. You been going on and on about some other way your brother's buried dead, so now I'm involved?"

"Sounds good to me, money is a motive enough for murder."

"Money? All I did was look the other way and let him do whatever he wanted. Look here, Emma, you've been snooping and digging around in the past until you can't see the light of present day. First, you say we're covering something up at the mill, and now you want to somehow blame me for what happened to your brother! But it's a big nothing, and you need to move on. Now, I told you a week ago to leave this matter be or you might find out something you didn't want to know and now you've gone and done it. Your big old hero brother could be a real SOB, and not everyone in town is sad to see him gone."

Chapter Sixteen

Sunday

It mattered more than I thought possible—Early not being the hero I wanted him to be. I couldn't believe the evidence against him. I'd known for a while that my big brother shone brightest in my eyes, and not everyone's. Even though he lived on an edge, I knew he'd never step off on the wrong side. Finding out how his life ended still mattered. It's a sad thing, a person dying early, not getting the chance to see kids grow, watch them start families, grandkids maybe, winter snow, summer heat, the crisp air hanging over a sunset-filled horizon. It's a terrible thing to rob a man of what he has left, of what he is due, robbed of the time, maybe, to atone for past sins.

A man's time shouldn't be taken without knowing who and why. The Shaws were involved some way. I didn't figure Early tattling on the mayor and his girl got him killed. Lordy, if so, half the men in the valley would be dead. Early discovered something, and if not the formaldehyde at the mill, and if not the mayor, then something else got him killed…and Granddaddy Shaw knew, so I just had to talk to him.

On Sunday morning, Pa put on his one suit again. Preaching at the Swannanoa Primitive Baptist Church started at 11:00, but Sunday school began an hour earlier. I found Pa up three hours before time, polishing up his shoes.

"I don't know who, Emma," Pa said, as I came into the room rubbing sleep from my eyes, "but someone once said a man feels better when his shoes are shined."

After a minute of heavy brushing, I asked, "What are you going to teach on today?"

"Forgiveness," Pa sang out. The overnight temperature fell into the freezing ranges, and even though a stiff breeze rattled the windowpanes, the wood stove kept the chill out of the room. Pa stroked those shoes vigorous enough to break into a sweat. "Pastor already gave me the passage, so I'm working on the lesson."

"What's the passage?" I asked him, taking a seat across the table, sipping hot coffee.

"Mathew 6:14-15…*For if you forgive men when they sin against you, your heavenly Father will also forgive you. But if you do not forgive men their sins, your Father will not forgive your sins.*"

"Now, that's a powerful word Pa, forgiveness."

"Yes, Emma, a powerful word, indeed."

"A hard row to plow, the forgiveness of others, don't you think?"

"It's hard, but necessary for entering the Kingdom of God, Emma. That's the lesson for this old town."

"How about His earthly Kingdom, Pa?"

"The good Lord rules over both and one goes with the other. Forgiveness begins in your heart, right here on the ground, Emma, that's the real lesson in this here passage."

After I washed up and brushed out my hair, I changed into slacks and the new blouse I'd bought, and exchanged my moccasins for my flats. I put face lotion on and rubbed some color into my cheeks. I applied some gloss to my lips to brighten them up and wrapped a blue scarf around my neck for contrast.

"You clean up good," Pa said when I came out of the bathroom and we headed to my Jeep.

"When it counts," I countered back.

We rode down to church with a strong fall wind blowing,

sending loose leaves rolling across the road like brown waves at the beach. A sky of broken clouds, the first daytime clouds I'd seen since coming to town, stretched over the blue horizon and I wondered if the day would warm up, or did the chill I felt signal the end of the Indian summer.

I saw the church steeple from a ways off, tall and white against the morning sky, standing proud above the tree line. Right when we came up to the church, the bell tolled the start of worship.

Based on age groups, the Sunday school classes congregated in eight different rooms arranged four to a side along an annex that the congregation built on to the west side of the church proper. They raised funds for construction through bake sales, a fall fair, and an annual Christmas tree lot. The annex connected the school classes to the sanctuary via a passage, and contained a convenient separate entrance/exit door to a rear parking lot that came in handy when, if you didn't want to stay for preaching, you could leave before and not be seen.

Pa spoke to his group from a battered podium, leaning on it for support—support in more ways than one, I imagined. His words of forgiveness carried a heavy message, and I could tell the men of the group listened because not an eye wavered during the lesson. An intense discussion on the topic followed, and I don't think I ever felt more proud of my father than right at that moment.

After class, we joined the other parishioners for coffee before going into the sanctuary where Pastor Bennett Shaw led the full congregation in several songs before he took the podium and repeated much of what we discussed in Sunday school, for emphasis, I imagined.

After the service, we filed out and greeted the pastor as we exited the double-wide doors.

"Pastor Bennett," Pa said when we reached the man, "you remember my girl, Emma Louise, Early's sister?"

139

"Of course," the tall man with short graying beard said, "I remember. We're all sorry about the chief, Emma, and you have our sympathies. Know we will be praying for him as he sleeps in wait for the next world."

"I appreciate that, Pastor." I reached for his firm handshake. The man's brilliant yellow aura engulfed him, the color a sign of great spirituality. "Although, I don't know if Early would appreciate the effort."

"No," the pastor said, raising his hand to his breast after the greeting. "I don't think the chief held the faith, much like your pa use to not, but like your pa, we hoped he'd come around in the end."

"Maybe he would have if he hadn't run out of time."

"We know not how much time the Lord has allotted us here on earth, Emma, so whatever it is, we must value it."

"Pastor, I didn't see any other Shaws in your congregation this morning."

"No, I'm afraid the Shaws, by and large, attend First Presbyterian down in town."

"That's unfortunate, Pastor, I wanted to catch up with Granddaddy Shaw."

"Have you been out to the farm?"

"No, I wanted to catch him in town."

"He's not able to come into town, Emma."

"No?"

"No, if you want to see him, you'll need to visit the farm."

"Pastor, I don't believe we'd be welcomed out to the farm."

"Why, Emma, you know any Shaw is welcome out at the farm on Sunday afternoon. You'll get the answers to your questions if you go out there."

The direct line of Shaw descendants began with the arrival

of Walter Shaw from Ireland in 1768. The lineage that spawned the current branch of Shaws started with his grandson, William Shaw, at the end of the Civil War. Recently returned to the valley and happy with his survival, William fathered twelve children, and every Shaw since traces their lineage to that clan although a scattering of other cousins stake claims to Shaw heritage based on William's five brothers, who also settled in the foothills of the Blue Ridge. Regardless of claims of ancestry, the current band of Shaws held title to the land and property that shaped the town and Shaw fortune. They founded most of the town's businesses, and what they didn't start themselves, they bought or stole.

After dropping Pa off at the house, I headed out to the Shaw farm. The Jeep bounced up the road, potholes peppering the way, tires splashing in puddles. I passed under the granite arch marking the beginning of Shaw Farm. The family house appeared at the end of the lane, tall and white on a heavy gray granite foundation, the green manicured grounds spread before me. The field to the north side of the lane held several military-straight rows of trellises stretching to the horizon, carrying heavy grapevines, growing where once cattle grazed in the afternoon sun.

Pulling the Jeep up to a spot behind a surprisingly long row of cars and other vehicles, I turned off the engine and set the brake. The two-story grand farm home looked much like I remembered it. A variety of Shaw progenies, poor and rich, old and young, roamed about the farm, their heads bent against the gaining cold marking the last warmth of the season. Some folk carried paper plates of food prepared for the weekly family visits or disposable plastic cups with who-knew-what liquor concoctions mixed in the outside kitchen behind the house. People I didn't recognize shouted a few words of sympathy or condolence as I made the long walk up the drive, across the lush lawn to the house and up the steps onto the front porch.

"Emma Louise Shaw," an older woman recognized me and greeted, seeing me approach the doorway. Though the years hadn't affected her bearing, she wore them in the wrinkles of her face, but even after my long time away I recognized Mrs. Mathias Shaw.

"Grandma Shaw," I acknowledged the woman, her aura oscillating between silver and white, a combination I see on those on their way to the next world.

"Emma, it's been so long."

"Yes, ma'am, the last time I came up here was…"

"Why, I can't remember when," she said.

"Yes, ma'am, it's been a while."

"Yes," she agreed. Moving to me and reaching out, she took hold of my arms, squeezing with a steely grip. She looked hard at me with unmistakable sadness in her voice and a blue aura emerging, swinging from light to dark about her, a sign a person is generous but critical at the same time. "And now, now poor Early. What a loss. We were devastated when we heard. You know, Lawrence cried when he heard the news, poor boy."

I didn't know which boy she referred to, Early or her son, Lawrence, the current Granddaddy of the Shaw clan.

"Emma!" Franklyn Shaw called from the doorway, "what are you doing up here?"

"Franklyn," Mrs. Mathias Shaw scolded, "where're your manners?"

"I apologize, Grandma, but Emma and I talked in town about this, after which I thought I made it clear for her not to come out here on business."

"Since when is the family farm closed to a Shaw?" the old woman asked. "The farm is open on Sunday to any Shaw who has business with Granddaddy, you know that."

"This business is between Emma and me, Grandma."

"Never-the-less," she ended her time with me, squeezing my arms again, "let's be civil to relatives, no matter how distant they are, shall we?"

"Sure, Grandma," he said to her as she drifted off down the porch, ready to greet another clan member, I'm sure forgetting about me after a few steps, her aura trailing her like steam behind a locomotive.

"Emma," Franklyn started in, "I told you not to try to talk to Granddaddy."

"Listen, Franklyn, there are a few questions I'd like to run by the old man."

"Now, I told you he wasn't up to visitors, and for some reason you don't believe me, but it is the truth and now you've gone and wasted your time driving out here."

"Who's wasting time?" a middle-aged woman asked coming up the steps from the yard. I remembered Franklyn's mother, the former Brenda Charles. Still pretty in her sixties, she looked regal in long black dress, flowing gray hair, and the bright turquoise aura of a care giver.

"Mother," Franklyn said, and introduced me, "this is Emma Shaw, Chief Shaw's sister."

"Oh, yes," she nodded, extending a hand which I reached for and held a moment. "Chief Shaw," she said. "How sorry we all are. You must forgive us, my dear, for not attending the services; you see, Lawrence has not been well these last few months."

"Yes, Mother," Franklyn said, "I explained to Emma, here, about how she couldn't see him, and how she wasted the trip out."

"Oh, yes, Emma," she said, releasing my hand and joining her son in the entryway of the house, forming a formidable roadblock. "Lawrence is unable to receive guests."

"I only need a few words with him."

"To what end, may I ask?"

143

"Well, it's about Early."

"Yes," she said, "what about him?"

"Emma…" Franklyn said in warning.

"Well, Mrs. Shaw," I began, ignoring Franklyn's intimation, but now unsure of what I wanted. "Well, I—"

"She's on a fishing expedition, Mother, nothing more."

"Oh…what's she fishing for?"

"She thinks the chief's death has something to do with the family, and she's been snooping around trying to find someone to blame."

"Why would someone in the family know something about your brother's death?"

"That's what I want to find out."

"Franklyn, I thought the chief died in an accident?"

"He did, Mother."

"They think an accident, Mrs. Shaw, but I don't think so."

Mrs. Lawrence Shaw paused on the porch of the house and after a minute said, "Emma, I know the town people find it hard understanding the Shaws. Why, it took me a while myself when I first came into the family, but we aren't monsters up here; in fact, we are quite generous with our many neighbors. We'd be the last to stand in the way of the truth. Franklyn, I don't see any harm in letting Emma in to see Lawrence."

"But Mother—"

"Now, let's not have an argument, after all, Emma did drive out here, so the least we can do is humor her curiosity."

Although I didn't like the way she said that, I welcomed the chance to see Granddaddy Lawrence Shaw.

Brenda Shaw turned, and beckoning me with her head, she led the way around Franklyn and into the house. A long hallway divided the first floor with a formal living room packed with ornate furniture on one side, and on the other, a library with walls of bookcases, and thick, leather chairs. The next set of rooms held a dining area and kitchen. The long dining table held a variety of serving pans and casserole dishes that displayed that Sunday's supper for the visiting clan.

At a room in the back, I found a gathering of family at a door entrance where a decided hush held sway. Both women and men stood about reverently, like waiting for a church service to start. Randall Shaw and several others were in the room arranged around a heavy hospital bed. Tubes and cords from a variety of monitors and other medical devices splayed across and connected to someone reclining in the bed.

At first, I didn't recognize the person, but upon entering and looking closer, I recognized Granddaddy Lawrence Shaw, comatose, his aura oscillating between the gray of sickness, and the black of death.

Doc Miller and Randall Shaw saw me standing there, gawking, and coming over, they took me by the arms and guided me out.

Doc Miller Shaw said, "I thought we told you not to come up here and bother us with your nonsense."

The group of us all started talking at once, but before the din rose, Mrs. Shaw raised a hand to the four of us, silencing the squabble. Waving everyone to follow, she led us back down the hall to the library where, after entering, she slid two pocket doors closed and sealed us off from the rest of the household.

"Now, Franklyn, Miller, Randall," she said, after taking a seat on a small brown leather sofa, "suppose one of you three tell me what this is about?"

Randall started the explanation. "This fool lady thinks we are connected to her brother's death."

"Who's connected?"

"The Shaws," Miller said, "but more precisely Granddaddy."

Turning to me, she said, "Is this true Emma?"

I hadn't expected the conference with Mrs. Shaw, and the unexpected situation took the wind out of my sails, but I ploughed in anyway, hoping I sounded professional; although, at the moment, I would have accepted coherent.

"You see, Mrs. Shaw, I can't see Early just running off that road like that. I think he was on police business and I want to know what."

"Like what?"

"That's what I wanted to ask Granddaddy Lawrence about."

"And now, after you see him in there?"

"Well, of course, now that I see his condition, I don't suppose he would know much about anything Early was working on. I assume he's been like this a while…"

"For a year and the last three months, comatose," Doc Miller Shaw said. "Oh, he comes around from time to time, Alzheimer's, like when we told him about Early getting killed, but only for a few minutes at a time, in fact since then, no more at all."

"Yeah, well, obviously he couldn't have much to do with it, but the family still looks suspicious to me."

"How so?" Mrs. Shaw asked.

"Why do you keep it a secret how bad Granddaddy Lawrence is, like you're hiding something? Would of saved a lot of questions if I knew back when I first came to town."

"We told you," Randall Shaw said, "several times."

"Just what is it you suspect?" Mrs. Shaw asked.

"I think Early was working on a case that involved you Shaws."

"What kind of case?"

"A case that gave Early enough evidence to use to blackmail Granddaddy."

"Blackmail," Mrs. Shaw asked, "but for what?"

"I think, for one thing, to keep his job…and maybe for money."

"Money?" the three Shaw brothers said, as one.

"You're nuts, Emma," Doc Miller said. "In his condition, Granddaddy Lawrence couldn't plan much of anything like that."

"Then why are you all trying to cover up what happened to Early that night?"

"What do you mean?"

"I'm sure Early was on police business that night, and that's how he ended up dead. I don't know why, but you all are trying to hide something, and it has something to do with Early's death."

"No, Emma," Mrs. Lawrence Shaw said, interrupting the discussion. "We wouldn't do anything against Early." Getting up from the sofa, she moved to the window and looked out at the lawn and extended family scattered about in different groups. "Boys," she directed her sons, "would you leave Emma and me alone for a spell?"

She led the group of grumbling men out, all acting like third graders, their communal muddy brown-green aura of jealously and greed flowing after them. After closing the doors on them she turned to me and said, "No Emma, you see, Lawrence wouldn't do anything against Early—not ever."

"What makes you say that?"

"Because, Emma, your brother, Early Shaw, he was Lawrence's son."

Chapter Seventeen

Lawrence Shaw

Mama's family, the other mill workers and blacks, lived in Mill Row back then. Her daddy worked at the mill, but how he died remained a mystery. The single barrel of his little 410 was empty when they found him. Her mama put the shotgun back up over the front door, and the next morning took on his shift at the mill. Mama, being the oldest, quit school to look after her younger sisters.

I've seen pictures of Mama back then; more than pretty, with hair the color of the crisp golden field hay after it dried in the sun. Up until the day she died, her eyes matched the high blue sky on a clear fall morning.

When young, Mama could chatter on non-stop. Used to be you couldn't get her to slow up, but with age, she settled into a quiet stage. She took to smoking a little cob pipe. She grew a patch of tobacco every year and dried it in a little shack on the south side of the barn. In the evenings, right before the sun set beyond the valley, Mama would step out on the porch and sit in her rocker. She'd light up the little pipe and stare out into the distance as she rocked, watching another day come to a close in the mountains.

I'd ask her then, about being so quiet.

She'd smile at me and say, "It's no bother, Emma Louise, one day you'll come to know, but it can wait for now."

"I'm sorry," I said to Mrs. Lawrence Shaw, "what did you say?"

"I said, Early's father is Lawrence Shaw—Granddaddy Shaw. Lawrence is daddy to our four boys…and your brother."

"What are you talking about?"

"You see," she said, taking a seat on the sofa, "Lawrence told me this story back before we married. He wanted to make sure I understood some things before I committed to him. So he told me of his hell-raising days growing up. He'd been thrown out of school more times than could be counted. His daddy—Granddaddy Mathias to the Shaw clan back then— tolerated it, spoiled Lawrence rotten. Gave him anything he wanted, and the young Lawrence ran rough shod over the town and everyone in it. The mill, back then, employed 400 workers and every family in town owed their livelihood to the mill, so there wasn't much anyone could do.

"Well, when your mother, Dot Brown, started at the high school, Lawrence met his match. The town girls envied Dot Brown, hands down, your mama being the prettiest girl in the mountains. I know, even though younger than me, you could see how special she carried herself, everyone knew."

"Mrs. Shaw—"

"No, let me say my piece, I owe it to Early, and you, Emma. Well, in his 12th grade year, Dot came to the high school for her first semester. It didn't take long for him to fall for her, but she, still young with more than four years between them, held him off as long as she could. Of course, Grandma and Granddaddy Mathias didn't feel it proper for Lawrence to be seeing someone from down Mill Row. They were snobs about it.

"One day, Granddaddy Mathias laid down the law and told Lawrence to give up the girl, but of course that was the worst thing he could do, because it bowed the young man's back and he kept right on seeing her, making the friendship intimate. Dot stayed out late one night, and her daddy took to looking for the two of them. He found them here at the farm, out in the barn. Mr. Brown brought along a little bird gun and he caught them up in the hay loft. He went wild with anger, I mean who could blame him, his little girl just out of elementary school and this old teen man been skipped over two grades, both hunkered down in the hay together.

"Well, Mr. Brown shot off a blast up into the rafters above the couple, and I'm sure the roar of the shotgun in the wooden barn about scared them to death. Lawrence told me he tried to talk to Mr. Brown, but the man loaded a second shell and blasted away into the rafters. Lawrence said he feared for his life and jumped from the hay loft. He hit the floor on his feet and flew to the barn door.

"Granddaddy Mathias, having heard the ruckus, came out to the barn and came through the doorway just then, toting a squirrel gun. To tell the truth, I'm sure Mr. Brown was only trying to scare them, but Granddaddy didn't know that, and in the dark, couldn't make anything out. All he saw was someone chasing his son and reloading a rifle.

"Well, God bless him, I don't blame him, back then—or even now. With his son apparently running for his life, he did the first thing that came to him and shot at Mr. Brown in the dark. He explained later that he thought he caught a horse thief in the barn getting ready to haul off one of his prized trotters.

"The first shot caught Mr. Brown in the shoulder and sent him down. In the glare of the blast, Mr. Brown fired back and missed everything, but the ricochet from the spread caught Granddaddy Mathias in the leg. Course, remember now, it's still dark in the barn with a faint light coming in through the loft window from a half moon, but Granddaddy could see the man getting to his feet, and I'm sure, he thought, going to shoot at them, so Granddaddy Mathias fired off a second shot that killed your grandfather.

"By this time, Grandma and Lawrence's brother, Michael, were up and coming out to see what was what. Someone found a lantern and put a match to the wick and the barn lit up, and then everyone could see the mess. Lawrence confessed to what happened, and poor Dot Brown, climbing down from the loft, hay clinging to her hair, her dress half off, ran to her pa lying on the soft barn floor, blood everywhere."

She paused for a minute or two and I waited, unsure of the end of the tale. Her aura wavered amid the green shades, indicating someone with the capacity to love greatly. She continued. "Well, Uncle William Shaw, the town sheriff back then, someone called him, and he came on out and looked at the mess. In retrospect, the family didn't shine its brightest that hour, but given the circumstances, he didn't see any need to officially carry it forward. He called it an accident and though the family made out, they still had Dot and her reputation to think about.

"Granddaddy Mathias apologized, but given the circumstances, he wouldn't take any blame since the man trespassed, and in his words, 'shouldn't of been slinking around the barn in the dark', to begin with.

"They got Mr. Brown up and put him in the back of the truck and delivered him back to his people in Mill Row.

"The family circled the wagons and not much more was said about any of this. I didn't hear anything about the whole episode until Lawrence told me during our engagement."

"What about Early?"

"The family wouldn't allow the match. Uncle Whitley Shaw sat on the county draft board then, so he changed Lawrence's status to 1A and they drafted him into the army. He left right after that to basic training. He spent two years in the army, including a tour in Vietnam.

"It wasn't until after he shipped out that they found out about the baby. That first year, Mother Shaw loved on Baby Early. They weren't sure what would happen when Lawrence came home, so treated Early like family. When Lawrence got his first leave, he came back, but he'd changed. He didn't even know about Early until he came home. Your mama tried to make it right by him, but Lawrence broke it off, denying the baby was his.

"So with the family and Lawrence against a marriage, they lined up your pa, Logan. He's a distant relative of the clan and just back from the war his self. He'd been bouncing around, with some problems of his own and not many prospects, so he agreed to marry your ma and they put him on at the mill. Though a few knew and others suspected Early wasn't his baby, no one said much about it. Your pa was smitten by Dot, of course, and I know she grew to love him.

"Soon after Lawrence got out of the army, we met and fell in love, and except for making sure he watched after Early when necessary, he's been loyal to me all these years."

I wondered if Early knew, so asked her and waited to see if her aura blinked dark pink. "Did Early find out about this?"

"I don't think so, Emma," she said, her aura a steady green. "Lawrence kept things to himself, and I take it your ma and pa did the same."

"Not a word, at least not to me, all these years."

"Well, it should have been left to your ma and pa for telling secrets like this, not me."

"I don't understand how they kept this from me, from us?"

"Well, if you hadn't insisted on talking with my husband today you could have saved yourself the trouble. Dear Lawrence won't be telling stories anymore, and Granddaddy Mathias passed away years ago. Of course, Mother Shaw can hardly make sense of her memories now days. Michael died in Vietnam couple of years after, and besides me and your pa, no one alive knows what happened that night so long ago."

"What about Mama coming up here all those years, on Wednesday nights?"

"Your mama couldn't afford regular doctor care, so the family arranged for Doc Horace Shaw, from Spring Lake way, to come out Wednesday evenings for a well-baby check, because of your mother's youth. They asked him to keep it quiet. Of course, your ma wouldn't see taking it as charity, so she insisted on doing some laundry when she came to make payment for the doctor visits.

"After Early was born, she came to do the work for pay. I know early on, she came up to be around Lawrence, even if for just a little, but it was over between them after Lawrence and I married. Lawrence remembered his obligation, Emma, and tried to be there for Early, at least…at least up until last weekend."

"Franklyn and Randall know about all this?"

"No, Lawrence reasoned it didn't matter. By the way, I have something for you. Mother Shaw been saving it for a while and now I believe has forgotten all about it, but I knew where it was all these years and now, well, I guess it can't hurt to give it to you."

"What is it?" I asked the lady when she handed me an old photograph album.

"Those are pictures of Early that first year he stayed here."

"Baby pictures," I asked opening the album and looking at a set of baby photographs taken of a just-born to one-year-old.

"Yes, Mother Shaw just loved your brother and insisted on pictures. Of course, when Lawrence came home, she lost interest. I thought that maybe you'd want them."

"I just can't believe all this."

"Truth be told," she said with a hint of disappointment, "I worry about just how many other distant offspring running around Black Mountain could lay claim to the Shaw name."

No telling.

It's not every day you find out something new about a dead brother. It wasn't so much that Early and I were half-siblings, but more that ma and pa kept the secret for so long. I don't expect they discussed it any, wanting to keep the façade up. If

Early knew, he never hinted at it with me, but I should have figured it.

Physically, we grew into polar opposites, although our active lives mirrored each other. I often wondered why Early's aura ran through shades different than mine. While my aura shown the bright violet of the gifted psychic, Early's throbbed amid the dark earth shades of brown, denoting a tendency toward greed, like all the Shaw men.

"Mother," I heard Franklyn call from beyond the door.

"Yes, come in," she answered.

"Is everything alright?"

"Yes, yes," she explained and getting to her feet said, "I've been relating a bit of Shaw family history to Emma, here, and she's satisfied of your father Lawrence's innocence in the matter. Are there other questions, Emma?"

"Just one."

"Yes?"

"How come you all are keeping Granddaddy's condition so secret?"

"Look," Franklyn began, "the mill has an important contract to be finalized with a national supply chain. My father set it all up before he became ill and we didn't want to upset the cart before they signed off on it. It's a hefty contract, Emma, and it will keep the mill in the black for years to come. We don't care much down here about the mill, one way or another. Oh, Mathew would like to see it continue for old time sake, but we've got the farm, and now the vineyard, which makes money, so we don't need the mill. The mill is a headache, Emma, but my father made us promise to keep it open for the people in town still working there. Now, look here, Emma—when Daddy dies, I'm going to be the new Granddaddy of the Shaw family, and I plan to keep that promise to him, but I'm going to need your help."

"How so?"

"Look, I don't know what all your brother got his self into, but it has nothing to do with the family. You need to stop your snooping. I don't know what it's gotten you, but if a crossed word gets out about some impropriety at the mill or in the family, we'll lose that contract—and as much as I'd hate it, we'd shut down the mill. "

"That bad?"

"Let's just say the fate of 100 good families at the mill and a bunch of businesses in town, not to mention the pensions of another 300 or so, are resting in your hands. Make sure you make good decisions from here forward, Emma, there's a lot riding on you."

The late afternoon turned toward twilight and the clouds the day brought looked like they were settling in for the night. I switched on the Jeep lights as I rode toward town after my visit to the Shaw farm. Needing a cup of coffee and some time to think, I rode back into town with the aim of stopping at The Coffee Bean. The revelations of Early's birth rights hung over me like a brewing storm cloud, and I needed to put some thought into what it all meant. Some thought on just what I would say to Pa about it all.

I parked in front of Saunders Studio, and climbing out, I notice that the door sign of the shop was turned over to the open side.

"Hello!" I shouted as I pushed the door open and entered the shop, happy with the diversion, thankful for any delay that kept me away from the confrontation with Pa over the revelation of Early's birth.

A little bell above the door rattled a weak ring as I entered, but no one came out to greet me.

The shop looked like it did the last time I spent time there during my early college years. I worked in the studio one summer when both Mr. and Mrs. Saunders went north on a grand car tour to Niagara Falls. They wanted to keep the shop open, but I think they just wanted me to have a summer job. I did complete a few sessions though, birthdays and anniversary shots, nothing complicated. Even then, I could tell I just had a way with a camera.

When Mrs. Saunders came back and saw my work, she told me I had a gift. I thought about explaining to her the aura thing, but the thing about magic like that is not everyone understands, so it's best to not be forthcoming. That's some advice Louise Looking Bird gave me, years before, and up to today, I tried to abide by it.

"Emma," Mr. Saunders said, coming out and seeing me standing there, "is that you?"

"Yes, sir, I saw your open sign and thought I'd stop in. I've been by a couple of times, but you're not keeping regular hours."

"Yes, girl, I'm not open as much since ma died."

"I'm sorry about Mrs. Saunders. I know you all loved each other for a long time."

"Thanks Emma, you know she asked about you some, there at the end."

Oh no, I thought, feeling guilty. "I didn't know that."

"Oh, yes, she stayed interested in you and real proud of your work and how you got your start here in our studio."

"Well, I'm thankful for the start."

"You know, she followed your career all this time, kept a book of your work."

"What…?"

"Yes, girl, she kept anything she could find published on you. Look," he said and moving to a counter he dug out a photo album. "Look, she put everything she found in this book. There's all your work from the national park series you did, and from every newspaper or magazine that ran a picture of yours. When she found out she could track your work by the internet, she took a course at Morgan Tech to learn how all that works. She collected the weekly series of photos you've been doing for your paper. She kept them all. She was proud of you."

I looked down at the collection of my work and felt even worst about not keeping up with the old couple.

"Sure sorry about your brother, Emma," Mr. Saunders said in a quiet voice. "It seems like just yesterday you and Early would be running up and down the street out here. It's hard to keep up with time as it flies by you."

"Yes, sir, I know what you mean."

"Do you?" he asked me, giving me a good look, a look like he meant for me to explain.

"Yes, sir, I know about time and how valuable it is. I see how some people get a full share of time and yet others get the short side. I saw a lot of young men in Afghanistan run out of time, bleeding to death on the desert sand. Dying before your time seems such a waste. No telling what their lost time meant to them, their families, their neighbors. What would those extra years have brought them…brought us?"

"No telling, Emma, no telling."

After a long minute, I broke the silence between us and asked him, "So, you working today, on a Sunday?"

"I had a shoot yesterday and thought I'd develop the film today, you know, get me out of the house for a spell. Sundays can get quiet around that old place without Mrs. Saunders."

"Still using regular film, Mr. Saunders?"

"You know about old dogs, Emma."

"Well, even old dogs will pick up a new bone every once and a while. You should at least look at digital."

"Oh, I have a digital camera on my smart phone, it takes okay pictures, but for my work, well, I wouldn't consider it. I mean, what art is there in digital pixel? No, for my work I'd prefer to use film. Of course, not a lot of us left that appreciate film anymore."

"No, Mr. Saunders, I'm afraid digital is here to stay. I'm

surprised you can even get supplies for developing."

"Oh, sure, it's used by photo artists still. I had to learn to use the internet just so I could find it and order for delivery. It's pretty convenient to order like that and then a man delivers it right to the door."

"A real miracle."

"Say, how would you like to help an old man out?"

"Sure, Mr. Saunders."

"Well, I promised the Shaws these photos I took during the Apple Festival."

"The what?"

"Oh, I take a bunch of shots of the Apple Festival for the monthly Black Mountain Post. You know, Randall Shaw is the publisher."

"Does that paper still come out?"

"It comes out on a monthly basis, covering the local community and major town events. I take a bunch of photos of the opening parade and the mayor puts some of the photos in the paper. That weekend turned beautiful, so I got some great shots. Well, it would help an old man out if you'd drop them over to Town Hall for me."

"Sure," I said looking through the set of 8 x 10 photos, all familiar shots of town officials in a parade of official cars, marching bands, and flat-bed trucks pulling floats, "I'll take them over first chance I get."

"Thanks."

"Sure, and say, why don't I buy you a cup of coffee and we can talk over old times."

"Okay," Mr. Saunders agreed, "but better make mine decaf."

After my coffee date with Mr. Saunders, I climbed the mountain toward Pa's house. The Sunday of revelations started the day and somehow ended it, as well. I didn't know what, if anything, to say to Pa. Did it matter at this point; was Early any less a son after all these years, any less a brother?

A three-quarter moon broke through the overcast sky under a star-filled heaven. I picked out a bright one, twinkling between clouds, low on the horizon; Early's star maybe, on its way to heaven.

That evening, over a pan of baked corn bread and fresh buttermilk, Pa asked me about my visit to Shaw Farm.

"Did you look over those the grape vines?"

I took a second piece of corn bread from the pan sitting between us and said, "It's an impressive operation, and they said they're making money with the wine."

"Did Granddaddy Shaw tell you they won a blue ribbon for one of their wines?"

"No," I said, breaking a hunk of corn bread into a glass of milk and using a spoon to scoop the mess into my mouth, "I didn't get to talk with Granddaddy."

"You didn't?"

"No, he's pretty sick. They let me peek in on him, but he doesn't look well. Doc Miller says it's only a matter of time."

"So the rumors are true, then?"

"What?" I asked finishing the last of the bread by drinking it down.

"Oh, people been saying he's been sick for months now, but you know how people talk."

"Lot of family there, paying respects."

"Yeah sure, the vultures circling, scavenging on their minds."

"He has that Alzheimer's, a terrible disease."

"So they say."

"Hard to believe, him lying there, all those tubes."

I took a quick shower and put on some old sweats I found in the high school clothes box. Picking up the album Brenda Shaw gave me, I plodded back out to the kitchen wearing old wool socks. I found Pa with his head down in the Bible.

"John 8:34," he said looking at me from over his bifocals.

"How did you know I was going to ask?"

"Every time you see me reading this here Bible, you ask me what I'm reading."

"Well?"

"Jesus said, *'Truly, truly, I say to you, everyone who commits sin is the slave of sin.'*"

"What does it mean, Pa?"

"For all the good they do, the Shaws are guilty of sin, guilty of accumulating wealth at the expense of others, and they'll pay for that sin."

"You're a Shaw, Pa."

"There's quite a few Shaws in the valley, Emma, but like men everywhere, some fall closer to the tree than others."

"How about Early?"

Pa paused and put down his Bible. He rose and walked to a table lamp Mama picked up at a flea market forty years ago. He turned the little lamp on against the approaching darkness of the night. Moving to the stove, he opened the fire box and began to shovel ash out, putting it into the tin bucket.

"You didn't speak with Lawrence this afternoon," he asked, taking some short pieces of oak and preparing the box for the night's fire.

"No, Pa, he's well out of it, but I spoke a spell with Brenda Shaw."

"Nice woman, Brenda Shaw," Pa said lighting the kindling and closing the stove box door.

"I know," I agreed. "She gave me this here photo album."

"Oh…"

"Yes," I said, and opening the album, I thumbed through the first few pages. "It's full of baby pictures."

"Who's baby?"

"Lawrence Shaw's and Mama's baby," I said, looking up at him and waiting for a response. When he only sat, staring down into his coffee I said, "They're Early's baby pictures."

Pa sat in his chair, looking down into his coffee mug, but I could see his brow furrow as he struggled with the information.

"Did Early know he was Lawrence's son?"

"Early was my son, Emma."

"I know you raised him your son, Pa, but …"

"Early may have come to us by a different route, Emma, but he was our son, and nothing, no pictures, no stories from the past, can change that. Your mama and I thought the same on this."

"Did Early know?"

Pa raised his hand up to me to be quiet and taking up his Bible and opening to a page marked by a thin piece of black ribbon said, "Listen to this. Galatians 6:8 – *'For the one who sows to his own flesh will from the flesh reap corruption, but the one who sows to the Spirit will from the Spirit, reap eternal life.'"*

It was a poignant passage, and I wondered at Pa's having it marked so. Marked to easily find and read, over and over.

Chapter Eighteen

Monday

In the morning, I dressed in my jeans, sweatshirt, and hiking boots. After washing my face and pulling my hair back into a ponytail, I went out and sat with Pa at the kitchen table. He made a batch of scrambled eggs and crisp bacon strips for our breakfast and I spent a good minute yawning and sipping coffee.

"What are you planning for today?" he asked me after giving me the proper amount of time to wake up clearly.

"I'm going into town. I've got something to drop at Town Hall, and after, I want to talk with Bobby Carson."

"What for?"

"Oh, just something the mayor said about Early, and all."

"What?"

"Oh, it seems like Early may have got his self into something. You know he and the Carson boys used to run together. I'm hoping Bobby may know something and can fill me in."

"I don't know, seems like Early kept things to his self lately. I asked him whenever I saw him, and he never shared much."

Before going to the Fish and Game shop, I spent the morning talking to some of the other Main Street merchants. I was sure Early had got into something, but didn't know what... yet.

I meandered up the sidewalk and visited every place I

thought he might have done business with and every one of the shops and stores said Early charged things, but he had come in recently and made good on his debts. Although the majority of merchants said Early could be heavy-handed no one disputed his honesty.

I walked back to Carson's Fish and Game where I saw Jeff back behind the counter loading shot into those hulls.

"Hello, stranger," he said, when he saw me come through the doors. "Where you been hiding?"

"Trying to stay out of trouble."

"How's that working out for you?" Bobby Carson said, coming from out behind some shelves full of stock.

"Not good, but I did want to ask you something."

"Oh, yeah?" he responded, and joined me at the counter. "Shoot."

"Well, it's about Early; seems like he'd been into something, and darn if anyone knows what."

"Why ask me?"

"Come on, Bobby, you and Early used to run together. Did he say anything to you?"

"Early and I hadn't been close in sometime, Emma."

"Why's that?"

"Let's just say there was water under the bridge."

"What's that supposed to mean?"

"You figure it out, you're the one playing detective."

"Come on guys, give me something. I promise it won't hurt my feelings."

Jeff Carson got up from his work bench and joined us at the counter.

"Emma," Jeff said, "this last year or so, your brother was out of hand. The mayor even threatened him about his job."

"Yeah, I heard something."

"Well, it was something serious."

"Yeah, yeah, but serious about what?"

"Look," Jeff said, "Early may have been running with

163

some of the backwoods boys."

"What do you mean?"

"Those boys who cultivate a crop of the weed, the backwoods are full of them. They run the green stuff dealing and all. Just like their pappies used to run liquor."

"Are you saying Early was into drugs?"

Jeff looked at his brother, like asking permission to speak, then said, "He got into *something*, Emma. I don't know what for sure, but something…and I tell you one thing, you'd better be careful where you go snooping; those boys like to keep their affairs private."

After leaving the Carsons, I drove up the mountain at a modest speed, taking my time, formulating a plan. I didn't altogether understand Jeff Carson's warning, but similar talk around town suggested something. Pulling into the circle drive in front of the Davis place, I saw Becky's SUV parked around the side of the house.

Becky came out on the front porch and called hello to me.

"Hello, back," I said, climbing out of the Jeep and walking up the brick path."

She said, "What's up?"

"Well, I think I stumbled on a little something with this case."

"Emma," she said, stepping to one side and letting me in the house, "I wish you'd leave that alone."

"Just wait," I said, "let me run something by you."

"Why are you dogging this so?" she asked me as I went into the small parlor to sit on their worn sofa. "What are you trying to find out?"

"How Early died," I said, noticing something in her voice, maybe urgency, her aura quivering around the pink range of color.

"We know he died in an accident," she said again, following me and sitting beside me.

"No, we don't!"

"But Franklyn said…"

"What are you talking about?"

"Franklyn said…"

"Franklyn can hardly put his pants on straight. What's wrong with you, anyway? You think Early just drove off that road?"

"What I'm saying is, I'm satisfied, and I want to leave it be."

"Becky, I've got something to ask you."

"What," she snapped, impatient with me.

"I was wondering if you might be able to tell me what Early had been working on. You know, what kind of case he might have been dealing with here lately."

"Early used to discuss his work with me," she said, "all the time. He said I had a head for police work. But he hadn't said much the last few months, like he was into something heavy. When I asked him, he'd only smile and change the subject."

"Are you sure?" I asked her again, hoping she could shed light on the whole thing. Although not easy to read, Becky's aura usually throbbed among the warm colors of the rainbow, but in the quiet of the room I saw her aura flare up in the light red, indicating, I hoped, her deep feelings for Early.

"Look, I don't know what Early was looking into, but maybe that is for the best…so why don't you drop it now."

I sat up, pulling myself straight and said, "Don't you want to know how Early died?"

"The mayor and Randall seem pretty sure it was an accident."

"No, it wasn't."

"How do you know?"

"Early wouldn't have just run through Moore's Curve. He'd been running that road since he was fifteen. No way would he just crash through there."

"How can you be so sure?"

I looked over her shoulder to make sure her boys weren't listening, then said, "Few days ago, Jeff and I went over to the city yard and looked at Early's cruiser."

"You what?"

"Yeah, I had to have a look. I jumped the fence to have a look at it, and guess what?"

"What?"

"I took a good look at it and I think I saw paint scrapes all along the driver's side."

"What?"

"Yeah, it was banged up pretty good."

"So maybe it got banged up during his accident."

"No, Early went in the river hood first, straight in. These marks are along the side panels."

"So…"

"So, I think its evidence that would prove Early was in pursuit of someone, and during the tangle, he got banged up and then pushed through Moore's curve, plunging down into the river. Carter says Early didn't have his seat belt on when he pulled him out of the river."

"So?"

"Early not buckling up when he took off proves he was in a hurry. He was chasing someone alright, working a case. The cruiser took a side beating, different bang up than from a nose-first fall."

"You're guessing on this, Emma," she said. "Where is all this coming from? I know you want a better explanation, but it was just bad luck for Early, and that's it. All those police cruisers been beat up for a couple of years now. That's one of the things Early wanted the mayor to do, buy a couple of new cruisers, but that Wendell Banks and the mayor told him the town couldn't afford new cars. That man, Banks, he runs the budget like it's his own money.

"Now, I'm ready to put this behind me. You're wonderful to do this, coming to the rescue thing, but Early's dead and nothing's going to change that, so I'm for moving on. Aren't you?"

I hadn't thought about it, the "moving on" part, so caught up in the hunt, I'd not thought about much else. Not work, not Jeff...

"Emma," Becky said loudly.

"Sure," I said, coming back to the conversation, "sure, I'd like to get on with things, but—"

"No *buts* Emma. There are no *buts* left. I'm putting this behind me and moving on. I owe it to the boys, owe it to myself, I wish you would, too."

At that moment, the younger boys came home from school. We heard JB's truck sliding into the gravel lot on the north side of the house as he pulled in. Becky smiled at me and rushed to greet her two youngest.

"Mom," Johnny called out, coming into the house, "what can we eat?"

"There're cookies in the bread box," came the reply from Becky as she headed to the kitchen, "Grandma made them this morning."

As Becky directed logistics in the kitchen, I got out my phone and connected to their Wi-Fi. With Pa off the grid, it had been a couple of days since I got a chance to look through my email messages.

"Any problem?" Becky asked when she came back and saw me frowning at my phone screen.

"Just work, they've been wondering if I've fallen off the face of the earth. I told them I needed a couple of more days."

"Emma Louise, I thought you were going to drop this?"

"I can't, Becky," I said, looking at her, hoping for a sign she understood. "I wish I could."

"I told you, Emma," she said, "I'm ready to move on, but I can't if you keep bringing it back to me. I don't think I can take much more."

"Look, Becky, I know this is hard. Hard on you and the boys and everyone, but Early was into something outside what he normally handled, and I think that might have something to do with his accident."

"Like what?"

"Like a special case or something. Did he mention a special case or anything to you?"

"No, like I said, nothing here recent. In fact, here lately, when it came to his work, nothing...almost..."

"Almost what?"

"Almost like he was afraid of something."

"Early, afraid?"

"Yeah, I know, I don't know anything that scared Early, but something was bothering him."

"Did he work from home any?" I asked.

"Sometimes. Why?"

"Maybe he left some notes on the case he was working on?"

"He worked on somethings here, but he put whatever he had into old backpacks and he'd drag the things back and forth between here and Town Hall."

"So he might have a few notes on what he was working on?"

"Sure, he scribbled stuff, names and places."

"Okay, then, I know my next move and I'm going to need your help."

"Doing what?"

Chapter Nineteen

The Caper

I didn't know if Becky would help me. I tried to give her a pouty lip when I asked her, but she didn't go for it.

"You want me to do *what*?"

"I want you to help me break into the Police Office."

"That's what I thought you said."

"Come on, it'll be fun."

"I don't know Emma; it appears our ideas on fun don't quite coincide. Have you lost your mind? Breaking into the police office?"

"Look," I explained, "I think Early was in the middle of a big case, and if so, I'm sure he had a file on the thing. I don't think those two deputies can add two and two, so if Early was running an investigation, the proof of that will be in his office. Now, I need to get in there—and I need you to help."

"What if I don't?"

"Then I'll stay up here in Black Mountain for the next three months making a pest of myself."

"And if I do?"

"Okay, if I don't find anything, then I'll drop the case and get out of Dodge."

"Well, with a deal like that, how can I refuse?"

"Okay, then…so do you think we could borrow Little Earl's old Jeep?"

The Town of Black Mountain closed up before six, the lone exceptions being the hospital and The Coffee Bean.

169

We drove slowly down to town; Becky in Little Earl's old Jeep and me in Pa's older truck. We pulled to the side of the road just outside of town and waited until darkness settled heavy on the street. I climbed in the Jeep beside Becky and went over the plan again.

"So remember, give me about five minutes to get over to Town Hall."

"You sure this will work?"

"Look, by the scheduling I figure Carter is on duty, so when he comes out to see what happened, the office will be empty for a couple of minutes. I can get into the office and grab whatever file looks important."

"What if there are no files?"

"No, there'll be files. Those two rookies in the office have enough to do, so I don't see them doing much tidying up after Early."

"Okay, so after you park your Pa's truck, I drive down the street and run the Jeep into it and make a racket."

"Yes, but remember, you have to back into it. If you bang him with your front you might damage the engine. Pull around to the opposite side of the street and back up. You'll hit Pa's back bumper, but that thing weighs a ton, so it will come out unscathed. When Officer Carter comes running out, make a fuss and keep him out there as long as you can."

"How am I going to do that?"

"Pretend like you are hurt. Here," I said to her, reaching over and unbuttoning her blouse three buttons down her front."

"Stop," she scolded me, slapping at my hand.

"No, leave it like that. When Carter comes out give him a look."

"I will not!"

"Becky, you got to keep him busy for a while."

"I'm old enough to be his mother!"

"No, you're not! Besides, I caught him looking at you the other night at the wake. He'll be more than happy to offer you comfort. Just don't get carried away."

"Did you?"

"Did I what?"

"Catch him looking at me?"

"Don't get a big head, it's just puppy love. Now, get a hold of yourself!"

When the night darkness fell along the street, I went back to the truck and rode into town, parking in front of Town Hall. I got out and pretended to walk towards The Coffee Bean, but ducked behind a row of holly bushes and snuck on back to the front of the building and waited. A minute later, Becky started down the street.

Pulling across the street, she hesitated and then, gunning the Jeep, she backed up and ran the rear of the Jeep into the right rear side of the truck's bumper. The resulting bang echoed up and down the street, and sounded a lot worse than I knew it was.

At the moment the Jeep slammed into the truck, I opened the Town Hall door, the crunch of metal covering the sound of the door opening. I stepped across the police office entrance door and waited around the hall corner until what I hoped would be Officer Carter rushing out to see what had happened.

I didn't have to wait long as Carter came running out the office door and headed to the exit. I rushed and slid into the office, just beating the door closing back into place. I didn't know if the door would have automatically locked behind him, but I didn't want to take a chance.

The overhead office lights were on and a small portable TV set sat on a pile of folders on an office chair at a comfortable height for viewing as Carter spent the night defending the Town of Black Mountain.

Moving to the rear office doors, I went into the one marked, *Chief Shaw*. I let my eyes adjust to the dim atmosphere, but enough outer office light filtered into the room so I could see. As befitting my brother, Early had left his

171

desk in a mess, but a desktop file holder stood full, from front to back. I started thumbing through what I hoped were all the recent cases Early had been working on.

As I worked through the files, I read several names I didn't recognize and cases I didn't see as having anything to do with Early per se, besides his investigating. After spending several minutes looking through the files, I came to the last one, but frustrated, I didn't find anything pertinent.

Sitting down in Early's chair I rocked back and reviewed my thought process. It looked like another dead end, and coming up empty handed gnawed on me. I figured time was short, so I got up to leave before I got caught. Leaving the desk, I looked at the file holder again and this time I saw an empty file divider among the others, indicating a missing file.

I wanted to get another look around, but I wasn't sure how much time I had, so I went over to the lone office window and looked out on the street just in time to see Officer Carter and Becky walking toward the building. I started to rush out, but there, hanging on the back of the office door were a couple of backpacks that Becky said Early carried back and forth.

I stopped and struggled with a zipper on one of the packs for several precious seconds before getting the thing open enough I could reach inside. I felt a thin cardboard folder, and even though I couldn't see exactly what in the dark, I yanked it through the pocket opening.

I spent precious seconds reading random pages beneath the light filtering in from the admin area. It looked like Early had written down several people's names and places in some order. I recognized the last person's name on the list and pausing read over the list again, only recognizing the last one. I stared down at the sheet of paper surprised at what I saw. The light wasn't good enough to read the details, but I saw enough to jump to a conclusion and decided that staging the fake accident warranted taking the file.

I stuffed it back in the backpack and retraced my steps

back through the outer office. I snuck over to the outer door and pushed it open and stepped out just as Officer Carter opened the building's main door and walked into the hallway leading Becky by the hand.

Engrossed in helping Becky, Officer Carter didn't look up just then and Becky, seeing me out in the open, faked a stumble which brought even more attention from Carter. This gave me seconds more to slip around the corner of the hall.

"Officer Carter," I heard Becky telling the young man, "I'm just fine, I only tripped on the door jamb."

"Now, Becky, let's get you in the office and sit you down. You may have a concussion or something."

"Don't bother," she told the young man, letting him lead her, "I'm just fine. I think I should be out there. You know that was Emma's Pa's truck I backed into?"

"Mr. Shaw's truck, are you sure?"

"I've seen it enough times. That's it, alright."

"Well, he must be in town somewhere."

After the two went into the office, I hustled over to the front door and opened it and nosily slammed it shut.

"Becky!" I called out, sliding the pack behind my back and partially covering it with my denim jacket.

"In here," came the answer.

I paused at the police office door, poking my head through the doorway just in time to rescue Becky from the attentions of Officer Carter, exclaiming when I looked in, "Becky, what happened? Are you hurt?"

Becky jumped up from the desk chair where Office Carter had cornered my friend with a wet hand towel, about to administer first aide by damping down her forehead.

"No, I'm fine," she said, rushing to me, "just a little shook up."

"What happened?"

"Oh, I backed up without looking, and ran into your Pa's truck."

Ruben D. Gonzales

"Yes, I saw that, but you're okay?"

"Yes, yes, let's go out and see what the damage is."

"Are you sure you should be walking around?" Officer Carter asked.

"I'm fine, Stevie, just fine," Becky said and grabbing me by the arm she pushed me out into the hall, leaving Officer Carter with his wet towel and daydreams.

"I hope you got what you were looking for." Becky squawked at me as we left Town Hall. "Another minute, and I think Stevie would have tried to perform mouth to mouth."

"I told you he was sweet on you."

"Shut up. Early's not even cold in his grave yet."

We joined a small crowd gathered at the scene of the fender bender and as previously arranged, Pa showed up in my Jeep and pretended to be surprised. As planned, the damage was minimal and after hooting about it some for show, Pa got in the truck, and muttering something about women drivers, drove it off, leaving my Jeep behind.

Little Earl's Jeep took the brunt of the collision but to tell the truth I was sure whatever new damage it sustained would get patched pretty quick. By the looks of the multiple patches on little Earl's car, he was an expert at filling in dents and scrapes on the vehicle.

Becky thanked everyone who had come out to help and gawk, and climbed back in Little Earl's Jeep. She headed out of town and back to the farm without looking back at me.

I was about to leave when Jeff Carson appeared and asked if I was okay.

"Sure, I wasn't in the truck. Becky just backed into the rear bumper. It made a lot of noise, but no one was hurt."

"Since when do you drive your Pa's truck?"

"It was handy when I headed out. Becky and I were going to meet for coffee, but you know how she can be when driving."

He looked at me, smiling wide, then said, "Well, as long as you're not hurt."

174

"No, I'm just fine," I said, and as long as I had him away from that darn hull loader, I asked him, "Say, since Becky's not in the mood, want to get a cup of coffee? My treat."

The Coffee Bean appeared about half full, but a game on the big screen drew the crowd gathered there, leaving the seating area near vacant. Jeff and I went to the counter, and with the lateness of the night, we both ordered decaf and he got a giant May Shaw chocolate chip cookie that looked as big as a Frisbee.

After we corralled a booth as far away from the TV crowd as we could get, a young gal brought our coffee orders to the table.

"You want to tell me what that was all about?" Jeff asked me through a half-full cookie mouth.

"What?"

"Alright, Emma," he said, sipping coffee to clear his throat, "what's going on? Your pa just wouldn't let you drive his truck, and I darn well know Becky would rather be caught dead than be seen in Little Earl's old Jeep. That was a set up out there, and I'm curious to know why."

I didn't know how much to tell Jeff, or even if I should confess anything at all. I didn't know who in town to trust with my amateur investigation swinging wildly in different directions. I wasn't sure who'd get in the way in the end. I knew Jeff, but I didn't know his brother all that well, and he and Early did run together once.

"I can't tell you."

"You can't or won't?"

"Can't. It's something I'm looking into, and Becky was helping."

"Something to do with Early, I'm sure."

"What else?"

"Well, let me know if I can help—you know, if you need someone roughed up."

"There's one thing, this thing about Early that Bobby said, you know—"

175

"I don't agree with Bobby about that. Early could handle those backwoods boys, he ran into them all the time. He couldn't help it because of his work, but he tried to look the other way, I'm sure."

"Why would he do that?'

"Most of those boys are friends of ours or know our families. Early would be hard pressed to come down on them. Knowing the hard times at the mill, well, he'd try to look the other way, if he could. There just aren't a lot of ways to make a living for a lot of men up here."

"What do you mean?"

"Look, the county has been trying to clean up the stuff for a couple of years, now. There's been a push from the new county manager to drop the hammer on any drug trafficking. He's trying to spruce up the image of the county and our little mountain town is a sore spot for him. He likes to think he's hip with the influx of tech people around the lake and he doesn't think Black Mountain is representative of the millennial generation's clean-cut look."

"So, where did Early stand on all that?"

"Early was on a tight rope, Emma. He had the county on one side of him, and then he had a bunch of good ole boys on the other, half of whom used to play football with him. We talked about it some. He said he was facing a dilemma, but he didn't lay it all out, so it's hard to say just what."

"Do you think he was taking money from the backwoods boys? Getting paid off to let them run free?"

"I don't see that…what makes you say that?"

"Just the way he'd been spending money lately."

"I don't see that."

"And look at this," I told him, pulling the folder from the backpack and placing it on the table between us.

"What's this?" Jeff asked, skimming through the pages in the file

"Just say I stumbled upon some information," I told him

as he got a good look at the file I stole from the BMPD. Apparently, Early had gathered some information on a number of people, and except for one, which was noted several times, I didn't recognize any of the names. He had drawn out several rough maps and identified road and street locations. They looked like routes of travel. The letters ATF appeared at several random spots. The ATF notations were double underlined I assumed for emphasis and worried me the most.

"What kind of information?"

"These are some notes that Early kept on a case he was working."

"Yeah?"

"Yeah, and although it is sketchy on details, there are some names and initials…see them? One, in particular."

"I see," Jeff nodded his head, reading through the file, I could see interested. "I wonder what this is all about?"

"I don't know Jeff, but I'll need to check it out, find out what the ATF is looking into."

Jeff turned quiet on me. I didn't blame him. I shouldn't have brought up the subject of my brother. I don't know that a dead brother is conducive to romantic talk.

I didn't enjoy the rest of my little *date* with Jeff, either, since my mind turned to the inevitable drive up the mountain to speak with Becky about why her father's name was written prominently in Early's notes on a case he'd been working.

Chapter Twenty

JB

Even though historically the onset of winter could be sporadic in the fall, the thought of a second Indian summer descending on Black Mountain seemed far-fetched, but as I climbed out from beneath the comforter on my bed I felt warmth in the air.

I dragged my body into the kitchen, and I joined Pa for coffee.

"So, did you get what you needed last night?"

I smiled at him, measuring how much to tell him, not wanting to get him too involved. Borrowing his truck to stage a traffic accident was one thing, but I didn't want to make him an accomplice. The whole thing with Early could end up serious if the ATF angle proved prominent.

"Well, let's just say I accomplished my mission. I hope we didn't bang up your truck too bad…"

"That old thing is built like a tank. It would take more than a fender bender to slow it up."

"Still, let me know if you want it fixed and I'll pay."

"Save your money, girl, you'll need it one day."

Going through my morning routine, I got ready and drove over to the Davis place. I didn't know a whole lot about JB Davis's past. Oh, I knew he served in Vietnam and I knew since returning from his duty, he'd been pretty much a kook. In addition to preparing for when the government might come and take his guns, he liked to talk about the Russians and how we needed to be prepared for the invasion.

JB and drugs didn't go together, but JB knew the mountains—and if anyone could escape an ATF posse, it was JB.

When I showed Becky the file with Early's notes, she couldn't have disagreed more.

"This is what you took from the police station?"

"That's it."

"Well, you're nuts if you think Daddy has anything to do with what happened to Early."

"Early had his name down here, on the notes of the case he was investigating."

"That doesn't mean anything."

"Well, let's just ask him. Where is he?"

"He's out plowing in the north fields."

"Well, we could go over there."

"No, I'll not bother him with this rubbish. Now, I helped you last night because it might of helped with Early, but not this. I can't believe Daddy would have anything to do with anything Early was investigating."

"His name is right here."

"I don't care what's written down there. Daddy wouldn't have anything to do with running drugs."

"I don't know, Becky…your pa pretty much knows every backwoods boy up here. If it somehow helped in his preparation for the absence of law and order, I can see him forming alliances with anyone. Your pa is pretty adamant that he won't give into the government when they come."

"He's changed now. He's not like he used to be."

"Well, from what I hear, men like that can't change. Oh, they can go to their grandkids' Friday night football games and all, but the reason they stay up in these mountains is because they need the space. From what I hear, it's better for everyone that they do isolate themselves."

Becky didn't have a lot to say to me after that, and in fact, asked me to leave. I knew she was hurt by my accusation, but

Early was onto something, and somehow, JB Davis was right in the middle of it.

I steered down the mountain to town and the mayor's office. I noticed the distinct warming in the air. A gentle wind blew through town, where yesterday it had whipped like a brewing winter storm. The cold seemed to have vanished, a fair southern breeze taking its place.

Pulling the Jeep up to the front of Town Hall, I parked in one of the police cruiser spots. I noticed a late year black truck parked in one of the staff spaces next to the mayor's Mercedes.

I found Shelby behind the reception counter, dressed like a night on the town loomed. She smiled at me when I came in.

"Where've you been, stranger?" she asked, looking up from her smart phone. "I thought you left town."

"Not yet!"

"Nice, the laughs keep right on coming with you around."

"Thanks," I said, ignoring the slight. "Franklyn available?"

"No, he's in with George Magill."

"Who?"

"He's the contractor that's going to renovate the old water mill."

"Will he be done any time soon?"

"I don't know. They're in there going over the construction proposal."

At that moment, the door to Franklyn's office opened and a burly man I took for Magill and the mayor marched out. The mayor was emphasizing something to Magill, but the man walked right past us and out the suite door without saying a word.

Turning back to the office and spotting me, Franklyn said, "Oh, great. Just what I need." Looking past me, he told Shelby, "Better get Randall on the phone ASAP." Looking at me, he said, "Well, what do you want?"

"Just a minute of your time," I said, trying to hide a smile behind my hand.

"What gives?" he asked. "You're not going on with this Early thing, are you?"

"I've got something interesting I think you should look at."

Seeing I was serious, he turned and said, "Okay, why not?"

He led the way back to his office and closed the door behind us. "Alright," he said, settling heavily into his seat behind the desk and motioning for me to take one of the chairs in front of him, "what's on your mind?"

"I understand Early was working on a drug case?"

"What makes you think that?"

"Here." I gave him the file. "We found some notes Early made on a case he'd been working."

"Notes, police business notes, just where did you get notes on police business?"

"Early left some notes at his home," I lied, "and Becky showed them to me."

"That's got to be against regulations or something."

"Probably, but it will be hard to punish Early now."

"Why are you looking at official police business notes?"

"Well, it wasn't intentional, but we saw JB Davis's name, so of course Becky was interested."

"What else does it say here?"

"You can read for yourself. I mean, it's pretty sketchy stuff but it looks like JB was involved with something to do with drugs that the ATF was looking into. I figure Early was involved somehow, but it's not clear. I thought you must know about it."

"No, Early ran his office like he wanted. I tried to stay out of the way."

"Is that a management good practice?"

"You knew your brother, Emma. He could be secretive when he wanted and as long as he kept the streets safe, he could do what he wanted behind that badge he carried."

"Well, I think this has something to do with his running off the road."

"What?"

"I think Early got close to something and got push-back; in fact, pushed right off that curve."

"You're still going down that path?"

"Look, Early didn't just drive off the road. I went over to the yard and took a look at his cruiser. I saw evidence of a collision."

"Says who?"

"It just looks suspicious. There were scrapes along the driver's side. I think you need to have it examined, maybe by the SBI, see if there's evidence of something other than an accident."

The mayor remained quiet for a spell, and then said. "We can't do that?"

"Why not?"

"Whitaker sold the chief's car for scrap."

"What? Who told him he could?"

"I told him. It was a total with all that river water. I told him to get rid of it, so it's long gone."

"It had damage, Franklyn, damage other than hitting that river head on."

"Well, now we'll never know."

"I've got pictures."

"What?"

"I took pictures of the driver's side of Early's car; it shows the damage."

"When did you get pictures?"

"I went over to the yard and took a look at his cruiser. There were red scrapes all along the driver's side."

"Oh, heck, you know Early, he couldn't care less what his vehicle looked like. Any scratch or dings you saw could have happened any time this last two years."

"Look, Franklyn, I think Early was run off that road."

"Don't know how you think you can prove that with pictures, or even if you had his car."

I waited a minute before firing back at the mayor. What I was thinking turned my stomach some, and I didn't know I wanted to go there, for a number of reasons. Seeing the mayor waiting on a response I said, "I think JB Davis might know something about this."

"Why do you think that? Just because his name showed up on a random piece of paper?"

"There's that, and the fact that JB drives a red truck."

The mayor paused a long time before saying, "Plenty of people drive red vehicles."

"What's up with you? Don't you *want* to get to the bottom of this? Do you know more about all this than you're letting on? What's going on here? What are you trying to hide?"

Before he formulated an answer, Shelby buzzed through on the inner office line to say she had Randall Shaw on the phone. Holding up a fat finger to me, and picking up the hand piece, he said into the phone, "Randall, better go over that grant agreement a second time and let me know what all is left to be done." After a brief pause, during which Randall must have asked something back, he continued, "Just double check. The contractor was in here and he wants some up-front money before he starts work, and that application deadline is fast approaching. Banks is dragging his behind on this and if he can't do it, we need to get someone in here who can. I don't want to lose that grant. I'm counting on it for next year's budget, and need to get it in so we can start on that mill."

He slammed the phone back in its cradle and for a moment forgot about me sitting there, but remembering, he responded, "Why do you think I'm hiding anything?"

"I don't know, Franklyn, that's what I've been trying to figure; why would you?"

"If I was hiding something, I'd be keeping it to myself."

"You might try, but it will come out."

"I can hold off a while," he said, slumping back into his chair, "that's all we need."

"Until after that big box contract is signed?"

"Maybe," he said, frowning.

"Does that contract mean so much?"

Pulling his heft up to the desk he grabbed up his ruler and waving it at me said, "Not to us, Emma, but to this town. You ready to sink this town because of some misguided notion of your hero big brother?"

"Not *misguided*, because I know Early was murdered."

"The heck you say," Franklyn smiled. "Which Shaw are you going to blame today?"

"Look, Franklyn," I said, "I know I've been a thorn in your side, but you'd do the same for your family. In fact, I think that's what you've been trying to do right from the start. Now, we have some information that can shed some light on Early's accident. Either you look into it, or I'm going over to the county sheriff."

"I wouldn't do that!"

"Look, just tell me why you've been covering all this up, what's going on?"

"Emma, there's more here than Early having a suspicious accident."

"What are you talking about? Is it the EPA thing up at the mill or what?"

"What makes you think that?"

"I questioned Doc Shaw about it, and he said the mill operated under the allowed thresholds—but I know he was lying."

"What makes you say that?"

I couldn't tell him I saw Doc Shaw's pink aura, so I said, "Just the way he answered…evasive-like."

"That's not enough."

"Come on, Franklyn, what's going on?"

"What do I get if I tell you?"

"Franklyn, I'm not going to put the mill out of business, I know plenty people here that rely on their pensions. I don't believe those pensions would be worth much if the mill closed."

"Not a dime."

"Okay, then, nothing you'll say will go beyond this room. So why you been covering up this thing?"

Franklyn lifted his wide body out of the chair and walked over to the windows, looking out on the manicured lawn that because of grow chemicals, still harbored a green luster in spite of the season. Looking at him from his backside, his aura beat among the darker shades of green which I've found indicated in some a lack of integrity, but not lying.

"Alright," he said turning back to me, "alright, so we ran into trouble with the EPA regs up at the mill. Mathew wanted to make some changes up there to get compliant, but the costs are high, making it hard to make a profit. We need that new contract to justify the expansion. We hired a local group to run a thin environmental study and Randall signed off on it, for just long enough to get that contract in place. You guessed right, Granddaddy loves that mill and would do anything to keep it open."

"What about Early?"

"You sure this is staying between us?"

"Just between us."

"I told you there was more to all this. I heard about Early and a drug investigation. Randall got word from his contacts back east that the ATF was launching a big investigation up here, and we'd better watch it. I didn't know what Early was into. I think he was working with the backwoods boys for money and protection, and about to get busted.

"You know JB is friends with all those boys, and they share the same disdain for government, so they were connected somehow. Well, it looked like a mess for the town if word got out we had a drug problem here. That ownership group for that hardware chain is head over heels law and order, and the political far right. They'll only do business with a clean town, so I need to keep the lid on everything until that contract is signed. After that, we'll get compliant up at the mill and clean house around here."

"So you've been covering up?"

"Any way I can."

"What about Early?"

"I don't know what happened to Early, and I'm not digging into it until after that contract is signed."

"What about JB?"

"Emma, I don't know what JB has to do with any of this, but whatever it is, it can wait."

"I hope you're right, Franklyn, but right now, he's right in the middle. I'd hate for it to come out true, but he's my best bet on finding out what happened."

"His name penciled on a piece of paper is pretty thin, Emma, don't you think?"

"If JB is mixed up in this, then the ATF might pick him up at any time. If you don't get to him first, they might beat you to the finish line and the whole story may come out in a big blow, get back to the hardware chain folks. Think about what that might do for that big contract."

"So?"

"Why don't you get JB in here and ask him, unless you can come up with another reason for the ATF to be investigating him."

"Will it keep you quiet about everything if I do?"

"Franklyn, I just want to know about what happened to Early, and right now, JB Davis is my best bet for information on that matter. How much trouble can it be to talk to the man, quiet-like?"

Franklyn didn't say anything right away. I'm sure he was debating over in his head the different options and outcomes on the best way to move on the whole matter. On the one hand, he could chance it and ride it all out and see what materialized in the end. That would be the easiest, but then he'd lose control of the narrative and maybe lose that contract.

On the other hand, if he jumped in now, he could control the spin and make sure the Shaw family came out the best they could.

"Okay, it can't hurt. Let's go out and talk to the man."

I offered to drive to save the wear and tear on the mayor's Mercedes and we headed up the mountain. The temperature higher up returned to a more seasonable fall bite as the wind picked up and grew heavy with damp moisture, rolling down the north face of the ridgeline.

Pulling up to the front of the Davis place, we met the matriarch of the clan, Mother Davis, rocking on the front porch, a double barrel 12-gauge shotgun resting across her lap. She did not get up to greet us.

"You got some nerve, Emma Shaw," Mother Davis shouted from her perch, her dark red aura of anger pulsing out from behind her. Getting to her feet and positioning herself at the top of the steps as we climbed out of the Jeep, she continued, "—bringing the law out here."

"Now, hold on, Mother Davis," the mayor said. "We only come out to talk to JB for a spell."

"He's not here."

"He's not?" the mayor asked back. "Where's he at?"

"Gone hunting!"

"Little early in the season for that, isn't it?"

"Not for the bow, it ain't."

"The bow?" I asked, not sure I heard.

"That's right, John goes out bow hunting this time every year."

"When will he be back?"

"Oh, no telling, why last year he stayed out for a week, maybe a little more."

"A week?"

"That's right."

"We need to talk to him before that."

187

"Well, mayor," the woman said with a smile, "I'm afraid you are out of luck. We'll be lucky if John comes back in a week or two."

"Do you know about where he'd be?"

"When John gets up in that mountain, no telling where he could be."

"Now, look here, Mother," the mayor said, "we need to talk to John, so you best be thinking how we can reach him."

"What's this about, anyway?"

"Becky didn't tell you?" I asked the shotgun toting woman.

"She told me some fool notion you had about drugs and stuff, but that's nothing to do with John."

"Well," the mayor said, "that's what we want to talk to JB about, sort of clear this up."

"Well, that's a problem, then," the woman said. "John's not here to talk."

"Mind if we come in and…"

"You got a warrant?" she asked, taking a step down the stairs, still cradling the shotgun in the crook of her left arm.

"Now, Mother Davis," the mayor said, taking a step back, "we didn't come out here to cause a problem."

"Mr. Mayor, if you put one foot on these steps you going to have a big problem, like a missing foot."

"Now, I need to have a word with JB, Mother Davis. The ATF has been running an investigation up here, and JB is involved somehow. Now, if it comes to it, I can get a warrant."

"Oh, Judge Shaw can fix you right up, I'm sure, but if you come, then better bring a good number of men, because we don't take kindly to trespassers. Now, I don't know what you are up to, mayor, but if you want to talk with JB, well, best come back around Christmas, I'm sure JB will be back by then. He wouldn't miss a Christmas with his grandsons."

The breeze picked up a notch then, blowing leaves across the gravel yard. The sun dipped behind the stand of trees and shadows began to take over the area from the sun.

"Now, what?" the mayor said turning to me, buttoning up his coat against the cold and reflecting on the standoff.

"I don't know, but I wouldn't step on her porch if I were you."

"You got that right. She got her hair up for sure."

"I guess you have to go look for him."

"Why?"

"He's run off."

"He's probably just hunting, like Ma Davis said."

"I don't think so, and you don't, either. If you want the truth before the ATF swoops in here and busts this thing wide open, you're going to have to go and find him first."

"Up there," he asked, looking up to the mountain.

"If that's where he's gone."

"You're kidding, right?"

"What do you mean?"

"If JB is up in that mountain it'll take more than a few men to find him."

"You can get up a search party."

"Search party…oh, sure," the mayor said, moving around the Jeep and getting into the passenger seat. "That would take fifty men."

"That many?" I asked, climbing in, shutting the door against the bite of the wind.

"Maybe more."

"You could turn out the men at the mill."

"Shoot, half those men are friends with JB," the mayor said with a laugh. "They'd as soon help him get away as catch him."

"You could bring the county in here."

The mayor turned and looked at me, and said, "On what? Some scratched out note in a worn file and a voodoo suspicion of yours?"

"He did run off…maybe feeling guilty?"

"Oh, heck, he's just off hunting."

"You don't believe that. JB was into something and I think Early knew it."

"You know, Emma," the mayor said, rubbing his hands against the chill air, "I don't know what to believe, but I'm not fool enough to go chasing John Davis up in his own back yard. If he's dug in up there, he'll be hard to flush."

"You could wait him out…he's bound to get hungry and cold."

"Maybe, but if there is something going on, I'd kind of like to find out sooner than later."

"So, what?"

Mayor Franklyn Shaw looked through the windshield, up into the bleak mountain hovering gray over the farm. "Okay, I'll get some local boys together. McDonald lives down a ways, raises tracking dogs. We can't do much right now, it will be dark soon, but I'll make a few calls and put a team together. We'll meet back here tomorrow, mid-morning, and see if we can pick up his trail. If we're lucky, JB might be here in the morning and save us all a lot of money and headache."

I looked out through the windshield, but Mother Davis sat back down on her rocker and began to rock in rhythm, a wry smile across her face, her aura settling into a faint rainbow, like she didn't have a care to worry her.

Chapter Twenty-One

The Night

After dropping the mayor off, I turned back up the mountain to Pa's place. The sun so bright with promise and hope a few hours earlier now set, taking with it the leftover warmth of the day and the light of a final resolution to the whole affair.

The aroma of a cooking stew greeted me when I entered the house. Pa sat at the table, his Bible open to a passage, but he looked to be dozing.

"Smells good," I said as I came in, surprising him awake.

"I put some beef and vegetables in the Dutch oven couple hours ago," he said, making like he hadn't been sleeping. "I thought you'd be hungry when you came in."

"I'm starving."

After Pa served up a bowl of the stew he asked, "So, what did you find out?"

Between stuffing spoons of stew into my mouth, I filled him in on the details of my day.

"You sure about JB?"

"I've been going over it and best case I can make is Mr. Davis knows something."

"Because Early made some notes on him?"

"That, and he run off up the mountain."

"Could be he's hunting, like Mother Davis said."

"Maybe."

"Any case, like Mother Davis said, you all best wait for him to come down.

"No chance to find him?" I asked.

"No chance," he said, retrieving a loaf of homemade sour

dough bread and putting it down on the table in front of me. "JB knows that area like the back of his hand. Lordy, you could walk right over him and not notice. Gal, I don't remember the last time I agreed with the mayor on anything, but he's right about this."

"That bad?"

"If you sent a search party up there looking for him, well, best case is they would come back empty- handed."

"Worse case?"

"Worse case is they'd come back short a few men."

"Could *you* find him?" I wanted to know, wiping up the last of the stew gravy in my bowl with more bread.

Pa took up his empty bowl and walked over to the sink. He ran the hot water for a few seconds, then after squeezing some dish detergent from a plastic bottle into a tin basin, took a brush and washed the bowl out. He returned to the table and picking up my bowl said, "Maybe, just depends."

"It might be necessary."

"Why not wait him out?"

"Too long, he could be out there until Christmas and the mayor wants it over sooner than later."

"Better safe than sorry."

"The mayor's an impatient man. He's going to put a search team with dogs and head out tomorrow, mid-morning, and try to find him."

"Girl, I hope you're not serious!"

"Mayor's dead serious."

"Well, then," he said, dropping my bowl down in the basin, "we'd better get going, then."

"Get going? Get going where?"

"Up that mountain."

"What…now?"

"If you want to find JB."

"But, tonight?"

"Yes, tonight. Chances are he hid close to the house when

you made your visit, but he'll be moving before morning."

"Can't we wait and join the search?"

"Emma, do you know anything about JB?"

"Besides being a wacky survivalist?"

"He has weird ideas, that's for sure, but do you know what he did in Nam?"

"No, but I heard he served."

"He served alright, Special Forces, trained to kill. If he wanted, he could come out and take that whole search party without firing a shot—and then disappear again."

The last time I'd been out in the woods late at night, Early and I chased a big old coon for three hours under a brilliant fall moon. Young teens then, full of life and spring in our legs, we followed our old dog, Butch, who caught the scent of the varmint and led us on a wild hunt through the thick summer woods. Exhausted and sporting a wide assortment of thorn scratched arms and legs, we caught up with the rascal when Butch treed the thirty-pound beast in a giant dead oak tree. The old coon snarled down at us from where he sat a good twenty feet above the ground.

Early brought his shotgun up to his shoulder to shoot the coon and I saw his finger start to squeeze the trigger, but he stopped short. Lowering the gun, he turned and smiled at me, and without saying a word, we started back home in the night, Butch leading the way. When I asked him why he didn't kill that old coon, he said, "Just didn't seem right after all the fuss."

"Any idea where to start?" I asked Pa as I put a few things in a canvas pack.

"We'll start out back and climb up to the ridgeline."

"Aren't we back far east of their farm?"

"No, he's back west a bit I know, but we need to stay above him."

I put my good wool socks on, high school jeans, and slipped into my moccasin boots. I took a light fleece for the trail, but stuffed my coat into the pack for putting on later when we stopped. Before leaving out the door, I filled a couple of two-quart water bottles at the sink and stuffed them into the pack, as well.

"Put these in, too," Pa directed, handing me a food bag, three tin mugs, and an old, battered camp coffee pot.

"Are we going to take the rifle?" I asked him, adjusting the pack's contents, storing my coat to the rear of the pack and the metal objects in the front, away from my spine.

"You plan to shoot something?"

"Well…" I said, pausing on the threshold, looking up at the rifle hanging over the doorway.

"Look, if we show up hauling a rifle we may as well say farewell to JB. He'd not take kindly to it."

Taking the trail that began at the edge of the property line we marched out and immediately began a moderate climb, heading west. At that altitude, Pa explained, we remained well above the surrounding foothills and above JB Davis, and chances were, we'd stay above him.

After an hour of steady walking we stopped to drink a sip of water. Pa knew the trail well, a trail he hiked a thousand times. Pa used to say he had Cherokee blood in him so even though the night stood pitch black under the canopy of trees, he recognized every foot of the trail.

After another hour of climb, the path flattened out and we found the way pretty level along the crest and kept a good pace. Sometime after another hour of walking, Pa said we had arrived.

"Where?" I asked, not noticing anything different between

that spot in the dark and any other spot in the dark.

"We're about a mile above the Davis place."

"Are you sure?"

"Oh, sure, it's right down there."

"It doesn't seem like we came far enough west."

"It's a longer trek if you go all the way down and then up again, but we came straight across the mountain's spine, and saved all but a bit of the time."

"So, now what do we do?"

"Now, we're going to gather some wood and build a fire," he said rubbing his hands, "and get some coffee going. It's cold out here."

"Won't JB see a fire?"

"I sure hope so," Pa said, as he started to pick up fallen limbs and branches. He pulled a pine tender from a pocket and built a little teepee of twigs in a slight indention on the ground under the clearing in the trees. Once he gathered a good amount of wood, he squatted and started the fire. He fed it other sticks and larger branches I'd gathered, breaking longer ones with his foot, stoking the flame so it gave off a sturdy heat. He poured water in the old pot and put it near the flame. After a while, he added coffee grounds to the pot. When ready, he poured coffee in two tin cups and handed one to me.

The night grew heavy with a thick mist settling through the trees. I pulled my hood up over my head and zipped on my coat. Pa stayed squatted at the fire, feeding it. He snapped the dry wood in his hands and that, along with the crackling of the fire, made the only sounds in a still night.

I gazed for a time into the bright flames of the fire, thinking about Early, about Pa, about Becky. I looked up and saw a bright forest green aura materialized out of the dark.

"Here comes JB," I announced to Pa and a few seconds later JB Davis came out of the mist and into the little camp.

"JB," Pa greeted the man, "coffee?"

"Logan," JB said, walking into the light of the fire, like

coming into the kitchen from morning chores, "don't mind if I do. Cold up here this time of year."

"Yeah, I guess winter setting in for good now," Pa said, reaching for the hot pot and pouring a tin mug full of coffee.

"Nice and pretty Indian summer, though." He put the heavy bow he carried on the ground and adjusting a small pack on his back, squatted across the fire pit from Pa. The fire cast a skittish light over the scene with John Davis in full night camouflage, his eyes peeking through black face webbing, beneath a floppy hat.

"Yep, real pretty," Pa said, handing him the mug.

"You been out long?" he asked, taking the mug and holding it in both hands, warming his palms.

"No, Emma filled me in some back about sunset, so we hiked out about then."

"I didn't expect to be up this high," he said, pulling the webbing back and over his head so he could sip from the mug.

"You hear what the mayor said down at the farm?"

"I could make out some."

"Is it true?"

The man everyone called JB sipped on his coffee, but didn't respond.

"Mr. Davis." I waited for his green aura to flow to the red side. "Why was Early investigating you?"

"Your brother didn't know to mind his own business."

"Sounds like you are guilty of something…"

"Nothing that can't be explained."

"So why are you running off?"

"Who says I'm running?" he smiled at me. "I'm out for a deer. It *is* the bow season, you know."

"The mayor says he's going to come looking for you tomorrow."

"I heard."

"JB," Pa said, "it'd be a lot easier on everyone if you come on down on your own. I know you don't want any trouble."

"I haven't brought the trouble, Logan, but if that's what they want…"

"Look," Pa said, shifting his weight from one leg to another, but continuing to squat at the fire, "so far, the mayor's guessing, but you running up the mountain here will only confirm his suspicions."

"What, that I had something to do with Early's investigation?"

I waited for Pa, but when he didn't continue the questions I asked, "If not, then what was it between you and Early?"

"This mountain, here, and the town hold lots of mysteries, and most of them best be left alone, for everyone's sake, right Logan?"

John Davis raised his mug and after finishing the last of his coffee said, "Thanks for the brew." He put down his mug and picking up his bow. Raising from his squat, he said, "I saw some deer sign up along that stand of trees," he pointed out into the dark, "just yonder. I don't know that we might face a long winter up here this year, Logan, so a little extra meat in the freezer would come in handy. What do you think?"

"Could be, JB," my pa said, as the man stalked out of the light of the camp and disappeared out in the dark of the forest. "Could be."

"Let's follow him." I jumped up after JB vanished into the night, dragging an orange aura after him. "Before he gets away."

"Girl, you best be settling down," Pa said, feeding more sticks to the fire, "If JB wanted to, we'd already be dead. He can hit a running buck at 50 yards with that bow of his, in the dark."

"Then what are we going to do?"

"Well, it's near morning, and we have a good walk back to the house. I'd like a hot breakfast after all this exercise you been making me do."

"And Mr. Davis?"

"JB is going to do what he's going to do."

"Pa, what did he mean about other secrets in the mountains?"

"Oh, that's JB talking wacko, but he's a nice wacko."

"You don't think he knows anything, do you Pa?"

"Not for me to say, Emma. I tell you, JB's been through some things these years, but I don't see him partnering with these backwoods boys. I doubt he knows anything about all that and Early."

"Then why'd we come up here?"

"I don't know, maybe to show him a friendly face. We needed to put the bug in his ear about the consequences. What's done is done, but maybe our little talk will help him make up his mind, go on down to town."

"Why would he?"

"Well, for one, if I found him so easily, he might figure this old mountain can't hide him so good after all."

Chapter Twenty-Two

Wednesday

Pa cut thick, near half-inch strips of bacon off a slab of pork been curing in the cellar for near a year. He layered the bacon in a cast iron pan and set a match to the gas, letting the meat slow cook on each side. In the meantime, I took a shower, letting the hot water run off my back and legs, loosening the stiffness after our all-night hike in the woods.

"Scrambled or fried," Pa called at me as I padded past the kitchen, a towel wrapped around me as I darted down the short hall to my room.

"Scrambled," I yelled, not even pausing, "two with cheese!"

"You think this is Shaw's Diner where you can special order?"

I put on another pair of my leftover underwear, old jeans, and flannel shirt. I used a towel to wring out the last of the shower water from my hair and combed it out. I put on the same wool socks I wore the night before and pulled my boots on again.

When I got back to the kitchen, Pa put my breakfast plate on the table and started on his bacon. I barely began eating when the house phone rang, the sound so unfamiliar it made me jump. Until then, I'd forgotten Pa even had a phone in the house.

"Emma," Becky's voice came softly across the line.

"Becky, I—"

"They just arrested Daddy."

"What?"

"The mayor and his search team were out here, and Daddy

199

came down the mountain and turned himself in."

I didn't know what to say, so I repeated what she said. "JB turned himself in?"

"You started this whole foolishness," she said. "You need to tell the mayor you were wrong about Daddy."

"Becky," I said into the phone, "I can't. I know it's hard to believe, but I think your Daddy knows something about Early's accident."

"You don't know what you're talking about. Daddy wouldn't know anything about what Early was up to."

"Why'd he give himself up, then?"

"He didn't want anyone to get hurt."

I didn't know that I didn't agree with her on that. After she cut me off, I said to Pa, "Becky says JB turned himself in this morning."

"I'm glad," Pa said from the sink.

"I wonder why?"

"The dark has a way of making you not see straight. Maybe when he woke this morning, he saw it different."

"You think so?"

Taking the Jeep, I coasted down the mountain to town. The sun, out for a tickle ahead of its disappearing act later in the afternoon, shot streams of light through the thinning canopy of tree leaves and the morning mist.

I didn't know what to believe about John Davis. He looked involved somehow.

In town I parked at Town Hall.

"Well, you stirred up the hornets now," Randall Shaw said, seeing me come through the door. "You need to stop and think about what your actions can do."

"What did Mr. Davis say?" I asked him.

"He hasn't said anything. He says he wants a lawyer."

"He did?"

"Right, he clammed up good after that."

"I don't get it. Why turn yourself in?"

"Do I look like a mind reader?"

"I'd like to see him."

"Why?"

"Just to ask if he knows anything about Early."

"He's not talking to anyone until we get a public defender in here to talk for him."

I didn't know what to do, but after my long night, I needed another cup of coffee. I made for the door and drove to the diner.

A sparse early lunch crowd occupied three of the eight booths along the glass wall with no one at the counter. A teenage girl with a name tag that said "Ruth" stood behind the counter with a pretty smile on her face.

"Where is everybody?" I asked the girl who seemed to be in charge.

"Rush hasn't started yet," she said, wiping down the glass display case with a fairly soiled rag.

"Um," I mumbled, looking over the different pie and cake selections filling the case, my stomach growling at the first hint of food within arm's length.

I took a seat at the counter and ordered a piece of apple pie and a cup of coffee, and before my morning treat arrived, I pulled out my phone to check my email messages.

My boss Ken, at the paper, had sent me an assignment—in bold font, no less—about covering the annual Brown Jug football game that coming weekend at Western University. He added a note about thinking I needed to get back to work. At that moment, I kind of agreed with him.

Ruth brought my order, and I ate three or four bites. After doctoring up my coffee with cream and sugar, I chased the pie down with a big gulp. I heard a heavy vehicle pull up outside and the customer warning buzzer sounded out in the room. A half-minute later, Jeff Carson walked into the diner. He ordered a glass of sweet tea and walked down the counter and took a seat next to me.

"My hero!" I said, pausing in my eating.

"I hear JB got himself arrested."

"Seems that way." I continued with my pie.

"I wonder what that's all about?"

"I don't know," I lied, forking pie into my mouth and gulping down more coffee, hoping Jeff Carson couldn't read the dark pink aura forming around my head.

"Maybe that drug thing with Early?"

"What makes you think that?"

"You're the one who started it!"

"Am I the only one?"

"Mainly you and the mayor, but there's other talk around town."

"Oh?"

"Yep, all which I find interesting."

Something about the way he said *interesting* stopped me with a fork full of pie halfway to my mouth. "Now, I don't know that I like the way you say *interesting*."

"Well…" he started, but when Ruth brought his tea, he paused to take a swig.

"Come on, what is it?"

"Best tea in town, here," he said, putting his glass down.

"What's so interesting, Jeff?"

"Well, I heard something about JB and the drug stuff going on around town."

"Yeah, okay…"

"Well, you know, all those backwoods boys pushing that stuff."

"I think everyone knows that."

"Well, JB doesn't cotton to the backwoods boys."

"How do you know that?"

"Oh, just some things he'd say when he came into the shop. He liked to pop off and spout stuff about those boys and their drug trafficking, how they made it hard on everyone in the hills. You know, giving everyone a bad name."

"So…?"

"So, I don't see JB against the law on this, siding with those boys."

"No?"

"No, ma'am, not JB; he didn't get along with those boys. Oh, he knew them now, every one of them certain, but he didn't like them."

"Then, what?"

"You tell me," Jeff said, and smiling, he got up to leave, adding, "you're the detective."

Then what was going on with JB?

I stalled at the diner for a few minutes, thinking over what Jeff Carson said. It started raining as I left, heading to town. The rain came down from way up high. The mountain rain came packed in dark clouds, scooting down the valley, lightning and thunder leading the way, pouring water as it moved. Summer or spring showers are like that, but not the fall. In the fall the rain seems to come from another place, higher up, over the mountains, like out of heaven, and thunder marking its approach. I didn't know if heaven controlled the clouds and rain, but right then, I prayed that the God in heaven would be on my side in all this.

I pulled the Jeep up in front of Town Hall and pulled my body out from behind the wheel and to the ground. The rain managed to soak me after just a couple of steps, but I shrugged it off.

"Oh, no," Shelby Stone said when I opened the glass door and entered the mayor's office suite. "I thought you left town."

"No," I said, wiping rain from my face, dripping water over the reception counter, "not yet."

"Well, what do you want now?"

"I want to see the mayor. Is he in?"

"He's back there with Randall and Doc Miller."

"Oh, now what?" came the reaction from the mayor when Shelby used the intercom to tell him I wanted to see him. "What on earth…"

"Tell him it's important," I told Shelby.

Ruben D. Gonzales

"She says it's—"

"I heard her," he shouted in the phone loud enough I could hear him over the phone and through the office door down the hall. "Tell her to come on back and join the party."

Opening the door to the mayor's office, I saw the three brothers situated around the small conference table, a scattering of note pads and other sheets of paper taking up the surface of the tabletop.

"I hope you are in here to say goodbye?" Franklyn Shaw said.

"No, not yet, but I did want to ask about Mr. Davis."

"What?"

"Did he say he had anything to do with Early's death?"

"No, he denied everything."

"But you don't believe him?"

"I don't know what to believe."

"But why turn himself in if he's not guilty of something?"

"I don't know, and he's not talking until the public defender gets here."

"Well, I don't know that JB had anything to do with that investigation."

"What are you talking about? You're the one that started this whole thing."

"I know, but I hear JB doesn't cotton to those boys and the drug trade."

"Where did you hear that?"

"Just something he once said to me," I explained, remembering an early conversation with JB, but leaving out what Jeff Carson said.

"So what of it?"

"So if JB wasn't in it with the backwoods boys, what was Early doing in all this?"

"Well, if JB has something to say, he's not talking. We called over to Morgan and they're sending a PD over. In the meantime, we wait."

204

◆◇◆

I didn't know what had happened between Early and JB Davis. The two were involved in something; either on the same side or on opposite sides. If Early was into something, it looked like JB Davis occupied the center space in the whole thing. Whatever it turned out to be, I just had to find out what.

"You got your nerve," Mother Davis said after opening the inner door and seeing me through the screen door, dripping rainwater on her doorstep. She stood there, shot gun resting in the crook of her arm and continued her comment, "Coming up here after what you've done."

I didn't know how to respond, but Becky came up from behind her and said, "Let me handle this, Mama, you go on back to the kitchen."

Mother Davis hesitated a second, repositioning the shotgun in her arm before relenting and leaving the two of us alone.

Becky pushed the screen door open, and stepping aside to let me in, said, "She's pretty upset, thanks to you. I started her on canning some apple butter to keep her mind off everything."

"I'm sorry about your pa," I said, stepping past her and moving into the room before she could change her mind.

"You should be." She closed both doors behind me, shutting out the cold.

"Look, I know it's hard to believe, but your pa and Early were into something."

"Oh, Emma, half the town could say the same."

"Becky, this is serious."

"Emma, you can't believe Pa knows something about Early's accident?"

"He knows more than he's saying."

"What makes you think that?"

205

"Why did he give up?"

"He didn't want anyone to get hurt."

"He told the mayor he wouldn't talk until he got a lawyer. That sounds like someone hiding something."

"Sounds like the smart thing to do. Daddy knows the law. He always said if you want to beat the law you'd better know the law."

"Becky, this thing with Early is just a puzzle to me, and now your pa is mixed up in the middle. I just can't seem to make any headway in this."

"Well, like I said before, maybe it'd better if you don't pursue it anymore. Enough people been hurt by all this."

"I know, you've said that a couple of times. Like you were worried of what I might find out."

She looked at me then, straight in the eyes, her aura beating a steady crimson, indicating she was hiding something, her face a mask against the truth. "I'm not worried."

In the pause of our talk, the sound of tires churning through the gravel on the driveway could be heard in the house. "What in the world?" Mother Davis said, coming out of the kitchen and going to the door. "It's Little Earl."

"Grandma," Little Earl called out as he rushed up the steps, dripping rainwater as he ran.

"What is it?" Mother Davis said, greeting him by opening the door before he had a chance to crash through it.

"They said they're going to let Grandpa go!"

"Who said?"

"The mayor and them said they didn't have anything on him, so they are going to let him go."

"When?" Mother Davis asked, closing the door behind her grandson.

"They're saying today!"

"Who says?" Becky asked, rushing towards her boy.

"Down in town," Little Earl kept explaining. "I went down

to Town Hall to see if I could visit Grandpa and I saw Holly Stone and she told me."

"What did she say?"

"She told me not to worry that her mama said they would let Grandpa go."

Mother Davis gave the boy a hug and casting a smug look in my direction, then led the boy off to the kitchen where I could hear them laughing and celebrating the news. I wondered if the County Public Defender got to town and arranged JB's release.

Becky watched her mama and Little Earl leave the room, and turning to me, asked, "Did you know about this before coming up here?"

"About what?"

"About this letting Daddy go."

When I didn't say anything, she said, "Did you talk to the mayor about Pa being innocent?"

I didn't know what to say to her. With JB in the clear, it somehow left Early holding that proverbial dirty bag full of money, he and those backwoods boys.

"Okay," she said, straightening her blouse. "So, I don't see how pursuing this is getting us anywhere, and since Pa is out of it now, you better think on what you are doing. Now, I asked you to drop this whole thing, and I think it best you mull it over before you go on. Now, if you don't mind," she said turning to leave the room, "Mama and I got some canning to get to."

I didn't know what I wanted Becky to say about the mystery between JB and Early. Becky just turned away without saying more, just walked out and into the kitchen to join her mama cooking up apple butter.

I showed myself out of the house and went over to my Jeep and noticed that Little Earl had parked his old red Jeep right next to me.

♦◊♦

When I got back home, I saw that Pa left out a half pan of cornbread and a stew pot sitting on the back of the wood stove. I filled a bowl with the stew and sat at the table spooning thick lumps of deer meat into my mouth and flipped pages in Early's baby album still sitting on the table. With each page I turned, a thought wiggled further out of my memory about something to do with baby photos.

When I finished, I took my bowl over to the sink and cleaned it up. I took the pot of soup and emptied it in an old plastic container and spent a few minutes looking through a drawer for the right lid to seal the thing before putting it in the refrigerator. I had just finished washing out the pot when Pa came in.

"Thanks for the stew," I told him. "It hit the spot."

"You're welcome."

"I just put it up, if you are hungry?"

"No, I ate a bowl just before I went out."

"Where did you go?" I asked him as I dried off my hands and went to the table for Early's baby book.

"I went up to Laurel Ridge to speak some with Louise."

"Oh, yeah?" I went over to the parlor chest that housed all of Mama's old family photos. I didn't know what she'd say about putting in Early's baby photos. I wondered if she'd mind. Back then, it just didn't interest me, baby pictures. While I was in the chest, I pulled a number of other albums of photos from Early's collection to browse through.

I hadn't remembered, but Mama had quite a collection of pictures of Early, arranged chronologically, starting from before his elementary school days and on up to college. In keeping with the order of books, I put Early's baby album I got from the Shaws into the first position at the beginning of his collection since they would be the oldest. When done, I pulled the first album from the lineup of my baby books and browsed through it.

After I opened and closed a number of albums I stopped, and looking up, started to ask, "Pa…"

"You won't find any of your baby pictures in that cabinet, Emma. At least, not any before you were one year old or so."

"Why, where are they?"

"You see, that's what I went up to talk to Louise about."

"What?"

"About you and your first year after you were born."

"What are you talking about?"

"You spent your first year living with Louise, up on Laurel Ridge."

"What?"

"Yeah, you being a baby, you don't remember it. You see, they didn't cotton to cameras up there, so they didn't take any pictures of you. They were afraid of that voodoo thing where an image on paper might be stolen and such."

"But why was I up there?"

"Well, you see, I'm your Pa, alright, but your mama was Louise's daughter. Louise Looking Bird is your grandmother."

"Mama was my mama."

"Mama was your mama, after the first year. But before that, Louise's daughter, we called her Wendy, she was your mama. Her Cherokee name was *Unole Gogayi*, it means Spring Wind, but we called her Wendy for the English short version."

I sat there on the cord carpet looking up at Pa as I searched for words.

"What are you talking about?"

"Wendy and me were your first parents, Emma. She got pregnant by me and then she gave birth to you. We were married there by her people…but…she died."

"What are you telling me?"

"I'm trying to say your mama and I didn't conceive you, but me and Wendy Looking Bird did. Wendy was young and she died in childbirth having you. Louise tended her. Tried her best with potions and all, but said there wasn't anything that could have been done. When Louise calls you daughter and explains about your aura-reading, she meant only someone born of Cherokee blood could read auras like you.

"Well, when Wendy up and died, I couldn't take it so started to drink. That was a dark year for me, Emma, up until I met your mama. When Dorothy came into my life with your brother, it settled me down, turned me around. We fell hard in love from our first meeting. I went to Louise then and asked for you back. Louise saw I meant well and since I was the father, and all, she let you go back to me. She had a house full of young grandkids so didn't mind much. She figured you'd be better off with us, anyway. That's why she kept up with you, showing interest all these years, teaching you about the aura- reading."

"Pa, are you saying—"

"I'm saying I'm your Pa, alright, but your birth mama was Wendy Looking Bird, a Cherokee woman I loved with all my heart. I still don't know why the Lord took her, but in her place, He put your mama. We raised you and Early like our own, and proudly so. If circumstances had been different, maybe this would have all turned out another way, but it is what it is and you and Early came to be ours; Early by your mama and Lawrence Shaw, and you by Wendy Looking Bird and me."

When I didn't say anything, Pa said, "I'm sorry we didn't say anything before, but both the Shaws and Louise's kin wanted it all kept secret. That's why I went up there today, to tell Louise it was time to tell you the truth. I promised her a long time ago I wouldn't say anything, but after our visit the other day, it's been eating at me. Then, too, when you found out about Early, well I just thought it was time to have both sides out."

"So, this aura-reading I have?"

"Only a person with Cherokee blood can read auras like

you, Emma, that's why the gift is so strong in you. Louise tried to tell you a couple of times, about your birth and all."

"Pa, I don't understand why you didn't say something."

"Between Louise and your mama, there just wasn't any way. Your mama loved you, Emma, from the first time I brought you home to her last breath on earth. You know she did."

Pa was right, of course, Mama loved Early and me, no doubting it. She'd do anything for us and did more than she should. In the end, did it matter? Did it matter that Pa wasn't Early's real pa? Did it matter that Mama wasn't my birth mama? In the end, it only mattered that Mama and Pa loved us and raised us up as best they could.

"Pa," I began, tears flowing down my cheeks, "tell me about my mama, my birth mama."

Pa sat back in his chair and looked out through the kitchen window, staring out, staring out into what must have been a dark past for him. "She was pretty like you, Emma, and when she spoke to me my heart beat in my chest like a pecker pounding on an old birch looking for food. When she died, I thought the world had come to its end, and the only way to survive it was to forget. Of course, I found out that forgetting about your mama was like trying to forget the sun rises in the morning. You look like her, Emma, the spitting image, just as pretty—and just as stubborn."

Chapter Twenty-Three

Thursday

The next morning, I explained to Pa about my assignment up at Western.

"Will you be gone the whole weekend?"

"I'll be back tomorrow night," I said, giving him a big hug and smile. "I want to see little Earl's last game, Friday night."

The morning radio weather announcement for the weekend called for cold and cloudy skies, with snow a possibility. I'd been to many games in the mountains that time of year and the prospect of cold weather didn't faze me as long as I would be dry. The only thing worse than cold weather, is wet cold weather.

The trees higher up surrounding the university stood bare against the cold and damp with a light snow falling. However, the prospect of four inches of snow didn't bother the fans of the two schools as they began to pour into the little town in four-wheel drive vehicles and big RV's.

The paper had sent a team to cover the game, and as usual, I was responsible for the photos the paper would use and the video of the game for the newspaper's web site. The team spent the afternoon visiting the various fan parties and gatherings, and interrupting diners in the middle of meals to ask about their passion for coming to the game.

After putting in a full day, we headed to the High Country Bed and Breakfast Inn situated in a mountain high grove of thick evergreen. Later, we all gathered at a local chain restaurant, but I know I wasn't much company as I lost myself in a long buffet that included barbecue ribs.

Chapter Twenty-Four

Friday

In the morning, we ate a late breakfast of homemade waffles and fruit served by Marge Nance, the nice lady of the home whose aura seesawed between the cooler reaches of the rainbow, befitting her earnest hospitality. Her small dining room faced a pretty yard covered with two inches of overnight snow.

Packing up, we reloaded our vehicles and slushed over to the university, for the scheduled interviews with coaches and players from the two teams. By 1:00, I completed my part of the assignment. Later, the team would add quotes from the one or two heroes from the game, and I'd shoot several minutes of the Saturday afternoon game, but at that point, I was done and anxious to get back to Black Mountain for the high school's last game of the regular season.

After the frigid temperatures of the higher elevation in Boone County, the cold of Black Mountain didn't seem as bad. The game time forecast didn't call for snow but said to expect freezing temperatures. I arrived in town with enough time to put on warmer clothes and meet the Davis family at the cold stadium. I didn't know how, but it looked like twice the amount of fans packed in the stadium than the week before. No telling how many more in the overflowing stands were past alumni of the school, but it made for a formidable scene, and was intimidating to the visiting team.

We found the Shaw family section in the stadium and the

kin navigated around to squeeze us in. It looked like everyone showed up for the big game. Franklyn and Shelby were there, May and Doc Miller, Mathew and his brood, and Cousin Evelyn, although I didn't see Wendell Banks.

Jeff and Bobby Carson sat nearby, sitting with a man dressed in a sheriff's uniform who looked familiar. I thought maybe the man came to provide extra security for game.

I acknowledged a number of greetings, but didn't know if the friendliness arose out of left over sympathy for Early or more associated with Little Earl. The fans knew his football prowess promised to bring the season to an exciting close, and a chance at the state high school playoffs.

The cold wind circulated around the stadium, but it couldn't cool off the Broncos. With Little Earl quarterbacking, they led twenty-eight to zero at halftime.

The halftime ceremony included a crowning of the homecoming queen and king. From a distance, I thought I recognized the queen. The two crowned winners climbed into a shiny classic red Cadillac convertible with a driver. Perched on the back of the rear seat, they were driven around the field in a victory lap that closed the halftime ceremonies.

As the car drove past our section of the stands, I recognized the homecoming queen, Holly Stone, and the red Cadillac owner and driver, Wendell Banks.

With the home team up by six touchdowns, the Bronco fans stood waiting for the game's end. When the last seconds ran off the clock, they hooked arms, and rocking to the rhythm of the band, sang the school song. I joined in on the last stanza:

'Friends together in thick and thin
We'll always be - until we meet again.'

We gathered up possessions and blankets and made our way to the parking area. I said goodbye to the Davis family and had just reached my Jeep when Jeff and the sheriff deputy intercepted me.

"Emma," Jeff said, introducing his companion, "this is my

215

brother, Lane Carson; he's on with the Morgan County Sheriff's office."

"Oh, yeah?" I said to the man, reaching my hand out for the greeting.

"Yeah, I've been with the county now about ten years."

"I remember, now. You used to run with Early."

"That's right, we used to hang out."

After jerking my hand nearly out of its socket he said, "Look, sorry I missed the funeral and all, but we've been working a big case and I just couldn't get away."

"Wait," I paused in the conversation, remembering something. "You're Lane Carson with the Sheriff's Department?"

"That's right."

"You work with the ATF over there?"

With that question, both Jeff and Lane paused for a minute.

"Jeff," I asked, "is your brother the Lane that Early wrote in his notes, involved in the case he was working?"

Jeff looked both ways to make sure no one was within hearing distance and said, "I told you she was smart, Lane."

I looked at both of them and asked, "What's this all about?"

"Okay, Emma," Lane Carson began an explanation, "Jeff saw my name in that file and called me about it. I filled him in on some details, and he told me of your suspicions. He said you were bound to find out, so he suggested I talk to you about Early and the ATF."

"Yeah," Jeff said. "I didn't even know."

"So," I asked the question that had been plaguing me since I got to Black Mountain, "what's this all got to do with Early?"

"Well, you know Early was involved with the backwoods boys."

"Now, don't be starting in with all that, Lane, I don't believe it for a minute. My big brother hated the drug trade."

"Now, hold on, Emma, I didn't say it like that."

216

"Like what?"

"Early was involved, alright, but he was working *with* the ATF."

"What?"

"Yes, Early worked for the ATF."

"He did?"

"That's right, they thought Early could infiltrate that group, you know work undercover, since he knew most of those boys."

"I'll be…"

"Yep, Early was a big help, been working right along on the investigation, off and on for several months now."

"For how long?"

"Several months, part-time but steady, and it was real important work. Dangerous too, you know, spying on those backwoods boys, he earned it working for them."

"Well, I'll be. Say would this have anything to do with JB Davis, too?"

"Oh, sure, the ATF said they used Mr. Davis's knowledge to track the main locations for the group. JB knows all the hiding places up on the mountain, so he helped in the investigation."

Still assessing the new information, I asked, "Did Early know about JB and the ATF?"

"No, I don't think he did. The ATF worked two sides on the case, two different teams, trying to get information through both sources, although as smart as Early was, he could have figured it out."

"So Early…"

"Yep, Early got in tight with the group, offering protection, you know trying to garner favor. The group thought they got Early on their side, but it was only a ruse. Once Early found out as much as he could, he gave it to the ATF. They raided several of their hangouts and labs yesterday and busted up the biggest drug ring in the history of Morgan County."

"Why didn't JB say something about this?"

"We told him to keep quiet because of the danger to his family. We didn't know who was involved. If those boys found out JB was informing on them, he knew his family would be in danger."

"So it was the drug ring that killed Early? They must have found out about Early informing on them, and in retaliation, ran him off the road."

"Now, Emma, Jeff's been telling me about your suspicions on all this, but we don't have anything definite on Early."

"I just don't figure Early's death an accident.

"Well, the ATF doesn't know for sure, and with Early's cruiser sold off for scrap…"

"What?" Jeff said, looking at me.

"Yeah," I confirmed the bad news, "mayor told me that couple of days ago."

Deputy Sheriff Lane continued, "Yeah, unfortunately the ATF boys had to time the bust, so they couldn't get into the junk yard to look at Early's car before the town sold it off."

"Oh, no…"

"Yeah, I guess now there's no way to tell for certain. They said for us to hold on a while, though, because they're convinced one or more of the gang will confess about Early. We'll all just have to wait on that."

Chapter Twenty-Five

Saturday

After the game on Friday night, and after the news about Early and the ATF, I went to The Coffee Bean for a celebration. It seemed like all the team members and their parents were there and spilling out into the street in front of the place, celebrating the team's win and making it to the playoffs. My own celebration centered on my big brother's return to hero status.

By the time I made it home, Pa had gone to bed. It wasn't until Saturday morning that I told Pa about Early and the ATF investigation.

Pa made me an early breakfast of eggs and sausage patties. We made small talk over coffee, about the game the night before, the celebration at The Coffee Bean, about my job for the coming day, and about the news out of the county on Early and the ATF. Pa was happy to hear that Early and JB stood in the clear of any wrongdoing. He did express hope that they'd find the guy who drove Early off Moore's Curve, but in the meantime, he looked content.

Light flurries greeted me as I drove up the mountain to Western University early enough to load in and cover the one o'clock game. At kick off the sky hung gray and overcast with the predicted scattered snow showers materializing around the end of the first quarter. I shot a quick sequence of the cheerleaders at halftime before the newspaper team retreated to a cup of hot coffee and bowl of steamy chili served up in the interior stadium press room. From the warm room we could hear the sound of the school bands outside playing as they braved the cold.

Most of the crowd in the strands stood throughout the second half of the game, either from the cold or the exciting play on the field. Both teams battled up and down the stadium, each scoring at will, and the snow increasing with every minute. On this particular Saturday, the home team scored last on a field goal that split the uprights with time expiring. The ball traveled through a light blizzard to get there. I got the whole play on video.

Even with security personnel protecting the goal posts, a crowd of determined students managed to skirt the guard and succeed in pulling down the north end zone goal post. I took some video of a mob of students carrying the post out of the stadium towards downtown in a then heavy falling snow.

We followed the game excitement with an hour of player-coach interviews, and before we were finished, we rode through town and I took some shots of a downtown celebration centered about a nice bonfire fed by freezing cold students. We gathered our equipment and notes and set up the laptop on a table in an on-street café with Wi-Fi, and along with my photos and video, sent the whole package in to the paper. They'd have to edit out what they wanted to run with.

We spent the rest of the afternoon and evening enjoying the high mountain town, and although I didn't know how, but with the news about Early not running a scam, those barbecue ribs tasted even better.

Chapter Twenty-Six

Sunday

We slept in Sunday, but by the afternoon we packed our things and said our goodbyes to the High Country Bed & Breakfast. A steady snow chased me to the highway for the drive down to Black Mountain. I decided to stop in town to get a cup of coffee before spending my last night with Pa. About two inches of fresh snow greeted me at twilight, covering the downtown in an unblemished white blanket, a reminder of the holiday season fast approaching. Several shops had already decorated their store fronts with colorful lights, looking festive enough.

I pulled into a parking spot in front of Saunders's Photography Studio and noticed a light on in the back where the old man worked.

"Working late again?" I asked when I entered the shop.

"Just trying to catch up, last minute rush yesterday."

"Well, if you're caught up, maybe we can get a cup of coffee?

"Sure, if you're buying."

We spent the time drinking coffee and eating cookies. Mr. Saunders told tales of his and his wife's travels, and I told him about my traveling out west. Sometime in the evening, Jeff joined us. Somewhere in the conversation, Mr. Saunders told us about his plan to close up the shop and head down to Florida to live closer to his grandsons.

By the time I left The Coffee Bean, I got out to Pa's house late, after he'd retired. I went on to bed, but tossed and turned through the night, thinking about Early and the whole mess, thinking about the photography studio, thinking about Jeff. By the time I nodded off, I had made up my mind that there was other unfinished business in town, other than Early's accident.

Chapter Twenty-Seven

Monday

Close to sunrise, I gave up on sleep, and when I went out to the kitchen area, I found Pa up with a cup of coffee in his hand.

"You sleep alright?" he asked with a smile.

I ignored his question, my body numb from the effects of a long two weeks, and asked him to just pour more coffee.

"You know it's snowing out," he said, making small talk as I sat at the table, shaking the cold, trying to come fully awake. "It's not much so you shouldn't have any trouble getting down off the mountain."

"That's good," I mumbled after yawning big.

I apologized about missing church the morning before and explained how we'd been tied up all day Saturday and couldn't get out of town until later on Sunday.

Pa told me not to worry about it since he figured there'd be other times when I could attend a service with him. He said this last bit looking at me like he expected a confirmation of sorts.

"Sure," I said, "I'll make it back more often and go with you."

My pa smiled like he hadn't smiled since I'd been home. Getting up to start breakfast, the conversation drifted back to Early.

"So," I said to him, "anything new come up on Early?"

"No, nothing, I guess we still don't know who killed your brother," Pa said as he mixed eggs and sausage in a big cast iron pan, the juice from the pork spitting grease.

"No, I guess not."

"So," Pa asked, putting eggs and sausage on two plates, "what about the case?"

223

"Those backwoods boys will have to answer for Early," I said getting up from my seat and taking the plates over to the table, "although it looks like we might have a wait on all that."

After breakfast, I dressed and packed up and loaded the Jeep for the trip down the mountain. The fresh snow looked several inches deep, but the bitter cold kept it from melting, so the white powder would mean an easy trip to the interstate.

"You know," I said to Pa as I finished packing up and stood on the porch for a final farewell, watching the pretty falling snow, "I can't see the good in any of this."

"What do you mean?"

"Oh, you know, the Good Lord must have a plan, but I can't see it plain just now."

"Well, Emma, the Lord does move in mysterious ways. I think it will all clear up in His time. So," he asked, "you heading straight out?"

"Well," I said to Pa, smiling, "I want to stop at the Fish and Game on my way out of town."

"Oh?"

"Yeah, I just have a little unfinished business to tend to."

We hugged long and I took a last look at Pa. We had missed out on a lot these last few years because of my attitude. Early passing reminded me how precious life is, so I promised myself then that I'd try to make the most of the remaining years the Good Lord had planned for us, try not to waste any.

I drove down the mountain to town thinking about Jeff Carson and what I was going to say to him, and parked in a street parking space in front of the Fish and Game and across the street from Town Hall. I reached over to the passenger seat for my ball cap when I saw Mr. Saunders's yellow 8" x 10" envelope I had promised to drop off days ago. Feeling guilty about my bad memory and not ready to talk with Jeff, I grabbed up the envelope and went over to Town Hall.

"Hello," Shelby greeted me from the reception desk when I reached the mayor's office, "you on your way out of here?"

"Yep, I've just got one more thing to do, if I could see the mayor."

"Well, he's busy right now. He and Wendell are meeting over the budget...which reminds me... Here," she said, handing me a white envelope.

"What's this?"

"It's the account of those reimbursements I got from the budget office. You remember, you asked for it last week. I tried to give them to you a couple of days back, but you rushed out of here in a hurry."

I had forgotten about wanting to see a copy of Early's account, but it didn't seem important just then, just as I was heading out of town. "Thanks," I told her, and handed her Saunders's envelope. "And this is for the mayor."

"What is it?"

"Photos of the fall parade, Saunders asked me to drop them off last week, but I completely forgot about them."

"Well, he's busy. You know the mayor, he's in there trying to squeeze another ounce of blood out of the town budget and Wendell is helping, but I'll give them to him."

I felt a range of emotions after my two weeks at home. The thought of Early's killer still running free gnawed on me, but I felt happy that I got to spend the time at home. Of course, there was still the unfinished business with Jeff Carson, so I waved bye to Shelby and headed across the street.

When I pushed my way into the shop, I found Bobby Carson working at the gun cabinet, arranging pistols along a display line. Jeff Carson was seated behind the counter, loading shot into shotgun hulls.

"Jeff," I called out as I stomped snow from my boots on the entryway mat, "are you still loading those hulls?"

"Got to save when I can, Emma," he responded, smiling, but continued his work. "I'll be right with you!"

Bobby Carson nodded stiffly at me and continued working, picking up a pistol and using an oil rag to wipe it down. With a minute to think of something to say to Jeff and with the envelope of Early's account in my hand, I opened it.

The account summary sheet listed some fifty items that Early applied for reimbursement for over the last year, most from the Fish and Game shop, but other town merchants as well…but something with the list didn't appear right.

Although my conversation about Early's reimbursement with Jeff took place the week before, I remembered he clearly defined what items were personal and which were job-related; so something was wrong with the account records. I noticed a line item for one reimbursement…*Shot gun …$200.00*. If I accurately recalled what Jeff told me, that was supposed to be a gift for Little Earl. I knew Early had an open account at some of the downtown merchants, and who knew where else, but everyone said he settled up. A nagging thought of where he got the money to settle up sprang back in my head.

Jeff filled the last few hulls to make some number that completed a small carton. When done, he got up, and carrying the box, approached me at the counter.

"Well, I guess you're ready to head out? I wondered if you'd drop by to say goodbye."

"You know I wouldn't leave without a last talk, Jeff," I said, putting the sheet of account paper down on the glass countertop that housed some of his inventory, "but besides that, I have something to clear up."

"Oh…"

"Yes, I was hoping you could explain something on this account here?"

"What is it," he asked, picking up the list and frowning while he held it up to read.

"It's the account from Early's reimbursements from the town. You know, you and I discussed how when he spent his own money on town-related expenses he asked to be reimbursed for."

"So," Jeff said, while continuing to review the list in front

226

of him, "what about it?"

"Well, you'll note that there are several items on the list that you said were personal items, and Early charged those to his personal account and not the town."

"Wait, are you saying this is a list of all his reimbursements?"

"That's what the town records show."

"This has got to be a mistake, we might be a little unorganized in the shop, but we keep good bookwork. Good enough to avoid a mistake like this."

When he said it, his aura didn't quiver from the blue ranges.

Jeff Carson lowered the account page and stared at me. Moving down the counter a few steps he placed the ledger on the counter in front of his brother.

"Let me see," Bobby Carson said, putting on a pair of reading glasses and bending down to inspect the list. "Could be we made a mistake with the account, but this can't be right. Early came in a couple of weeks ago and settled up for what he charged. We can pull the receipts if we have to."

"I figured you all have detailed records here on every purchase and every sale you've ever made. I just know that's the kind of records you all must keep, all neat and tidy, just like your shop."

"We try to be accurate," Bobby said, and when he straightened up from the counter, I noticed he had removed his reading glasses and held the pistol in his left hand.

"I know," I went on, trying to avoid staring at the barrel of the revolver, "and that's why these over-charges are not mistakes. You hinted that business was off these last few years, so what…were you and Early trying to get a little extra back from the town, or was it something else?"

"That's a serious allegation, Emma," Bobby Carson said, tapping the account page with the barrel of the pistol, his aura swinging wildly between brown and dark green. "You'd better have more evidence than this sheet of paper to make an accusation like that."

I turned to Jeff and asked, "Was Early getting some type of kick back from you all?"

Jeff walked back down the counter to where I stood and eyed me carefully. During the pause, his brother casually started rubbing down the pistol again, his aura pumping dark and brooding, but not pink.

Jeff picked up the freshly packed carton of shells, and turning away from me, started moving boxes around on his shelves, I assumed to make room for another box. "Why would your brother do that?"

"I know Early ran up accounts at shops downtown. Maybe this has something to do with his death."

"Lane explained about the ATF investigation, Emma. If Early ran into trouble out on Moore's Curve working that ATF case, they would know."

"No, the evidence isn't clear on that, so someone with a different motive could be involved."

"There're a lot of people out in the back country who ran up against Early after all his years as chief," Bobby said, moving down the counter with the pistol and stopping right in front of me. "There'd be no shortage of suspects up there."

Jeff kept working, straightening and fussing over the boxes on his shelves, but Bobby hung out at the counter. Tall and powerfully built like all the Carson boys, Bobby and his black aura of anger loomed over me.

Jeff finished straightening boxes on the racks, and he slipped the new box into a just-created space. Turning around to face me, he said, "I don't know about Early's reimbursements, Emma. We pretty much stay out of the town's business."

"Where were you two the Friday Early was killed?"

"Do we need an alibi?" Bobby asked.

"It might help."

"Well," Bobby explained, "it just so happens we were down in Fayetteville that Friday and Saturday. They run a fall gun show down there, one of the biggest in the southeast. Thirty dealers will swear we spent the whole weekend manning our booth during the day and drinking beer at night. We sold quite a few things. Even a bunch of our logo shirts."

"Emma," Jeff asked me, "do you think I could have something to do with Early's death, me knowing how much you loved your brother?"

I looked at him and I didn't need to see his steady blue aura to know he was telling the truth. He didn't need an alibi. I couldn't have been that wrong about the man, about the way I felt about him…but about his brother, I hadn't been so sure.

Bobby was big and tall, and left-handed. Of course, I couldn't tell them about their auras and how I knew by looking at them they were telling the truth. I doubt the two would have understood what I was talking about.

"No, you wouldn't do that, especially after you've come to my rescue."

"What rescue?" Bobby asked.

"I roughed up a couple of guys giving Emma a hard time about her investigating Early's death."

"Yeah?"

"Yeah," I answered, acknowledging Jeff's good deeds. "He even broke some guy's jaw last week," I said, and noticed no visible damage to Bobby's jaw line, "when I got mugged in the only alley in town, right next to Town Hall."

"Well, Jeff, Bobby," I said picking up the account sheet and stuffing it back in the envelope, "I hope you both don't hold this against me, this asking you about Early?"

"That's okay," Jeff said, "you do what you got to do. I hope you find out what happened to your brother."

With that thought to gnaw on, I asked Jeff one more question, "Say, how did Early pay for his purchases? Cash?"

"No," Bobby said, "Early used a card. He said he liked to

229

keep a record of things, and using his monthly bank statement made it simple for him to track and submit."

"What do you mean?"

"He told me he would highlight on his monthly statement those items to be reimbursed and submit the whole thing. It was just an informal way for him to account for his spending."

I thanked the Carson brothers for their patience and smiling at Jeff, waited a beat. Jeff smiled back, and when he went around the counter to walk me to the door, he said, "I hope you plan on coming back up here more often."

"I might be working on a plan for that."

"Oh, something to do with photography?"

"Maybe…We'll just have to wait and see."

When we reached the shop door, Jeff said, "One thing to think about on all this."

"What?"

"If that account is accurate," he said, pointing to the envelope in my hand, "then someone in Town Hall knows about it."

I left the Carsons' shop with Jeff's last words in my head. If Early somehow cheated the town I didn't know if I wanted to know anything about it. My emotions on the whole thing had swung around in a circle from Early guilty to innocent and now, back to guilty. I was tired of the roller coaster and wanted off.

I walked up to my Jeep, pulled the door open, and climbed in. I looked for a place to stash the envelope with Early's account and saw his old backpack I stole from his office. I pulled it up off the floorboard, and when I unzipped an outer pocket to stick the account in, I noticed a business-size envelope in there. I pulled the envelope out and discovered a stack of check stubs inside. The stubs dated back several months, a whole year's worth, one for each month. The amounts varied, but were all consistently around $4,000. Printed along the top line of each stub was a number and the seal of the - *United States Bureau of Tobacco, Firearms, and Explosives.*

I found another stub in the stack, this one still connected to a check. A check Early had not cashed, a Town of Black Mountain check. The check was made out to Early and the account noted it was for *reimbursement.*

Apparently, not only had Early been working with the ATF, but he'd been working for pay. So Early did come into some money, but it wasn't by reimbursement. It was for law enforcement work. So if Early came to his recent cash via his work with the ATF, where was the money going that was paid out via his reimbursement statements? And w*hy did he have a single uncashed reimbursement check?*

I sat back in my seat and looked out the windshield back toward Town Hall. There, covered in a fresh dusting of snow, sat the Mayor's Mercedes, and down the alley, another car I hadn't noticed before, Wendell Banks's red Cadillac convertible with the roof up against the weather.

Seeing the Cadillac in the alleyway reminded me of the night I got mugged. I got out and walked over to the spot in the light of the day. The whole event came back to me then, including what the man said, how he choked me with his left arm, and how the man ran away down the alley. I walked to the Cadillac.

That night the man warned me, saying Early's luck had run its course, but he didn't have a chance to say much more, because Jeff showed up and socked him. I remembered how the man ran and disappeared, like he vanished into thin air.

Next to the red car, I saw a door on the side of the Town Hall building. Painted gray, it blended into the granite wall. I stood in front of the door, and taking a deep breath, I reached up and tried to turn the knob—but it didn't open. I turned and looked at Bank's Cadillac and noticed it had been recently painted. The first time I saw the car, I thought it needed a good painting, and I remembered from the homecoming game it looked better, at least from the stands. I stopped and ran my hand over the surface of the recently painted passenger door.

Moving on, I walked around and entered Town Hall. Navigating down several hallways I found the one leading to that end of the building where I passed an office and found the door. A dead bolt held the door solidly shut, but to make sure, I turned the bolt knob over and opened the door, finding the alleyway and the Cadillac between buildings.

Turning about, I closed the door and retraced my steps, following the narrow hall just a short way, back to the office I'd passed. I could see a lady through the glass door sitting at a desk in the entry area of the office suite. I opened the door part way, and sticking my head in, said, "Sorry." I read her name, *Mable Stokes*, off a desk plate on her desk. "I came in off the alley, is this the way to the mayor's office?"

"No, you were lucky to get in that way, Mr. Banks is the only one uses that door. He likes to come and go without being seen. The mayor's office is around front."

When I got back to the mayor's office, I found Shelby thumbing through her phone.

"Oh, no," she said, seeing me come through the door. "I thought you left town."

"I'm on my way," I told her, "but I wanted to ask you another question."

"Oh, now what?"

"You know that account you got for me?"

"Sure."

"What took so long to get it?"

"I don't know. Mable in budget ran it for me last week when Wendell was out with that bug. Why?"

"Something I'm working over. Say, that is Wendell's car parked in the alley?"

"Sure, looks pretty nice since he had it painted, don't you think?"

"Why did he paint it?"

"I've been after him, what with the homecoming court, and all. I thought it looked a bit dingy. I told him I couldn't have my daughter riding in an old faded convertible. He surprised me and got it painted last week."

"Are the mayor and Banks still back there?"

"They sure are, still going over that budget."

I entered the mayor's office and found Franklyn and Wendell Banks with their heads down over a bunch of printed spread sheets and other items scattered across Franklyn's worktable, including the envelope of photos I had just dropped off. I figured the financial looking graphs and such contained the town's yearly budget projections. By their grim faces, it appeared the town was in for another year of austerity. Franklyn looked like Banks was trying to squeeze 5% more from his liver. Banks looked drawn and thinner than the last time I saw him, like he hadn't eaten in a week. He held a red pencil in his left hand that shook as he drew circles around budget lines.

"What are you doing here?" the mayor asked.

"I wanted to ask you and Banks a question."

"Question about what?"

"About this," I said handing him Early's account ledger.

"What's this?"

"That's the account of Early's reimbursements for last year. Notice anything unusual about it?"

"No," he said, his aura beating steady in the brown range. "Banks, what is this?"

When Banks didn't say anything I took a good look at him and noticed bruising up along his right jawline beneath a thin layer of some type of makeup, like someone had socked him good there, and he was trying to cover up the bruise

"I tell you what it is, Franklyn, someone's been falsifying Early's reimbursements. It looks like they were drawing on Early's account."

"How's that possible?"

"Someone in the budget office had authority over the process."

"Who?"

"Banks!"

"Who?"

"I think Banks, here, has been juggling the accounts and somehow pocketing the money."

"I didn't have anything to do with Early's scam," Banks mumbled between narrow lips, his aura trembling in the pink range, showing Banks was guilty of something.

"This wasn't Early's scam. Early didn't have an extra dime until he started working part time with the ATF, working on the drug ring back in the woods."

"What drug ring?" the mayor asked.

"Early had been working with the ATF on busting up a drug ring, he and JB Davis—that's what they've been working so mysterious on."

"Says who?"

"Lane Carson with the county sheriff's office told me. They set it up."

"Didn't they think of informing me of this?"

"They kept it a secret from everyone. But Early was on their payroll. Until then, Early didn't have an extra dime to spare. He charged a lot of things around town, but he made good on his debts when he started working for the ATF boys.

"You're behind this alright, Banks, and I think Early caught on and threatened the whole scheme. What was it, Banks, you need extra money to keep up with the Shaws? I figure that water mill grant you all got approved for turned everything on its head."

"What's that got to do with this?" the mayor asked.

"If you recall what you told me, in addition to all the other stuff you need for that grant, you said you need an audit of the town's finances. Banks knew an independent grant audit like that would uncover his scheme. I figure he was cooking the books to cover up his scam. Early got hold of a check made out to him, must have come to him by accident, but he figured Banks was running false receipts and paying out money that went in his own pocket. Banks figured he needed Early out of the way, figured he could cover the paper trail with accounting tricks to beat that audit, but he had to get rid of Early first."

"I didn't have anything to do with Early's running off Moore's Curve," Banks mumbled, his aura pulsing in the dark pink range of lying. Then, he said, "Early's luck just ran its course."

"Didn't you say you were waiting on the audit to complete that grant request?" I asked the mayor, remembering those words from Banks, words I'd heard before. I needed another angle on proving Banks guilty. I couldn't claim I saw the truth in Banks's aura, that he was lying. If I tried that in Black Mountain, I'd probably be burned at the stake for witchcraft.

"Right, it has to be an independent audit and I've been waiting on Banks, here, to arrange a time for the CPA firm we hired over in Morgan to come in here and start."

"So, Banks, what's holding you up?"

When Banks didn't answer, I asked him, "Having some trouble talking, Banks? So…how'd you get that broken jaw, anyway?"

"What broken jaw?" the mayor asked.

"Last Saturday night, I got mugged in the side alley, but Jeff Carson rescued me and punched out the guy, broke his jaw—his right jaw. Were you out all last week, Banks?"

"I had a bug."

"Or maybe that broken jaw of yours kept you out, the reason you lost some weight, being on a liquid diet, and all. That's when Mable ran that account. Until then, you wouldn't run it because you knew what it would show.

"Was Banks out all week?"

"Yep," the mayor confirmed, "he called in Monday morning and said he had the flu and was out all week."

235

"So, with you out, and Shelby asking for the account, Mable ran it herself. Early used a debit card for his purchases and submitted his monthly statement for his reimbursement. Instead of just pulling Early's legitimate reimbursable off the statements, Banks used other items on the account statements to inflate the totals and pocketed the difference. I'm sure the historical grant audit of the town's accounts will turn up enough irregularities to prove you've been cheating the town. Early loved this place, Banks; loved it so much he couldn't cheat it. The only task left for me, is proving you killed him."

"You might prove I was cheating the town, Emma, but not that I had anything to do with Early's death."

"No, I'm on to you now. You planned to get rid of Early so he couldn't testify against you. I found an uncashed reimbursement check Early had stashed away. He found out what you were up to and probably confronted you. Once that audit started, you knew your scheme would come out, so you killed Early alright, to try to cover your tracks—and, I'm sure, to somehow blame it all on him."

"You're crazy about this, Emma. You've been accusing everyone in town and now, me? I didn't have anything to do with your brother driving off that curve," Banks mumbled through a stiff jaw. I didn't need to see his dark pink aura to figure him guilty.

"Is that your car out in the alleyway, Banks?"

When Banks didn't answer, I said to the mayor, "You know I thought there was something fishy about that car, something about the paint."

"Yeah? Banks just had it painted."

"Why?"

"Why," the mayor said, "because it needed it."

"No, he painted it to cover evidence."

"What evidence? He painted it the same color as before."

"Banks and Early got into it, and Banks knew his time was short before his scheme would unravel. Banks must have run and Early chased him down in his cruiser. They got in a tussle there at Moore's Curve, and Banks used his big, heavy Cadillac to force Early's cruiser over the side and down into the river. A big Cadillac like that is about the only thing could win a tug of war with a police cruiser."

"You're dreaming!"

"No, I got a good look at Early's cruiser over at the junk yard and it looked like he'd been sideswiped on the driver's side. Sideswiped by a red car."

"Early's car was a mess," Banks said. "There were plenty of dents and dings on that car before Early went off that curve."

"No," I said, and smiling at the men, I remembered the photos of the Apple Festival. I reached down to the desk and took the envelope with the photos that Saunders had shot of the parade. I also remembered one of the 8" by 10" glossies showed Early in his police cruiser, riding in the parade. "No," I said, leafing through the photos, and finding the one with Early's car, said, "Early's cruiser might have been showing its age, but you can see from this photo taken just before he died, there are no dents or scratch marks anywhere on the driver's side of his vehicle. He only got those when you ran him off the road."

"You'll can't prove that!"

"Oh, no? Well, just look at these."

"What are these?" the mayor asked.

"They're a couple of photos of you riding in Banks's Cadillac during the Apple Festival Parade. Notice anything?" I asked the mayor.

"No, what?"

"You don't see any damage to the sides of Banks's car, at least, not enough to warrant a paint job. Banks only got it painted after the run-in with Early, trying to cover up the evidence."

"Shelby had been after me for a while to get the car painted, so I did. Besides, Early's cruiser has been sent off for scrap… you don't have it for evidence."

"I've got digital photos of Early's cruiser, Banks. They show the red marks, the fresh marks from the run-in with a big red Cadillac. That should be enough for the county to take a look at your car. Once they dig through the top layer of paint, they'll find the evidence."

"Won't the paint job have destroyed the evidence?" the mayor asked.

"No, like I was saying, that paint job looked funny to me. Banks must have gotten a jack leg shop to paint his car last week when he was out with that jaw. They did a crummy job on it, Banks. You shouldn't have gone cheap on that. They just painted over the old paint without sanding the old surface smooth and filling the holes with bonding. I think the county lab will be able to dig beneath the new top surface and find paint from Early's tan cruiser underneath.

When Banks didn't answer, I said, "It was you Banks. You mugged me that night trying to scare me off the case, taking hold of me with your left arm. I thought I recognized your voice, what you said about Early's luck running its course. Then, after Jeff slugged you, you got away by slipping in that side door off the alley by your office. I'm sure we'll find a key to that door when we search you. You killed Early, Banks, because he found out about your town scam."

Wendell Banks got up and moved toward the door, but I stepped in front of him. Bigger than me by a hundred pounds, he easily shoved me out of the way, and bolted for the exit. He had just opened it and started to step through, when he ran right into Jeff Carson who punched him full in his left jaw, sending the man down on his behind.

"I thought you might need a little help," Jeff said, smiling at me. "You know, rough someone up."

"Banks," the mayor directed the man, "why don't you just sit right there a spell." Taking up his phone, he hit a button for an internal line. "Carter, come on back here to my office and bring your handcuffs. That's right, your handcuffs!"

238

Chapter Twenty-Eight

Spring

On an early spring day, with the sun high in a cloudless sky, the story ran in the bi-monthly *Black Mountain Post.* The Post's publisher, Randall Shaw, wrote the story which appeared on the fourth page in the Community Section, between the gardening piece on how to get ready for spring planting and a story on several area Boy Scouts who earned their Eagle Scout awards. The story said that Wendell Banks killed Early Shaw, after a heated argument:

On the night of the incident, Early Shaw met with Wendell Banks and argued about Banks defrauding the town. Accused of a long-term scheme, the Budget Director, Wendell Banks, tried to escape apprehension by driving away, and Chief Shaw followed in pursuit. Wendell Banks collided with Chief Shaw and drove him over the top of Moore's Curve. Chief Shaw's car ended up in the Swannanoa River, the force of the wreck killing him. Walker Shaw, town magistrate, at the conclusion of a meeting in his office, accepted Wendell Banks's guilty plea to the charge of manslaughter, and Banks is awaiting sentencing by the Morgan County court.

In a related story, Black Mountain Town Mayor, Franklyn Shaw, announced that under a five-year contract, beginning on April 1ˢᵗ, the Morgan County Sheriff's Department would begin providing law enforcement services in the town. Please refer law enforcement questions to Lane Carson of the County Sheriff's Office, who will have an annex office in Town Hall.

That edition of the paper carried another story on an announcement from Mathew Shaw stating that: *Shaw Mill signed a contract to provide plywood sheathing to the Factory*

Hardware store chain. Mathew Shaw, general manager at the mill, said the contract would allow the mill to stay profitable for many years to come.

The Post's front-page story was a full biography and history of Lawrence Shaw, who passed away over the Christmas holidays. At the end of the lengthy obituary, Franklyn Shaw asked that, in lieu of flowers, all remembrances please be donated to the Black Mountain High School College Scholarship Fund.

Pa told me later that a regular Tuesday morning group down at the diner passed a copy of the paper around the day the story came out, and a few mentioned the case, but he said people appeared more interested in the article the County Agriculture Extension Service put out on the decline of the honeybee swarms, and how that might affect the apple crops come the fall.

That summer, after the years of futile escape, I found myself daydreaming of Black Mountain. It seemed like the mountain's allure beckoned me, its voice in the wind, a whisper of the past and the future come together in one bright aura of light, leading me back home.

About the Author

    Ruben D. Gonzales was born and raised in East L.A. but has called North Carolina home since 1976. The Black Mountain Mystery series is developed out of his love for the heritage and mystery of the North Carolina mountains. After college, Ruben spent five years with the Peace Corps in various capacities and stations including two years as an elementary school teacher in a small African village without electricity or indoor plumbing. Ruben spent evenings reading and writing by candlelight and during this time he wrote a short story that was bought by the BBC for world broadcast. His first published novel, *The Cottage on the Bay*, a historical novel, takes place on a fictional plantation outside of Wilmington, NC, and his second book, *Murder on Black Mountain*, the first in his series, takes place in the foothills of the Blue Ridge Mountains. Since retiring from full-time work, Ruben spends his time writing and teaches part-time with the local community college.